A DEAD HERRING

A RIGHT ROYAL COZY INVESTIGATION MYSTERY

HELEN GOLDEN

DREW BRADLEY PRESS

BOOKS BY HELEN GOLDEN

A Right Royal Cozy Investigation Series

Tick, Tock, Mystery Clock (Free Novelette)

Spruced Up For Murder

For Richer, For Deader

Not Mushroom For Death

An Early Death (Prequel)

Deadly New Year (Novelette included in an Anthology)

A Dead Herring

I Spy With My Little Die

ISBN (P) 9781915747129

Edited by Marina Grout at Writing Evolution

Published by Drew Bradley Press

Cover by Helen Drew-Bradley

First edition May 2023

To Elizabeth E.

From sitting in our prams together to swooning over Donny Osmond. Haring through the vicarage garden on our 'horses' and riding the cable car in Capri. Drinks on a submarine, racing in Newmarket, and walks with dogs in the Lakes. Separate 'kids' tables, reading gravestones, sneaking into your father's study and running out again scared by the man with the sword. Our parents drinking and playing games, us running around trying to find secret passages. The excitement of them filming Wilt in the grounds at Horning, the peace of Uncle Hugh's boat drifting down the river. So many memories as we reach another decade together. Thank you for your friendship.

NOTE FROM THE AUTHOR

I am a British author and this book has been written using British English. So if you are from somewhere other than the UK, you may find some words spelt differently to how you would spell them, for example Scottish whisky is spelt without an e. In most cases this is British English, not a spelling mistake. We also have different punctuation rules in the UK.

However if you find any other errors, I would be grateful if you would please contact me helen@helengoldenauthor. co.uk and let me know so I can correct them. Thank you.

For your reference I have included a list of characters in the order they appear, and you can find this at the back of the book.

1

1:25 PM, SUNDAY 10 JANUARY

Detective Chief Inspector Richard Fitzwilliam wiped his mouth with his napkin and pushed his plate away. "That was just what I needed," he said to the two women sitting opposite him across the wooden dining table that sat along one side of the wall in the living room of the small cottage.

"Thanks for bringing the wood in, Fitz." Emma McKeer-Adler shifted in her seat. "It's normally my job, but…" The petite dark-skinned woman looked down at her right leg, which was stuck out in front of her and slightly to the side, resting on a chair. She grimaced as she studied the heavy white cast covered in scribbles. 'It suits you, ma'am.'; 'Talk about taking one for the team, boss.'; 'My other leg's a mini!'; 'Is it too soon to call you Hop-a-long?'; 'The Cast and the Furious.'; 'Itch here.' She looked back up and shrugged.

"I could have done it," Isobel McKeer-Adler pointed out as she picked up her wineglass and raised it to her lips. "But I always fall over in the snow. I've got no sense of balance. You may have ended up with two broken legs on your plate." The woman with short blonde hair smiled, her green eyes shining.

"And she'd be an even worse patient than me." Emma patted her wife on the arm. "Wouldn't you, Izzy?"

Izzy grinned and nodded. "As unbelievable as that sounds —" She stopped as Fitzwilliam's mobile phone buzzed and vibrated on the tabletop in front of him.

'Blake' flashed up on the screen, and Fitzwilliam sighed. "Sorry, it's the boss," he told them as he put down his wine-glass and picked up the phone. *He's calling me while I'm on leave; this can't be good.* He hit the call accept button. "Nigel, what can I do for you?"

"Richard, we have a problem at Drew Castle. Are you at Adler's yet?" Superintendent Nigel Blake of the Protection and Investigation (Royal) Service didn't mince words.

Fitzwilliam rubbed his hand across his forehead. "What sort of problem, sir?"

His chest tightened. He knew Lady Beatrice and her business partner were at Drew Castle working on a refurbishment project. Drew Castle was only a mile from the cottage he was staying at while visiting his injured friend and colleague, but he was only planning on being here for a few days. There would be no need to see Lady Beatrice *unless…*

"There's been an unexplained death."

Fitzwilliam's heart skipped a beat. *She's okay, isn't she?*

"Who died?" Fitzwilliam blurted out quickly. Emma raised an eyebrow as she and Izzy leaned across the table, their mouths slightly open.

"A chap called Ben Rhodes. Businessman. He was there as part of a shooting party organised by Lord Frederick Astley."

"Was he shot?"

"No. It looks like he drowned in his bath."

"So it's murder then, sir?"

Adler and Izzy were now so close he could hear their breathing.

"Yes, it seems like it."

Well, of course it will be! Lady Beatrice was a trouble magnet, especially when it came to murder. Fitzwilliam frowned. *But what has this got to do with me? I'm on leave.* He opened his mouth, but his boss got in before he had time to ask.

"The problem is, Richard, they're completely snowed in at Drew Castle. It's unreachable from the outside at the moment. A local lad and the Drew Castle security guys are doing what they can to secure the scene, but I need someone up there overseeing it all and looking out for the family. The Queen Mother is there, along with Lord Frederick, and of course, your *friend*, Lady Beatrice." Could he detect a slight chuckle from his boss? Blake knew full well Lady Beatrice would hardly describe Fitzwilliam as a friend.

"I can't have them up there on their own with a potential murderer running around and no one from PaIRS to keep them safe," Blake continued. "But I can't get anyone to the area until the weather improves. So I think it's serendipitous you're only a short walk away, don't you?"

Serendipitous? Bad luck, more like... Fitzwilliam twisted to look out of the window behind him. It had snowed heavily since he'd been out to collect logs from the wood store behind the cottage, and now a thick blanket of snow smothered everything, leaving only a few outlines of trees looking like large blobs of ice cream. *A short walk?* Not in this weather. He sighed.

"I'm aware you're on leave, Fitzwilliam, and I wouldn't ask if I had any other options." Blake's voice was unexpectedly apologetic.

3

"Of course, sir. I understand. I'll get there as soon as I can."

"Good-o, Richard. I knew I could count on you. Send my kind regards to Adler, and when this is all over, extend your trip so you still get to spend some additional time there. Detective Sergeant Spicer will be available to you via phone and video, and as soon as the weather gets better, I'll get the local CID over there. Keep me posted."

The line went dead. Fitzwilliam placed his phone back down on the table and rubbed his chin.

"What's happened?" Two pairs of eyes stared across the table at him.

"There's been a murder up at Drew Castle. The boss wants me to take charge. They're snowed in, and no one else can get to them. Although having seen out there" —he gestured towards the window— "I'm not sure I can get there easily either."

Izzy nodded. "You won't be able to drive. The snow's too deep, and it'll be impossible to see where the road is." She got up. "But I think I saw some stuff in the boot room that might be useful."

"Can I come too?" Detective Chief Inspector Emma McKeer-Adler struggled up and gingerly put her weight on her cast.

"No!" Fitzwilliam and her wife cried in unison.

SEVEN DAYS EARLIER, SUNDAY 3 JANUARY

The Society Page online article:

Fifteen Years on from the Death of the Earl of Rossex, Lady Beatrice Sees Their Son Back Off to Boarding School.

On the fifteenth anniversary of the car accident that killed the Earl of Rossex James Wiltshire and his passenger Gill Sterling, his son Samuel (14) is returning to the exclusive Wilton College in Derbyshire, the same boarding school his father and paternal grandfather attended. Samuel's mother Lady Beatrice (36), the Countess of Rossex, waved goodbye to her son at Francis Court, where they live along with her parents Charles, the sixteenth Duke of Arnwall, and his wife HRH Princess Helen, sister of King James. Lady Beatrice entrusted the delivery of her son to her elder sister Lady Sarah Rosdale, whose son Robert Rosdale (15), also attends Wilton. Meanwhile, Lady Beatrice marked the anniversary of her husband's death with a quiet day at home preparing for her upcoming trip to Drew Castle, where she and her business partner Perry Juke (34) are managing the refurbishment and interior design of several family suites at the King's private residence in Scotland. Accompanying them is Perry's partner, crime writer and celebrity chef Simon Lattimore (39).

Lady Beatrice has been keeping a low profile since the tragic death of her ex-beau, Sebastiano Marchetti, three months ago. The recent inquest into the chef's death recorded a verdict of accidental death after he lost control of his car along a dangerous stretch of coastal road in Fenshire and drove off a cliff. Lady Beatrice and Chef Seb, as he was known to his army of fans, were no longer an item when he died.

Lady Beatrice will not be the only royal at Drew Castle this week. The countess's maternal grandmother Queen Mary The Queen Mother (82) is staying at Foxhall, her home on the estate, and Lady Beatrice's brother Lord Frederick Astley (39) is hosting a shooting party there that is rumoured to include entrepreneurs and identical twins Max and Ben Rhodes (38).

Multi-millionaire, Max Rhodes, has famously split from his Swedish super-model girlfriend Elger Hinz (29) recently and has been keeping a low profile ever since. Meanwhile, Ben Rhodes has been in the press repeatedly over the last month since he controversially purchased the football club, Urshall United, in what was considered a hostile takeover from the consortium that owned it. Fans of the London club have been up in arms about the takeover, and the new owner is reported to have received several death threats. A social media account titled 'We hate Ben Rhodes' was this week closed down because of the graphically violent nature of some videos being posted by fans under the subject 'How would you kill him?' Ben Rhodes and his wife Gemma (35) have employed round-the-clock security at their home in Surrey.

3

BREAKFAST, FRIDAY 8 JANUARY

"Holy moly, it's freezing out there," Perry Juke said as he walked into the Breakfast Room at Drew Castle, rubbing his hands together.

Lady Beatrice, the Countess of Rossex, smiled at her tall blond friend as he made his way across the room towards the self-service table along the back wall. Even though they were in Scotland in January, Perry was still surprised every day at how cold it was. "It's due to snow this week coming," she told him.

"It feels too cold to snow," Perry replied, helping himself to a large coffee from the coffee pot on the end of the long table.

"It's a myth that it's ever too cold to snow." Simon Lattimore strode into the room and dropped his laptop bag down by the table where Bea was sitting. "Morning," he said as he leaned in and kissed her cheek. "Do you want anything?" He looked over at the table where Perry was now plucking strips of crispy bacon from a bain-marie and placing them inside a roll.

She shook her head. "I've got a coffee, thanks."

He nodded and walked over to join his other half at the serving table.

"What do you mean it's a myth?" Perry asked him, adding some tomato sauce to his roll.

"It's not about temperature with snow; it's about how wet or dry the air is. So while it's true that the colder it gets, the drier the air gets, any moisture can turn into snow." Simon picked up the coffee pot and poured a large coffee, then added milk. "In fact," he continued. "In this country, we most commonly get snow at about two degrees."

Perry picked up his plate and coffee, then stared at Simon. "How do you remember such boring stuff, my love?"

Simon grinned. "It's a gift." He winked at his partner, and Perry laughed.

"So where's everyone?" Perry asked Bea as he wandered back to the table, looking around the empty room as he moved.

"They've been and gone. Fred and the shoot manager wanted to get out early and look at the birds." Her brother Lord Frederick Astley was hosting a shooting party over the next few days and had already started fretting the weather wasn't ideal for the game birds. It was too wet apparently. She had no expertise in this area, so had simply sympathised. "Grandmama's cousin and her daughter left last night to return to Sterling." As soon as Queen Mary The Queen Mother had seen her relatives off, she'd returned to Foxhall, her own house on the estate. "It will be quiet around here now until Fred's shooting guests arrive later today." At least it would give the staff time to clean rooms and prepare food before the next wave of visitors descended on the castle.

"And what are you two up to this morning?" Simon asked as he sat down opposite Bea and placed his latte and a plate of pastries in front of him.

"We're up on the second floor in the family wing, going through what we want to use and what needs to go into storage."

"We also have some wallpaper samples and paint arriving today so we can check it all goes together," Perry added as he took the seat next to Simon. "I have to say, as lovely as it is having a cottage to ourselves, I'm so glad we come here for breakfast." He took a huge bite from his bacon roll.

Bea smiled. She was glad Simon and Perry were comfortable where they were staying on the estate, but she was happy they joined her for breakfast each morning. She loved starting her day with them.

"Hold on," Perry said, scanning the room. "Where's Daisy?" He bent down to look under the table.

"She spent the night with Grandmama. Since Pluto died, she's been missing having a companion, and so I've lent her Daisy." The Queen Mother's Chihuahua-pug cross had passed away at the ripe old age of eighteen a few days before Christmas. Her grandmother had told everyone she was too old to have another dog, but Bea suspected she would change her mind once the rawness of her loss subsided.

Perry shook his head. "I'm not used to having a bacon roll all to myself." Perry was a sucker for the pleading eyes of Bea's little white West Highland Terrier.

"Well, make the most of it. She'll be back later." Bea turned to Simon, who was finishing a pain au chocolat. "What about you, Simon? How's the writing coming along?"

He wiped his mouth with a napkin and huffed. "Slowly. I'm at the awkward middle bit where I know where I need to go, but I'm not sure how to get there." He rose and grabbed his coffee cup and laptop bag. "And talking about writing, I need to get on. I'll see you later."

She watched the stocky man with short brown hair leave

the room and turn left towards his temporary office two doors down. *I hope accompanying us to Scotland won't stop him from meeting the deadline to finish his novel and get it to his editor.* Simon had been reluctant to come at first, worried that being with them would be too much of a distraction. It had taken both her and Perry to persuade him they would let him work undisturbed for him to agree to the trip. But was he regretting it now? She frowned as she turned to Perry. "Is he doing okay? He's not regretting coming with us, is he?"

Perry shook his head as he swallowed the last of his bacon butty. "No. In fact, he was saying last night he's finding the environment here really conducive to writing. He loves the aspect of the room you've given him to work in. The view sweeping over the fields with the forest in the background is inspiring him so much, he's moved some of the action in his book to Scotland."

"He didn't sound too happy just then."

"Oh, don't worry. He's always like this when he's in the middle of a book. Once he gets over the hump, he'll be fine."

"Are you sure you don't want to eat here in the evenings? It would mean Simon wouldn't have to cook, giving him more time to write."

Perry reached out and patted her hand. "Thank you for the offer, but cooking is his de-stresser. He needs it to unwind and clear his head. And he's loving getting to select ingredients from the kitchen here. He says the produce is amazing as it's mostly locally sourced from around the estate." He raised his hand to his chest. "You know me, Bea. I'm just as happy with stuff from the supermarket, but Simon gets excited about things like that."

She nodded. Perry was picky about wine, clothes, and shoes, whereas although Simon also appreciated good wine, he didn't care about clothes or shoes ("Function over style,"

Perry complained with an eye roll whenever Simon went shopping unaccompanied and proudly displayed his new purchases). But with food, where it came from and how it was treated was important to him. *They're so different, and yet somehow they complement each other so well.*

Just as well, as there was another excellent reason Simon had agreed to come to Drew Castle. She suppressed a smile. Simon was going to propose to Perry during their stay here. Butterflies filled her stomach. *I think I'm more nervous than Simon.* Not, of course, that she had any doubts Perry would say yes. They'd talked about it during their last job at Fenn House in Fenshire, and Perry had made it clear that although he didn't think it was right for *him* to ask (he was old-fashioned that way), should Simon go down on one knee, he would say yes. Definitely. Without a doubt.

I want it to be perfect for them.

They had all been so busy since they'd arrived four days ago that she and Simon had had little time to discuss it properly yet, other than to agree he should wait until Fred's guests dispersed later this week. And, of course, Perry didn't know, so they could only talk when he was otherwise occupied. Which seemed to be never.

She sighed gently. Her vision was for Simon to ask Perry on the balcony of the Upper Drawing Room late one afternoon to make the most of the magnificent sunsets the room afforded as a background.

Perry prodded her arm. "What's up? Your eyes have glazed over."

"Er, nothing." Heat rose up her neck. *It's so hard keeping this from him.* "Right," she said, getting up. "We really need to get on. That room won't rearrange itself."

Four hours later, Lady Beatrice and Perry Juke descended the sweeping tartan-carpeted stone staircase that led to the vast space of the main foyer of Drew Castle. As they reached the bottom of the stairs, a man with short sandy-coloured hair stepped into view.

"My lady, Mr Juke. We have set a buffet lunch out in the Breakfast Room." William Featherstone, the head footman and deputy butler, gave a barely perceptible nod and held his arm out towards the corridor to their right.

"Thank you, William," she said with a smile, then turned to Perry. "I'm going to pop into the kitchen and see Mrs Wilton. I'll meet you in the Breakfast Room."

"Sure. I'll see if Simon will take a break and join us for lunch," Perry replied as he branched right, disappearing around the corner.

Turning left, Bea followed the panelled corridor a short way, then went down another set of stone stairs leading into the basement of the castle. Clattering pans and the delicious smell of roasting meat pulled her along a wide corridor and into the kitchens.

On her left, a short round woman dressed in a full-length white wrap-over apron had her head in an enormous range oven, the top of a meat thermometer visible in one of her hands. In the middle of the room, her back to the cook, a slightly taller curvy young woman was bending over a massive wooden table, rolling out pastry. She glanced up and spotted Bea. Stopping what she was doing, she straightened up and wiped her hands down the blue overall that covered most of her outfit.

"My lady. Is everything okay?" she asked as Bea stopped on the other side of the table and smiled.

"Yes, Maddie. I just popped down to see how things were going. Are you all set for tonight?"

Maddie Preston opened her mouth to reply, but a voice behind her piped up. "We're all good, thank you, my lady." Erin Wilton unfurled herself from the oven, closed the door, and turned to face Bea. Her slightly damp fringe stuck to the side of her face, and her glasses were steamed up. She took them off and, grabbing the bottom of her apron, wiped them clean. "The beef's coming along nicely, and Maddie is getting the pastry ready for the apple and cinnamon tarts."

"Indeed. Well, it certainly smells good. How are you managing? Did Mrs Kettley arrange some extra help for you?" Bea asked.

When she, Mrs Wilton, and Mrs Kettley, Drew Castle's head housekeeper had met last night to check the arrangements for the shooting party guests and discuss the menu for the next few days, Bea had been concerned the cook, with only Maddie to help, might struggle with the extra mouths that needed feeding. Fred's decision to host the event had been rather last minute, something to do with the availability of one of the party, and there had not been time to send staff from Francis Court or Gollingham Palace to help.

With only a skeleton staff kept at Drew Castle in the winter, it was normal procedure for any of the family who wanted to bring guests to bring help with them too. In fact, in the summer, when the king and queen travelled up to Scotland for their annual four-month stay at Drew Castle, they packed up house and home and covered everything at Gollingham Palace in dust sheets. Then a huge procession of trunks packed with clothes, china, silverware, crystal, wines, household goods, and toiletries made its way from Surrey to Scotland via the Royal Train.

"Yes, the housekeeper at Foxhall is lending us a couple of girls for the duration." The Queen Mother, in residence at Foxhall and expecting to stay at least three months, had brought a handful of staff with her from Francis Court. Her stay was an opportunity to train new employees; Her Majesty was an exacting taskmaster.

"Perfect. Did Lord Fred tell you The Queen Mother will join us for dinner tonight?"

The cook nodded. "I'm doing her a nice piece of river trout that was caught this morning, my lady."

Bea's eighty-two-year-old grandmother had recently pronounced meat in the evenings was too heavy for her aging digestion. "She'll love that. Well, it looks like you have it all under control, as always. I'll leave you to get on." Her stomach gave a low rumble. She hadn't realised how hungry she was until the mention of food.

"Lunch is sandwiches and soup, my lady."

Bea nodded. There was too much preparation going into tonight's dinner to allow time for a cooked lunch as well. "Thank you, Mrs Wilton. That sounds great. If you need anything, just let me know."

"Thank you, my lady."

Bea turned on her heels and hurried out of the kitchen, eager to tuck into her lunch.

4

LUNCHTIME, FRIDAY 8 JANUARY

Walking into the Breakfast Room five minutes later, Lady Beatrice spotted her brother sitting at a table in front of the vast windows overlooking the formal castle gardens. Perry and Simon sat opposite him. Simon and Fred were in deep conversation while Perry scanned the room. He saw her and waved frantically.

Weaving her way across the room, she nodded at the other occupied tables as she headed towards him. Perry shot up as she drew near. "Thank goodness you're here. I'm starving, but Simon insisted we wait for you. Can I get food now?"

Simon rose and nodded. He grinned as Perry lunged towards the white-covered table against the wall that was set out with two platters of sandwiches, a large tureen of soup, and a basket of rolls and grabbed a plate from the stack at one end.

"Thank you for waiting," Bea addressed Fred and Simon. "I just wanted to check Mrs Wilton was all set."

"And is she?" her brother asked as he pulled his tall lean frame up from his chair.

"Yes. She and Maddie have it all under control."

"Are you and Perry eating with us tonight?" Fred asked Simon as the three of them made their way toward the serving table where Perry was now adding a handful of small sandwiches to his plate.

Simon shook his head as he picked up a plate. "No. I have some trout Mrs Wilton gave me, along with some fresh dill from the greenhouses, so I'm cooking it with celeriac chips, roasted sprouts, and honeyed parsnips." He picked up two cheese sandwiches.

Bea's mouth watered. "Can I come—"

"Can I come—" Fred said at the same time.

They both grinned.

"I think you're both required to be here, aren't you, to welcome your guests?" Simon pointed out as he grabbed a glass of orange juice.

Fred sighed, his well-trimmed eyebrows forming a frown. "I guess so."

"Well, *I* don't have to be…" Bea smiled at her older brother as she opened the lid of the soup bowl, a waft of curry and butternut squash teasing her taste buds. "I mean, it's not my shooting party, is it?" She picked up the ladle and filled her bowl.

"Hold on there a minute, little sis. You're my hostess, remember? You need to be here to make sure everything runs smoothly while I chat up our visitors." He took the ladle from her hand.

She huffed. "I suppose so. But you owe me one." She grabbed a roll and a small dish of butter and joined Perry at their table.

"Sorry, I couldn't wait," Perry told her through a mouthful of food.

"Indeed. Anyone would think you'd been busy all

morning moving furniture around." She gave a slow smile. "Oh wait, you have."

He grinned and took another bite of his sandwich. Simon and Fred arrived, and the four of them ate in silence. Bea took a mouthful of the warming soup and looked out of the large bay windows, her gaze skimming over the neatly laid out formal gardens to the edge of the forest behind. The trees glistened as the sun melted the earlier frost, but the ground below remained covered in white. A movement in the trees caught her attention. A Scottish red deer came into view, his large branching antlers almost camouflaged within the trees. He stared at her. He was magnificent. Then with a flicker of his pale tail, the russet-brown creature disappeared out of sight.

"So who do you have coming to stay besides the famous Rhodes twins?" Simon asked Fred when they finished their food.

"A couple of contacts of mine through work and a local family called the McLeans. They live about twenty-five miles away."

"McLean as in McLean and Co?" Perry asked as he peeled a satsuma.

"Yes, do you know them?" Fred took a sip of his coffee.

"No. But I know about them. They make the most exquisite cashmere scarves." He turned to Simon. "I bought you one for Christmas. The black one with a fine red line through it."

Simon nodded, then looked away. Bea suppressed a grin. Wasn't that the one he'd lent to her son Sam to wrap up an injured kestrel they'd found while on a walk with Daisy a few weeks ago? *I wonder what happened to it?* She thought it wise not to ask Simon in front of Perry. She was sure it had been beyond saving by the time Sam had finished with it.

"Yes. They do many textiles, including tartan. Hector McLean semi-retired a few years ago so he and his wife could go travelling, but unfortunately, she died last year. His son Fergus and his son-in-law Ed run it on a day-to-day basis now." Fred put down his coffee cup and looked out of the window. "I hope it stays dry like this for the next few days. There's a threat of snow but not until mid-week."

"I haven't seen Hector McLean for years. I didn't realise his wife had died. What happened?" Bea took a sip of her coffee.

"Apparently, she disappeared one afternoon. When Hector got back from a business meeting and she wasn't there, he raised the alarm. The police found her body the next morning washed up on the banks of the river in the next village. Seems like she fell into the water somewhere near their estate and drowned."

Bea raised her hand to her chest. "That's awful, Fred. I don't remember anyone mentioning it."

"I think the family kept it quiet. She'd had a few drinks at lunchtime, so…"

She nodded. She recalled the last time she'd seen Fergus McLean at a drinks party hosted by her cousin, Lady Caroline Clifford, at Kensington Court. He'd made some jokey comment about his mother being a drinker. "Anyway, the McLeans are experienced shots. They won't mind a bit of snow, will they?" she asked.

Fred shook his head. "It's not the McLeans I'm concerned about. Hector's daughter Rose isn't shooting, and Hector, Fergus, and Ed are all excellent marksmen. It's the Rhodes twins I'm thinking about. I hear Max is an accurate shot with clays, but birds are very different. And Ben is inexperienced. It will be easier for them if it's clear. Rain and snow make it hard to pick the birds out against the sky."

Perry, finishing his last segment of orange, picked up his coffee cup. "So are you worried about having Ben Rhodes here? If the papers are anything to go by, the man has a target on his back after his purchase of the football club."

Perry, like Bea, wasn't a big sports fan, but they both tolerated it for Simon's and her son's sakes. Many a winters weekend when Sam had been home from boarding school, Simon and Perry had walked the short distance to Francis Court on a Sunday afternoon and joined them on the second floor. While Sam had taken Simon off to watch F1 racing or an international rugby game on the sixty-inch television in the room opposite her apartment that he'd now turned into a games room, she and Perry had flicked through home interior magazines and shared their favourite looks.

Fred sighed, rubbing his stubbled chin with his thumb and forefinger. "It's a real pain, to be honest. I originally only invited Max. It was him who asked if Ben could come too. He'd thought it would be good for his brother to be here, in a remote area, to get away from the hounding he's been experiencing. I could hardly say no, could I? At least he's bringing his own security, so it won't fall onto our guys here to keep an eye on him."

A man cleared his throat, and they started. "Excuse me, my lord, but I have it on good authority a car is coming up the drive. I suspect it may be some of your guests?" The clean-shaven grey-haired man gave a curt bow and stood to one side.

"Thank you, Brock. I'll be there shortly."

The butler nodded and glided out of the room.

Fred looked at his watch and rose. "They're a bit early, but I'd better greet them. I'll catch you all later."

"See you later," Bea responded as he left the table.

"How does he do that?" Perry asked, a frown creasing his smooth forehead.

"Who? Do what?" she asked.

"That butler chap. I didn't see him there. It's like he appeared by magic."

Bea smiled. "It's part of their stealth training."

Perry tilted his head to one side as if he wasn't sure whether to believe her or not.

"A butler would make an expert killer, you know, Simon," Bea said.

"I'll bear it in mind," Simon said, getting up, a grin on his face. "I'll work until about four," he said to Perry. "If it suits you two?"

They nodded, and he left.

"Well, I suppose we'd better get on," Bea said as she rose from the table.

Perry jumped up. "Okay, just let me grab something for an afternoon snack," he said as he headed towards the overflowing fruit bowl resting on the end of the table.

5

EARLY EVENING, FRIDAY 8 JANUARY

Wrapping her navy-blue dressing gown tightly around her body and tying the belt in a knot, Lady Beatrice hurried from her dressing room and through the sitting room to open the door. As she approached, a short sharp bark made her smile. *Daisy must be back.* A tall olive-skinned man holding a squirming white bundle of fur greeted her when she threw the door open.

"Daisy is back from your grandmother's, my lady," the footman said as he handed the small terrier over to her mistress. "I've walked her, and she's been fed."

"Thank you, Owen. You're a star," Bea said, trying to avoid the licks her little dog was attempting to plant on her partly made-up face.

"You're welcome, my lady." Owen Buckey gave a small bow before turning and drifting silently down the corridor.

Shutting the door, Bea kissed Daisy on the head, then placed her on the floor. "Did you have a lovely time, Daisy-Doo?" she asked as she walked back towards the dressing room, Daisy trotting by her side.

She sat back down on the peach satin stool in front of the

mirror, and her little dog jumped up to join her. Chatting away to her canine companion, she finished her make-up and brushed her long straight auburn hair. Rising, she moved to the wardrobe and took down the green evening dress that had been hanging up over the door since someone had pressed it this afternoon. She sighed. If she was totally honest, what she'd really like to do right now was curl up with Daisy on the sofa and watch a film. She shook her head. *It's not an option. I promised Fred I'd make an effort and be sociable while we have guests.* She sighed and slipped into the long fitted dress. *Not much room for dinner in this,* she thought as she held on to the side of the wardrobe and pulled her gold Chanel sandals on.

"I'm sorry I can't take you with me to dinner, Daisy," she told her little dog as she grabbed her evening bag. "But I'll come and get you straight after, okay?" The terrier tilted her head to one side. Reaching down, Bea patted her on the head, then taking a deep breath, she headed for the door.

Outside her room, the half-wooden-panelled half-wallpapered corridor was lit by double mock-candles wall sconces. As she turned the corridor and walked onto the landing, she came to an abrupt halt as voices drifted up from the floor below.

"I can't believe he's here. Of all the cheek!" The woman's voice was shrill, and the owner seemed agitated. Bea recognised the plumy tones. "I mean, after all he's done to us, especially you, are we really expected to spend the next few days with him?" *Rose McLean. Well, not McLean anymore. She got married years ago. Now…what is her husband's name? Ed, that's it.*

"Look, I know it's not ideal, but we hardly have a choice. Dad won't want to leave; he's really looking forward to this weekend—" *Ah, Fergus, Rose's brother.* Bea hadn't seen

Rose for many years, but she knew the woman's younger brother better. He lived in London, and they had mutual friends. She'd been pleased when Fred had told her Fergus was going to be here. He was the only other person she knew well enough to feel relaxed around.

"And what about you, Fergus? How do you feel about seeing him face to face?" Rose's voice was full of concern.

I wonder who they're referring to?

Her brother's aggressive voice cut through the hushed hallway. "I want to punch his smug face in."

Rose gasped. "Fergus, be careful—"

"Don't worry," he cut in. "I won't do anything stupid, sis. I just want to find out why he used me…" He trailed off, and it was silent for a few seconds.

"I'm so sorry, Fergus."

"Thanks, sis." His voice perked up. "Come on. Let's put on a brave face even if deep down we're working out a thousand painful ways for him to die!"

There was a giggle from Rose and then the sound of muffled footsteps. Bea leaned over the wrought-iron and stone balustrade and watched the two siblings descend the wide stairs leading to the ground floor.

She frowned. *What was that all about?* Clearly one of their weekend guests wasn't welcome as far as Rose and Fergus were concerned. She sighed. *I hope there's not going to be trouble.* After last year, when she'd inadvertently got involved in a handful of murder investigations, she just wanted a quiet life where she could concentrate on her and Perry's burgeoning refurbishment and interior design business. And she absolutely did *not* want to go head to head with the boorish Detective Chief Inspector Richard Fitzwilliam from the Protection and Investigation (Royal) Services ever again. The embarrassment of their last case together, where she'd ignored all the signs of who the killer was because of her personal feelings, still hung around her shoulders like an especially clingy monkey who wouldn't let go.

Someone clearing their throat brought her out of her musings.

"Are you okay, my lady?" A thin woman dressed in a navy-blue dress stood on the top step of the stairs, looking up at her with worried blue eyes.

Bea smiled. "Yes, I'm fine, thank you, Mrs Kettley. Just day dreaming."

The head housekeeper's look of concern turned to one of amusement. "Well, I hate to be the one to tell you, my lady, but everyone else is already downstairs, including your grandmother, so…"

Oh no, I'm going to be late. Grandmama will be furious. "Rats! I'd best go." Bea grabbed the stone banister and hurtled down the stairs as fast as her tight dress and sky-high heels would allow.

6

STILL EARLY EVENING, FRIDAY 8 JANUARY

Entering the Red Drawing Room six minutes later, Lady Beatrice took a deep breath to calm her racing heart. She quickly scanned the room and was relieved to see Queen Mary The Queen Mother deep in conversation with a grey-haired man wearing glasses. Bea hurried away from the doorway and made her way slowly along the wall on the opposite side of the room from where her grandmother was. As she passed a low coffee table, she grabbed a glass of champagne from the tray on the top of it and took a sip. *If I can just look like I've been here all along, maybe she won't notice…*

"Bea!" Her brother, resplendent in a grey-and-green kilt and fitted green jacket, shouted from the other side of the room where he was standing with a slim man in a dinner suit. He gestured for her to join them. Her head down, she slinked across the room, taking a quick peek at her grandmother as she arrived by her brother's side. The Queen Mother shot Bea a look that told her in no uncertain terms she knew of her lateness and would deal with it later. *Rats!* Blushing slightly, she turned to Fred and his companion and smiled.

"Brett, this is my sister, Lady Beatrice, the Countess of Rossex. Bea, this is Brett Goodman. We know each other through work."

Bea smiled at the round-faced, clean-shaven man and took his outstretched hand.

"A pleasure to meet you, Lady Rossex. I've heard a lot about you," he said, his deep and drawling accent suggesting he was from one of the southern states of America.

"Well, I hope it wasn't all bad, Mr Goodman. By contrast, as my brother refuses to tell us what he really does as a job, I'm afraid I can't say he's mentioned you at all." She dropped his hand gently and continued, "But please don't take it personally. There's a consensus amongst the family that he's a spy, so we don't expect him to reveal any details of the people he works with."

"Well, please don't ask me to enlighten you, my lady." He raised an eyebrow, his brown eyes sparkling as he grinned. "I'm afraid if I told you, then I'd have to kill you."

Bea laughed. *He seems nice…* "Please call me Beatrice."

"Only if you'll call me Brett."

She nodded and took a sip of her drink. "Have you been to Scotland before, Brett?"

He glanced quickly at Fred, then nodded. "Yes, I was based in London for a while when I was younger and still come over on a fairly regular basis, so I've been to Scotland a few times over the years. I'm actually over here on vacation at the moment, and when Fred found out, he kindly asked me to join him here."

"So you shoot, do you?"

He hesitated briefly, then smiled. "Only when I have to."

What an odd thing to say. She stared down at the man in front of her. A smirk appeared on his face, and as he took a sip of champagne, he raised his left eyebrow in a James Bond sort of way. *Is he flirting with me?* She felt a slight flutter in her stomach. She studied him closer. His white teeth showed through his full lips as he drank, standing out clearly against his brown skin. He lowered his glass as his eyes met hers, and he smiled. *He's a tad short, but he's got a pleasant smile...* She mentally shook herself. *You're off men, remember?* She dropped eye contact and took another sip of her drink. After the disaster that had been her last relationship, she was resigned to the fact men either wanted the publicity of being with her, or the public scrutiny would overwhelm them. Eventually they couldn't handle it. Why would she put herself through the pain of getting to know someone, knowing that was how it would end? Suddenly, she wished Perry and Simon were here.

"Er, Bea." Fred nudged her other arm. "I think Grandmama wants you." He nodded at the thin elegant woman standing in the corner of the room. Her green eyes immediately caught Bea's, and giving a barely perceptible nod of her head, the older woman gave a clear signal she wanted her granddaughter to join her. Now.

Feeling heat rise up her neck, she glanced at Brett Goodman, who was still smiling at her. "Er, nice to meet you," she mumbled as she picked up the bottom of her dress, pivoted on her heels, and headed off towards her grandmother and her companion.

"Ah, Beatrice." Queen Mary The Queen Mother gently rested her hand on her granddaughter's arm as she addressed the man next to her. "Do you remember my granddaughter, Hector? I believe she and Rose went to the same school?" Without waiting for a response, she turned back to Bea. "Isn't that so, darling?"

"Actually, Grandmama, I think Rose went to the same school as Sarah. She was a few years below her."

"Yes, yes, of course." The older woman waved her other hand around dismissively. "But you must remember Hector McLean, Beatrice. He lives at Invergate House just down the road."

Bea smiled at the stocky man in the red tartan kilt. "Yes, of course. Nice to see you again, Mr McLean."

He bowed his head. "It's been a few years, Lady Rossex. You and your husband came for dinner not long after you were married. My wife was all of a flutter that you wouldn't like the raspberry dessert she'd made after someone had told her that morning you didn't like raspberries." He gave a sad smile. "She worried about things like that, did Stella."

"I was so sorry to hear of her death, Mr McLean. Please accept my sincere condolences."

"Thank you, my lady." He indicated to a group standing across the room. "I believe you know my son Fergus?" Fergus McLean, dressed in the same tartan as his father, looked over and waved. Bea waved back. Next to him stood his sister Rose, looking stunning in a long red dress that suited her petite frame, her wispy blonde hair resting on her shoulders. Next to her stood a pale grey-haired man with a goatee and large glasses. He looked like a science teacher, but Bea assumed he must be Rose's husband.

"And that's my son-in-law Ed next to Rose," Hector said, confirming her assumption. "He runs the business these days, along with Fergus."

"You must be extremely proud, Hector," Queen Mary said.

"Yes, ma'am, I am."

As her grandmother and Hector McLean continued to chat, Bea slowly scanned the crowd. Owen, the footman, circulated the room with a fresh tray of drinks, and she followed his progress. He stopped by Brett, who had been joined by a woman she didn't recognise. She had very short brown hair and was wearing a silk jumpsuit in midnight blue. *Fred's other colleague he mentioned?* Brett looked her way, and she quickly averted her eyes.

Looking up a few seconds later, she saw Owen had moved on to where Fred was deep in conversation with two men just a fraction shorter than his six foot one. Even if she hadn't already met one of them at a dinner party last summer, there was no mistaking the tanned-skinned brothers. The Rhodes twins, Max and Ben, were the epitome of cool, with their slightly-curly dark-brown hair scraped up into man buns and their eyebrows well-trimmed. They looked like models. And they looked *exactly* the same. From their brown eyes to their polished black shoes, it was impossible for her to tell them apart.

I wonder if Fred is talking to them about twin stuff, she thought, suppressing a smile. Having grown up with twin siblings, Bea was used to their almost telepathic way of communicating and their incredible ability to know exactly how to wind each other up. She'd often been caught in the middle of Fred and Sarah when they had all been younger, desperately trying to broker a peaceful resolution to whatever silly dispute they'd been having. When Fred had gone off to boarding school at thirteen, Bea had selfishly been pleased that she would now get her older sister all to herself, and that had been when they had formed the strong bond they still shared now. Not that Sarah and Fred weren't close; it was just their lives had gone in different directions — Sarah staying close to home to help run Francis Court, and Fred first into the Army and then into his current job in London. In fact, these days, Sarah often complained that Bea and Fred were more alike, both being more emotionally driven than the unflappable Sarah.

Standing just behind Fred and the twins was a thick-set man with a shaved head, wearing a black suit. His legs were slightly apart, and his hands were behind his back. He looked like a stereotypical heavy in an action movie. *Is he Ben Rhodes's security chap?*

A gong sounding from the hallway made her start, and she looked towards the door as Brock, Drew Castle's stately-looking butler, stepped into the doorway, the large felt-headed mallet still in his hand. "Ladies and gentlemen, dinner is served."

Fred immediately made his way over to his grandmother, his arm outstretched as the older woman took it, then turned and offered his other arm to Bea. She smiled as she joined them, and they led the procession of diners out of the drawing room.

———

As they walked into the Grand Dining Room, it took Lady Beatrice's eyes a few seconds to adjust. The subtle lighting coming from wall sconces and a candelabra in the centre table, combined with the walnut-panelled walls, the dark-blue ceiling, and the deep-red tartan carpet, gave the room a dramatic, spooky atmosphere. The highly polished table in the centre of the room, which could comfortably hold up to twenty-six diners, was set for eleven, with the top place reserved for The Queen Mother, her being the most senior royal who was present.

As everyone took their places, Bea sat down and smiled at the man taking his seat next to her. It was one of the Rhodes brothers.

Returning her smile, the man's brown eyes twinkled. "Good evening, my lady."

Ben? Surely if it was Max, he would have said something like, "Good to see you again," to acknowledge their previous acquaintance. *Yes, it must be Ben.*

"Good evening," she replied, grinning. *I have a fifty percent chance of getting it right anyway!*

She leaned away from the table briefly to let William drop her napkin onto her lap. "Thank you, William," she whispered to the head footman as she continued to ponder if she was talking to Ben or Max.

Her grandmother rose, and a hush descended over the room.

"Ladies and gentlemen. I'm delighted to welcome you to Drew Castle for a few days of good food, good whisky, good company, and good sport." A ripple of applause ran around the table. "And now, Hector, can I ask you to say our traditional Scottish grace courtesy of Robbie Burns, please?"

Hector McLean, sitting on The Queen Mother's left, rose as she sat down. His sing-song Scottish accent, with its lulling harmonious tones, rang out loudly around the room. "Some hae meat and canna eat…"

As his soft voice washed over her, Bea looked across the table at the other Rhodes twin. He was listening intently to his dinner companion, his head on one side, his face solemn as he occasionally nodded. As if sensing her stare, the man raised his chin, and their eyes met. The same rum-coloured eyes as his brother. *Blast!* He gave her a small smile and a barely perceptible nod of the head. *Max! Is that a look of recognition?* She thought so, therefore… it had to be Max.

"… Sae let the Lord be thankit." Hector McLean gave a low bow, and the table burst into applause.

She turned to Ben Rhodes and, holding out her hand, said, "I'm Beatrice." Her shoulders relaxed, and she leaned back into her chair. He tilted his head to one side and stroked his Greek nose with his forefinger.

As Owen, the other footman, placed her appetiser in front of her, she picked up her napkin. Her dinner companion smirked and took her other hand. He flipped it around and raised it to his mouth, whispering. "It's good to see you again, Beatrice." He kissed her hand lightly, then continuing to hold on to it, said, "How's your son? Last time I saw you, you were rather dreading him going off to boarding school the following year, but his grandparents were most insistent."

She let out a sigh. *Max!* And she'd been so sure he was Ben. She gently removed her hand and smiled. "My son Sam is fine, thank you, Max. It turned out they were right, and he's absolutely thriving at his school." She picked up her knife and fork.

"Did you think I was my brother?" he whispered as he cut into the smoked salmon topped with crème fraîche resting on its pressed bread base.

Feeling heat rising up her neck, she ignored his question. After taking only two mouthfuls of food, he placed his knife and fork on the plate and pushed it to the side away from him.

"Don't you like your starter?" Bea asked, spotting his discarded plate.

He shrugged. "Er, no, it's not that. I try not to eat too much. You know, keep myself trim and all that."

"I find running does that for me."

He shuddered. "I'd rather not eat than run."

Wasn't he secretly training for a marathon to raise money for prostate cancer in memory of his father? "You were enjoying it when I last saw you. Did you give up on the idea?"

"I'm afraid so. Turns out me and running just don't get on."

"That's a shame. Personally, I love to be outside and moving, but it's not for everyone."

He leaned towards her and whispered, "Of course, I could be persuaded to give it another go with the right company…"

What's going on with the men here tonight? Is it something in the water? Her heart skipped a beat. He suddenly reminded her of her ex-boyfriend, Sebastiano Marchetti, with his olive skin and enchanting smile. *Remember how that turned out? Never again!* She turned and said politely. "I believe it's going to snow tomorrow."

"I reckon it's too cold to snow," he said.

She smiled smugly. "Actually…"

7

EARLY MORNING, SATURDAY 9 JANUARY

Walking into the Breakfast Room the next morning, Daisy by her side, Lady Beatrice was surprised to see the room was empty except for the woman with the buzz cut who had been talking to Brett Goodman last night. Where was the shooting party? She'd assumed they would have an early breakfast before they left. Or had she missed them already?

"Good morning, my lady. Can I get you anything?" William asked as the head footman glided across the room from the serving table along the opposite wall where he'd been filling up the coffee pot.

"No, thank you, William. I'll help myself to coffee. Has the shooting party not come down yet?"

Having bent down to pet Daisy, the footman straightened up. "They've already left, Lady Beatrice. His lordship wanted them on-site early, ready for when it got light. Owen accompanied them with bacon rolls and hot drinks."

Pressing her lips together, she nodded and made her way towards the coffee pot. She glanced at her watch. Perry and Simon wouldn't be here for a while. Pouring herself a large black coffee, she turned and paused. It would be rude to ignore the only other occupant of the room. She sauntered towards the table where the petite woman was gazing out of the window.

"Hello. Do you mind if we join you?" Bea asked as she and Daisy stopped by the side of the table.

The woman jumped up. "No, not at all, your ladyship. Please do."

"I'm Lady Beatrice, Fred's sister," Bea said, holding out her hand.

The woman nodded as she took it. "Hi. I'm Eve Morrison."

"And the little monster sniffing your leg is Daisy." Bea bent down and gently pulled Daisy away from the woman's black trousers. "I'm sorry, she's particularly attracted to colours she can noticeably leave hairs on."

Eve grinned and squatted down in front of the little white dog. "Hello, Daisy. I'm pleased to meet you." She ruffled the rough hair on Daisy's head. "I have a white cat at home, so I'm used to it." Daisy threw her head up and licked the slim woman's hand, making her laugh.

I like her already.

Eve straightened up, her blue eyes still sparkling with delight, and returned to her chair while Bea sat down opposite. Daisy curled up on the floor by her feet. "So, Eve. Are you another person who can't tell me what my brother does, or you'll have to kill me?"

Eve's thin eyebrows rose sharply, then a smile slowly spread across her face. "Fred told me his family thinks he's a spy."

"And is he?"

"No."

Bea caught her breath. In all the time she'd been asking everyone who knew Fred if he was a spy, this was the first time someone had given a direct answer. She looked down at her right hand and twirled her rings. *I didn't really think he was, but...*

"Are you okay, Lady Beatrice?" There was a hint of amusement in the woman's voice.

Bea glanced up at her. The twinkle in the woman's eyes as she met Bea's gaze made her think again. "Wouldn't you say that anyway, even if he was?"

Eve Morrison smiled coyly. "Of course." She picked up her tea and took a sip.

I bet she's a spy too.

"So you're not shooting, my lady?"

Bea shook her head. "No, I'm not a big fan, to be honest. In my experience, it's a lot of standing around in the cold and wet, interspersed with shouting and loud bangs. Half the time it seems like it's potluck if they hit anything. The dogs do most of the work." She looked down at Daisy by her feet. She couldn't imagine her spoilt little dog running around in muddy wet fields. Daisy let out a gentle snore. "You didn't fancy it then?"

"I have a report I need to write up this morning. I was going to join them this afternoon, but after your description, I might give it a miss…"

Bea raised a hand to her chest. "Oh no, please don't let me put you off. I'm dreadfully biased. It's years of sitting in a cold draughty Land Rover looking out over stark fields that's led me to avoid it. I tried it once. The shoot manager described me as 'not a natural shot,' and my father called me a 'blasted liability' after I was distracted by a dog when it appeared out of the long grass limping, and I nearly shot the King of Norway. But do give it a try. You may love it."

Eve grinned. "I might do then." She glanced at her watch

and rose. "Please excuse me, but I must make a call. It was nice to meet you, Lady Beatrice."

"You too." Bea watched the slim woman leave the room. W*hy do I feel like she found out lots about me, but I found out nothing about her?*

"Morning!" Simon entered the room, with Perry just behind him. Daisy ran up to greet her two favourite people. Simon bent down and scooped her up, giving her a kiss on the side of her face. "How's my girl?"

Perry, having patted Daisy on the head while she was in Simon's arms, hurried over to the table. "Who was that?" he asked. "She looks scary."

Bea smiled. "That's Eve Morrison. She works with Fred."

"Another spy then?" He looked behind him at the door.

"Who's a spy?" Simon said, returning Daisy to the floor and joining them at the table.

"That woman we just passed with the shaved hair," Perry told him.

"We don't know she's a spy," Bea jumped in. "I just said she works with Fred."

"Ah." Simon nodded. Placing his mobile on the table, he headed off to the breakfast table.

"Do you want anything, Bea?" Perry asked.

"I'll have another coffee, please." She handed him her cup, and he followed his other half across the room, Daisy trotting beside him.

Looking out the window, Bea was glad she wasn't outside. The mist still hadn't cleared, and it hung heavy in the air like static rain. In the distance, the forest appeared as a dark-grey mass, the trees barely distinguishable in the murky gloom. *I wonder if they're able to see anything out there?* Fred would be devastated if the first day was a write-off

37

because of the weather, especially as the forecast for tomorrow was for snow.

Simon sat down opposite her with a thud. "I've been looking forward to this," he said, unfolding his napkin and picking up his knife and fork. "I love a good Scottish breakfast." He looked lovingly down at his plate of crispy bacon rashers, square sausage patties, tattie scones, a fried egg, baked beans, mushrooms, tomatoes, and haggis, then sighed contentedly and tucked in.

Bea looked away. Just the thought of that much food this early in the day made her feel slightly nauseous.

"I don't know how you can eat all that," Perry said as he sat down next to his partner. He pushed a fresh cup of coffee towards Bea, then placed a plate of bacon down on the table, along with two bread rolls on a separate plate.

Simon emitted a grunt but said nothing as he continued to eat.

Perry picked up a knife and, cutting a rasher of bacon in half, leaned down and fed it to a waiting Daisy.

"Perry!" Bea cried. "She can't have bacon every morning. It's not good for her. I'm going to get into all sorts of trouble when we get back to Francis Court if she puts on even more weight." Daisy had been on a strict diet since the summer after the vet had announced she was "too stocky" for her height. Recently, they had all been slack with sticking to it (especially Perry), and there was a distinct thickening around the little terrier's middle again. Bea had been determined to start the new year getting her dog back on track, but Perry was such a sucker for those huge brown pleading eyes. "I'm going to have to leave her upstairs at breakfast time if you can't control yourself," she scolded her friend.

Perry raised his hands to his chest. "Okay, okay. But it was only *half* a rasher."

"I can tell by how much you have on that plate that it wasn't going to be just that one piece you were planning to give her."

Perry leaned down and whispered under the table, "I'm sorry your mummy is being so mean, my love."

Bea rolled her eyes at Simon, who, still eating, looked like a hamster storing food for later. He grinned back.

Perry straightened up and made himself a bacon roll. "So how was dinner last night? Did you talk to the gorgeous Rhodes twins?"

"Only one of them. I sat next to Max at dinner."

"Isn't he the one you met before?"

She nodded.

"So?" Perry raised an eyebrow. "How was it?" He took a large bite out of his bacon butty.

"It was fine. He was charming and a little flirty. The perfect dinner companion."

"Flirty?" Simon said as he picked up his napkin and wiped his mouth.

"Oh, nothing serious; you know, just dinner chat."

Perry smiled at her, pushing one shoulder forward and leaning to the side. "He'd be a real catch—"

"No. He wouldn't. I'm not looking for a catch, real or not. Not after what happened with Seb. I'm off men…" She liked Max Rhodes. He was interesting to talk to and there was no denying he was handsome. But she'd been down that path before, and she didn't like where it had led. However, she couldn't deny she *had* felt a shiver of excitement talking to Brett Goodman. There was something about the self-assured American that made her want to—

"But you can't give up—" Perry cried.

Simon cut him off as he rested his hand on Perry's arm

and subtly shook his head. "If Bea's off men, then we need to support her, not try to persuade her otherwise."

Her cheeks grew hot. *Thank you, Simon, for the reminder. I'm off men!* Pushing all thoughts of the man with the sparkling brown eyes and white teeth out of her head, she nodded and took another sip of coffee.

"So is there anyone else interesting among the guests?" Simon asked, pushing his plate away and picking up his latte.

"Well, now you mention it, I overheard a rather strange conversation between Fergus McLean and his sister Rose." She told them what the siblings had said the night before on their way to dinner.

"So who were they talking about?" Perry asked, his eyes wide.

She shrugged. "No idea. I kept an eye on them both all evening, but I didn't see them giving anyone an evil look, and they didn't seem to avoid anyone in particular."

Simon absentmindedly stroked his well-trimmed beard. "But they definitely said 'he'?"

She nodded. "So it could be any of the men here. I didn't really get time to talk to Fergus properly last night, but I'll see what I can find out next time I get a chance."

Perry made a squeak-like sound that made Daisy jump up under the table and go to stand by his leg. He whispered, "What the—" as the butler appeared noiselessly beside them.

"Will you and your guests be requiring any more of the hot food, my lady, or can we clear the table?"

She looked at her friends, who both shook their head. "You can clear, Brock. We won't be much longer, anyway."

"Thank you, my lady. I'll leave the coffee pot and some pastries out for the moment just in case you or the gentlemen want to take any away with you." He looked pointedly at Simon before bowing his head, then signalled towards the door. William walked in pushing a large stainless-steel trolley and wheeled it up to the serving table, then the head footman and butler removed the bain-maries from the table and stacked them on the trolley.

Simon glanced at his watch. "Well, I can't put it off any longer. I need to write." He rose and picked up his coffee cup. "I'll just get a refill. See you both later."

"Have a good morning, love," Perry said, then turned to Bea. "Is it down to the dungeons for us today?"

They needed to select some pieces currently kept in storage in the basement for the Red Room Suite's sitting room. Perry kept referring to the giant storage area under the north wing as the dungeons. She grinned. *Maybe I'll take him to the* real *dungeons later today. That will give him a fright!*

8

LATE AFTERNOON, SATURDAY 9 JANUARY

Detective Chief Inspector Richard Fitzwilliam of the Protection and Investigation (Royal) Services stepped off the train at Drewcory in Banerdeenshire and immediately pulled the edges of his coat together with one hand as he grabbed his small wheeled suitcase with the other. *Blimey, it's cold.* Over the years, when the royal family had been at Drew Castle for their summer holidays, he'd been a frequent visitor. Though one year he'd had to oversee an investigation into the disappearance of The Queen Mother's dog during the winter (a feared kidnapping for ransom that had turned out to be a case of accidental poisoning that fortunately hadn't killed the little dog but had made him too poorly to move from the outhouse he'd crawled into). The biting wind had whipped around the estate as they had conducted their search. He was pleased that this time, it would be unlikely he would need to go far from a warm fire.

As he strolled out of the station, a stout blonde woman standing next to a messy 4x4 motioned to him from the car park across the way. He waved back and made his way towards her.

"Izzy!" As he reached her, he bent down and, hugging her, almost lifted her off her feet.

Laughing, she mumbled into his chest, "I'm so glad you're here, Rich."

He released her, and she steadied herself on the side of the vehicle, still smiling as he stepped back. "How's the patient?"

"Dreadful!" she replied, shaking her head and pressing a button on the set of keys in her hand. The boot sprung open.

His brow wrinkled. *Oh no, has something happened that Adler hasn't told me about?* His mouth was dry. If there was a problem, why hadn't she told him? "Is the leg not healing as it should? Is there an infection?" he asked as he slid his case into the back and flicked the button to close the tailgate.

Isabella McKeer-Adler reached out and patted his arm. "Oh no, sorry, Rich, it's nothing like that. In fact, the checkup she had before we left London was really positive. Physically, she's doing really well."

"Oh, I see," he said, moving around the car to the passenger's side. *Mental health issues then?* Not something he had a lot of experience with. Sure, he knew after traumatic events—

"She's being the biggest pain in the backside you can imagine!" Izzy told him as they got in.

Oh... Fitzwilliam's shoulders relaxed. He grabbed his seatbelt and secured it.

"Honestly, Rich, she just won't sit still and rest. I thought taking this cottage on the estate would give her a chance to breathe and relax. You know, away from work and the temptations of the city. But she's worse because now she wants to be outside and chop wood for the fire or pick flowers. Honestly, she's driving me crazy." She rested her hands on the steering wheel and slowly shook her head.

He smiled wryly. *So Adler is just being Adler.* He should have expected the hardworking, determined, and ambitious

Emma McKeer-Adler he'd known for fifteen years wouldn't take kindly to the limitations of a broken leg.

"I'm so sorry, Izzy," he said, turning to Adler's wife. "While I'm here these next few days, I'll do what I can to distract her so you can have a break."

Izzy heaved out a long breath. "Thank you. You're a life-saver and probably a marriage saver too."

"So how's the cottage?" he asked ten minutes later as they turned off the main road onto a small country lane. A light mist descended on them as Izzy drove down the middle of the deserted thoroughfare, thick hedgerows on either side broken occasionally by field entrances.

"It's great. The main bedroom is downstairs, so that's making life much easier for Em."

He nodded. He knew their three-storey townhouse in Clapham well, and even if Adler hadn't been bending his ear ever since the accident about how she'd kept getting stuck on the top floor and had to rely on Izzy to help her down, he could imagine a cottage with a downstairs bedroom must be giving her so much more independence than staying at home would have.

"And actually, the corridors are much wider than you would imagine for an estate cottage." She momentarily took her eyes off the road and turned to smile at him. "I can't tell you how grateful we are to you for arranging this, Rich. As much as I'm complaining about her wanting to do too much, she's much happier here than she was at the flat, and Hope has already been to visit twice in the last week."

"You're welcome, Izzy." It hadn't been a big deal for him to call up the royal estate manager to ask if there were cottages free on any of the estates for a senior PaIRS officer injured in the line of duty to go to recuperate. He'd just been lucky one had been available at Drew Castle, only thirty miles from Edinburgh, where Adler's daughter Hope had a research fellowship.

As they rounded the corner, Izzy slowed down as a precession of black Land Rovers with the Drew Castle logo on their side piled out of the gate ahead. The last vehicle, pulling a large metal trailer, left the field while a man wearing green rain gear and a flat cap waved from the gate, then jumped into the passenger side of the car as it picked up speed.

"That must be the shooting party done for the day," Izzy commented as she sped up and joined the back of the convoy. "According to the papers, Lord Frederick Astley is here with some guests, including Ben Rhodes. You know, the one who bought the London football club last year."

Fitzwilliam nodded. Even though he was on leave and his visit to Adler and Izzy was a private one, he'd checked before he'd left to find out who was staying up at the castle and on the estate. Call it professional curiosity. He wasn't planning on seeing them, of course. In fact, with Lady Beatrice working here at the moment, he had every intention of keeping his visit under wraps completely. The last thing he wanted was for her to find out he was close by.

When he'd last seen her in October, he'd inadvertently let slip that there had been a few inconsistencies around the investigation into her husband's fatal car accident fifteen years ago. Ever since then, he'd been worried she would dwell on it and maybe even convince herself there was more to it than there actually was. He'd been able to brush off her questions about what those inconsistencies had been and had hopefully convinced her to move on. But she was tenacious and curious — a tricky combination when you want someone to leave things alone. He couldn't blame her either. After all, she'd been the one who had found the new information pertinent to the investigation into her husband's death that had begged questions he hadn't been able to answer, and he hated loose ends. Even the unofficial digging Chief Superintendent Tim Street had been doing for him had come to nothing. He reluctantly acknowledged they had done all they could now, but even after fifteen years, it still left a nasty taste in his mouth.

"Rich?" Izzy's voice dragged him out of his musings. "Are you okay?"

"Yes, sorry. I was miles away." Having turned off the road, they were still following the precession of vehicles along a dirt track. "Where are we?" he asked.

"This is the back way into the estate and the quickest way to get to the cottage." She flicked the wipers on, the mist having left a wet film on the windscreen. She turned up the heating. "It's just as well you came today. They're predicting heavy snow tomorrow."

They slowed down as the vehicles in front came to a halt by a gate with a security office at the side.

"Do you have your ID handy?" Izzy asked, taking a pass out of the glove box in-between their seats. "I've told them about your visit, but if you have your PaIRS pass, then you won't need to fill in any forms."

"Sure," he said fishing out his ID card from his wallet.

As the gate opened, the group ahead went in one by one, slowly disappearing into the thick fog. Izzy stopped by the barrier and wound down her window.

"Hi, John," she shouted into the booth as she flashed her pass. "I have my guest, Richard Fitzwilliam. You should have him on your list."

A muffled voice replied.

She nodded. "Yes, he's a chief inspector with PaIRS. Do you want to see his ID?"

Fitzwilliam held it out to her, and she handed it over. A hand reached out from the booth and took it. They sat in silence for a few seconds, then a door on the side of the booth opened, and a man in a navy-blue uniform hurried out and crossed in front of the car, stopping by the passenger window. He held up his hand and made a sign for Fitzwilliam to open the window.

"DCI Fitzwilliam, welcome to the Drew Castle estate," the man said, handing Fitzwilliam's ID back to him. "Enjoy your stay, sir." He nodded, and before Fitzwilliam got the full, "Thank you" out, the man scurried back into his booth.

As Fitzwilliam closed the window, the barrier rose and Izzy moved forward slowly, waving at the security hut as they passed. Before them on their left, rose a dark shape obscured by the mist.

"That's the back of the castle," Izzy told him as she slowed down again and took another dirt lane off to their right. "We're about half a mile down here," she said, switching the wipers on again and speeding up, the fuzzy outline of the castle disappearing in the car's back window.

9

EARLY, SUNDAY 10 JANUARY

"Sis, I wasn't expecting to see you this morning." Lord Frederick Astley grabbed Lady Beatrice by the shoulders and kissed her on both cheeks. "Morning, Daisy," he bent down and patted the little terrier on the head.

"I have an early express delivery of bedding and linen due," she told him as she walked over to the table in the Breakfast Room and poured herself a large black coffee. She glanced over at the window, dismayed to see flecks of white fluttering in front of the external lights. "But now it's snowing, I think there's a real risk they won't make it."

"It was heavy overnight in Edinburgh. If they're coming from there, then I think you're out of luck." He picked up a small bunch of grapes from the fruit bowl and popped one into his mouth.

She looked down at her phone. No messages.

"Anyway, I must get on, Bea. We're out in forty minutes, and I need to check on the dogs."

She frowned as she walked towards the window where Daisy was already lying under a table and sat down. "You're going out in this?"

Fred shrugged, heading towards the door. "It'll be fine. It's only light snow. The heavy stuff isn't due until this evening," he said over his shoulder. "See you later."

She waved at him as he disappeared out of the room. There were muffled greetings from outside the open door, then two men entered.

Now which one of the Rhodes twins is he? She couldn't immediately tell, so she studied the other man as they both walked towards her. The same height as Ben or Max (*whichever it is*), his stocky build and short hair was in contrast to the slim curly-haired man beside him. She hadn't actually met Clive Tozzi yet but had seen him the previous evening. He was Ben Rhodes's security. *Ah, so this is Ben.* She smiled, pleased to have worked it out for herself.

Daisy scrabbled up when Bea rose to greet the men as they arrived at the table.

"Lady Beatrice, may we join you?" Ben Rhodes smiled, his brown eyes twinkling in the light.

She smiled back. "Yes, of course... Ben." He raised an eyebrow, but before he could say anything, she turned to the other man. "And you must be Mr Tozzi?" She held her hand out to the slightly tanned man.

"A pleasure to meet you, Lady Beatrice," he said, taking her hand and shaking it briefly.

"And this is Daisy." The little terrier sat and wagged her tail as both men greeted her. "Do help yourselves, gentlemen." Bea gestured towards the serving table along the wall. "There's hot food in the covered containers and tea and coffee at the end closest to us." She sat down again and picked up her coffee as the two men made their breakfast selections.

Ben Rhodes was the first to return to the table, carrying a small plate with some ham, a couple of slices of cheese, a boiled egg, and an apple on it. He sat down opposite her and put down his plate. "Are you joining us today, Lady Beatrice?"

She shook her head. "Please, call me Beatrice, and no, I'm not. Is it pathetic of me that I'd rather stay indoors where it's warm and dry rather than stand around in the snow and mud?"

He grinned. "No, not at all." He took a mouthful of egg, then looked down at an ever hopeful Daisy sitting by his feet. "Your dog is very sweet. Can she have some of my ham?"

Bea tilted her head to one side. It was nice of him to ask. "She's on a diet, so she really shouldn't…"

"But how can I resist those eyes?" His brown eyes glinted in the daylight just peeping through the snowy landscape.

Their gazes met. Heat rose up her neck. *How indeed…*

"This looks great." Clive Tozzi dropped his plate onto the table. "I've never had haggis before, so I thought I'd give it a go."

Ben continued to smile at her. *There really must be something in the water here.* She smiled back, then cleared her throat. "She can have a small piece."

"So will you be able to shoot in this weather?" Clive asked Ben.

"As long as it doesn't get too heavy, we should be okay, according to Lord Fred." Ben straightened up from feeding Daisy.

"Did you have a successful day yesterday, Ben?" Bea had had dinner with Perry and Simon the night before at their cottage, so she'd not caught up with any of the guests after yesterday's shoot.

"I'll be honest, Beatrice, I'm not much of a shot. Max is much more accomplished in that area than I am. I don't think

I have the killer instinct." He smiled again, his white teeth standing out against his tanned face.

But you *do* have a killer smile... *Stop that, Bea! Remember what happened the last time you fell for a pair of sparkling eyes and a dreamy smile?* Ignoring Ben Rhodes's enticing look, she shifted her attention to Clive. "Do you shoot, Mr Tozzi?"

"Not for pleasure, my lady," he replied through a mouthful of food. "A bit of a busman's holiday for me if—"

"Gents!" Fred's head appeared around the door. "We're leaving in two minutes."

"Blast!" Clive shovelled an enormous scoop of food into his mouth, dropped his fork, and picked up two pieces of toast. "That was really tasty," he mumbled, standing up.

Ben rose too, grabbing the uneaten apple from his plate. "Sorry we have to dash, my lady." He bent down. "And, Daisy, it was a pleasure." Daisy wagged her tail furiously.

Bea stood. "Well, have a good day out there. I hope the snow holds off." They both nodded and headed for the door. As she watched them leave, Ben Rhodes stopped in the doorway, twisted his head towards her, and smiled before giving her a wave and was gone.

She let out a sigh of relief. *What's wrong with me? I swear off men, and within a few weeks, I'm flirting with three men in as many days. Although does it only count as one men when two of them look the same?* She hadn't talked to Brett Goodman since the night of the dinner party, but she'd glimpsed him walking down the corridor into the library when she'd returned home last night. It had taken a lot of willpower not to follow him and say hello. She'd found the American strangely intriguing and had been so tempted... but she'd pulled herself together and had headed up the stairs to her rooms instead. And now Ben Rhodes. She picked up her coffee. *Just as well my determination to avoid charming men is still strong...*

————

Peeking out of the window of the Blue Bedroom Suite sitting room, Lady Beatrice gasped. Enormous flakes of snow streamed out of the light-grey sky, blanketing everything in a thick layer of white. *When did that start?*

"What is it?" Perry Juke rushed over, pausing when he too caught sight of the heavy snow. "But it was hardly snowing at all when I last looked," he cried in excitement.

"I know!" A wide grin spread over her face. *What is it about snow that makes me feel like a child again?* Bea continued to stare out of the window, fascinated by the speed the snow was drowning out the details of the landscape and replacing it with large blobs of white in varying sizes.

She sighed, the childish elation she'd felt a few minutes ago replaced by the adult reality of the impact it would have on them now that it looked like they would get snowed in. For a start, she needed to make sure someone was implementing the estate's snow plan.

Is Fred back yet? She moved to the door. "Sorry, Perry, but I must check what's going on. We have a plan for when the snow gets bad, but with Fred and the others possibly still out — or hopefully on their way back, I need to make sure Brock and Mrs Kettley have it all under control. We'll also need to get Grandmama and her staff up here before the snow gets so bad we can't reach them."

"Oh my giddy aunt, that sounds serious. Can I help?" Perry said, following her out of the door.

"We get cut off here when we have heavy snowfall, so we

move staff and anyone staying on the estate to the main house if they're too far away to walk or ski." They hurried down the corridor and entered the foyer at the top of the stairs. "I know your cottage is close, but if you want to get some clothes and come back to stay here for the next few days, then you're more than welcome."

Perry rubbed his chin, then shrugged. "I'll see what Simon says, but I expect he'll want to continue writing, and if the castle is full of extra people, then he might prefer to be at the cottage."

Bea laughed as they descended the stairs. "We have six hundred and fifty rooms here, so I don't think it will be too crowded. But I get it. If you want to stay at the cottage, then I suggest you and Simon go back now before it gets much worse. Go via the kitchens and make sure you have enough food for the rest of the day. If you change your mind, then there are heavy coats, boots, snowshoes, and skis at the cottage. You can grab your things and come back. Just let me know."

Perry nodded as they reached the bottom. "Okay, I'll find Simon and see what he says. I'll text you." As he turned right, towards the office Simon was working in, Bea turned left, heading towards the basement, where the senior staffs' offices were.

As she opened the door to access the stairs to the basement, footsteps made her halt and wait. A few seconds later, a curly-haired head appeared.

"Ah, Mrs Kettley, just the person," Bea called down.

The head housekeeper looked up. "My lady, I was just coming to find you."

Bea held the door open as Mrs Kettley reached the top and emerged into the panelled hallway.

"I've just called Foxhall, my lady, and requested they

prepare to move here as soon as possible. Brock is organising some of the gardeners to clear a path for them to use. That should be sufficient if they use the snow tracks on the vehicles. If not, we'll send the tractors and trailers up. It seems to have eased up a bit, but the forecast is for more to come later today."

Bea nodded. As she suspected, the staff had it all in hand.

"I've got the maids making up The Queen Mother's suite and the staff bedrooms ready for their arrival. I suggested to Mrs Wilton she and her husband move up here too." She tilted her head to one side. "What about Mr Juke and his friend? Do you want me to make up a room for them?"

"I'm waiting to hear what they want to do, so can I let you know?"

Mrs Kettley nodded. "Of course, my lady."

"I also think we need to be prepared in case Lord Fred's guests won't be able to leave tomorrow morning as planned. Does Mrs Wilton have plenty of food if they need to stay a few more days?"

"Yes, she has a well-stocked pantry, plenty of fruit and veg in the cold store, and duck, goose, pheasant, and venison that was shot over Christmas and the New Year in the freezer."

They were lucky the Drew Castle estate was so self-sufficient. "Do you know if the shooting party is back yet?"

The head housekeeper shook her head. "Owen radioed Brock to tell him Lord Fred had abandoned the shoot, and they're putting the snow tracks on to get everyone back quickly. I'm expecting them any time. I've warned Mrs Wilton they'll be wanting lunch here now, so there will be sandwiches and soup in the Breakfast Room, time to be confirmed depending on when they get back."

"Perfect, Mrs Kettley; you're a star. I'll ring Grandmama now and chivvy her along."

"Thank you, my lady. The sooner we can get them here, the better."

10

11:30 AM, SUNDAY 10 JANUARY

"Are you sure you have everything you need, Grandmama?" Lady Beatrice asked as she and her brother stood in the sitting room of their grandmother's suite while The Queen Mother placed a picture of her late husband on the side table by the sofa looking out onto a snow-covered vista.

"Yes, yes. I'm fine. Now, are you two going to sit down and keep an old lady company while I wait for my lunch to be brought up?" She lowered herself onto the edge of an upright armchair and, grasping her hands together, rested them on her lap. "Daisy!" she commanded, and the little terrier trotted over from Bea's side and sat down at Queen Mary's feet.

How does she do that?

Bea glanced over to Lord Frederick.

"We need to be downstairs in the Drawing Room at twelve-thirty for pre-lunch drinks, but yes, we have until then," he said as he sat on one side of the dark-green three-seater sofa opposite her.

Conscious of her grandmother's scrutiny, Bea perched on the edge of the other side of the sofa, bringing her knees together and placing her hands lightly on them. Acclaimed as one of the most beautiful girls in that year's 'crop', Queen Mary The Queen Mother had made her debut in 1956. She was therefore a stickler for etiquette and appropriate behaviour, and she expected her grandchildren to act with decorum. "I don't care how casual things have become outside of this family. You are members of the royal family, and you must behave as such," was her frequently repeated saying when she observed the younger generation not following strict royal practices. She had a pet peeve of what she described as "young ladies sitting with their legs akimbo like they're about to give birth", and both Bea and her sister Sarah had frequently been at the end of her sharp tongue when they'd been younger and had failed to meet their grandmother's exacting standards of what she considered suitable behaviour for young ladies.

"So, Fred, how's the shooting been?" her grandmother asked.

Bea sat still, throwing daggers at Daisy, who was resting her head on crossed paws as if butter wouldn't melt in her mouth (*I bet she thinks she's a princess now*) while Queen Mary and Fred discussed yesterday's sport. Rotating her head slowly ("A lady never does anything quickly, Beatrice."), she took in the view from the imposing bay windows and smiled when she recalled a few years ago when she'd been here for the New Year with Sam, her sister Sarah, Sarah's husband John, and their two children Robbie and Charlotte. They'd been snowed in, much like today, and John, with the help of the head footman William, had repaired two old sledges that had been rotting in the basement. They'd taken them out onto the front lawn where it had a natural camber, and the children had taken it in turns sledging down the slopes, squealing with laughter. Wet and flushed, they'd been dragged away two hours later to enjoy

Mrs Wilton's homemade hot chocolate topped with marsh-mallows before having showers and getting into their pyjamas before tea, something unheard of in normal circumstances at Drew Castle. The snow had allowed an informality normal weather didn't. She suppressed a giggle as her mind was flooded with thoughts of Fred's guests in their nightwear sitting in front of a roaring fire, eating venison stew and mashed potatoes on their laps. *Not on Grandmama's watch, that's for sure!*

Hearing the name Brett, she zoned back into the conversation just as her brother said his colleague had bagged the most birds yesterday. "Max Rhodes came in a close second with Fergus McLean not far behind."

"And how is Fergus?" The Queen Mother asked, taking a sip of water from a glass resting on the table beside her. *Why does she want to know about Hector's son?*

"He seems fine. He's working hard running the family business and enjoying the role of man about town in London, it seems."

"He's a friend of Caroline's, isn't he?" Queen Mary's eyes focused on Bea.

"Yes. I've seen him at a couple of dinners at Kensington Court." Bea's cousin Lady Caroline Clifford was famous in London for her dinner parties. Invitations were much sought after.

"And is he courting anyone?"

"I really don't know, Grandmama."

"Hector was vague about it, but of course, I have heard rumours…" She trailed off and took another sip of water.

Rumours about Fergus? Surely she doesn't mean with him and Caroline? His taste ran in the opposite direction, didn't it?

There was a knock on the door.

"Come," shouted Bea's grandmother, and they all stood as her butler entered.

"Your lunch is ready in the Small Drawing Room, ma'am."

"Thank you, Paul." The Queen Mother turned to her grandchildren. "Well, it's been nice to chat with you both. Don't worry about me; I'll be fine. After lunch I'm going to settle in and watch *Fiddler on the Roof*. I've wanted to watch it again for ages, and Paul has kindly found it on one of those satellite channels for me. So go off and enjoy your drinks. I will see you both later."

Fred nodded.

"Thank you, Grandmama." Bea gestured to her little dog sitting patiently by her grandmother's side. "Daisy, come on—"

"Do you mind if I keep her here with me, Beatrice? It's probably not a good idea to take her into lunch with you, anyway. Not with all those people. She'll be much better here with me." She had a steely look in her eye that meant she wouldn't broker a disagreement.

Bea looked at Daisy, who hadn't moved despite of her earlier instruction. *If dogs could look smug...* A nagging suspicion tugged at her. "Yes, but please remember not to feed her any of your food. She's getting podgy, so she's on a strict diet."

Queen Mary looked down at the little white dog. "Nonsense, she's not podgy. West Highland Terriers are a sturdy breed, that's all."

Bea stifled a sigh. Remembering how 'sturdy' her grandmother's recently departed Chug had been, she feared she was fighting a losing battle. *No wonder Daisy is glued to her side.*

"Come on, Bea; it's gone twenty past twelve, and we need

to greet our guests," Fred said over his shoulder as he headed for the door.

"All right. I'll come and get her later, Grandmama," she said as she followed him.

"Thank you, darling." Her grandmother's words followed her as she left the room.

———

Entering the Drawing Room five minutes later, Bea was surprised to see the room full already. Maybe after such a busy morning, they were all keen for lunch.

The head footman approached. "Lady Beatrice, your lordship, can I get you a drink?"

"A whisky for me, please, William. Bea?"

"Just a sparkling water, please, William."

William gave a brief nod and moved over to the drinks bar set up in the corner.

Bea scanned the room. The McLeans stood together, Rose with her arm through her husband's as she spoke to her father and brother. *I must try to catch Fergus on his own over lunch and see if I can find out who it is he and Rose are so upset to see here.*

Further along by the giant marble fireplace, Clive Tozzi stood, his arms behind his back, staring into space while beside him, Ben Rhodes (she assumed it was him as he was with Clive) rapidly scrolled on his phone. As she moved to join him, Fred strolled in front of her and made his way across the room, beating her to it. Carrying on, her gaze fell on Brett and Eve, who were both looking at something on his phone. *Should I join them?* At that moment, Brett looked up and caught her eye. Her stomach gave a wobble, and she looked away. *No, I best not.* She ambled across the room to the McLeans. "I hope you've all warmed up after this morning's adventures?"

"Ah, Lady Beatrice. Yes, thank you. The estate team were quick to get the snow tracks on the vehicles, and it didn't really feel like we had to wait long at all," Hector replied.

William appeared at her shoulder and whispered, "Your drink, my lady." He held the silver tray out in front of her, and she took the glass of water. "Thanks," she whispered back.

"Yes," chipped in Ed, Rose McLean's husband. "It was well organised, much like the rest of the shoot has been."

"Well, I'm glad to hear it. I'm just sorry the bad weather cut it short." She rotated her head and glanced out of the window. It was snowing heavily again, all the track marks and cleared paths now covered once more in a blanket of white. Just as well they'd got everyone here safely. She thought of Perry and Simon at the cottage, hoping they were warm enough and had everything they needed. She'd been disappointed when Perry had texted to say they were going to stay put. Now she would have to navigate lunch and no doubt coffee afterwards without them or Daisy to save her from flirty men and her own weakening willpower to avoid them.

Rose was telling them she'd been out just before they'd got back and had taken some great photos of the snowy landscape when Ben Rhodes walked past her and left the room, followed a few seconds later by Clive Tozzi. *Are they off to lunch already?* But Brock hadn't sounded the gong. She twisted around to look for Fred. He was standing alone by the fireplace, so she excused herself and hurried over to him. "Are we lunching already?"

He shook his head. "No, I want to wait until we have everyone. Max and Clive have just gone to chivvy Ben along."

She rubbed her forehead. "So that was Max, not Ben?"

Fred shook his head, an amused smile on his face. "Ben told Clive he'd see him down here at twelve-thirty for drinks."

"Isn't the point of having a bodyguard is that they stay with you?"

Fred shrugged. "I don't think Ben feels threatened here. In fact, he told me when we were out this morning, he didn't think he'd really needed to bring Clive, but his wife and Max had insisted."

At that moment, Brock appeared in front of them. "Excuse me, my lord, but Mr Rhodes has asked if he could have a quick word with you in the hall."

Fred frowned, then put down his drink. Bea's stomach churned. The look on the butler's face told her something was wrong. She hurriedly placed her drink on a side table, and they followed Brock out of the room.

"Max, what is it?" Fred asked as they approached the man pacing the tiled floor at the bottom of the staircase. He was pale underneath his tanned skin and sweating, as if he'd been running. Just behind him at the bottom of the stairs, a stunned-looking Clive Tozzi was not moving.

Max turned wild eyes on them. "It's Ben. He's dead."

11

12:45 PM, SUNDAY 10 JANUARY

Coldness hit Lady Beatrice's core as she stared hopelessly from her brother to the shaking man before them.

"Dead?" Lord Frederick Astley ran his hands through his short brown hair. "What happened?"

Wringing his hands, Max Rhodes blurted out, "He's in the bath. It looks like he drowned."

She followed his gaze up the stairs, then pivoted around to find Brock, the butler, standing discreetly to the side. "Brock, please take Mr Rhodes and Mr Tozzi into the Blue Salon and get them a drink. Then call security and tell them to call the police. My brother and I will go up and take a look. Please make sure everyone stays where they are down here until we come back."

"Yes, my lady." Leaving him to gather the two men and lead them away, she grabbed her brother's arm. "Let's go," she said, dragging him towards the bottom of the stairs.

Had it been an accident? *Can you accidentally drown in a bath? Oh no, please don't let this be murder. I've had more than enough of murder to last me a lifetime.* They bounded up the stairs, then paused as they arrived on the first floor landing.

"Where's Ben's room?" Fred asked.

She closed her eyes, trying to remember which side Mrs Kettley had allocated the Rhodes brothers' rooms. "West wing," she said, branching left and running ahead. She yanked open a wooden door inset with frosted glass at the end on the right, and the lights came on as they entered the corridor. "I don't know which side," she told Fred. "I'll take the left." She hastened down the green carpeted hallway, checking the typed cards inserted into brass nameplates on each guest-room door.

"Found it!" Fred shouted, a little ahead of her on the right. She took a deep breath as she joined him by the door. *Come on, Bea; you're used to seeing dead bodies these days*. Fred looked at her, and she gave him a quick nod. Where was Perry when she needed him? They normally discovered bodies together. *Normally?* What was she thinking? *I must be in shock. There's nothing normal about finding a dead body.* She took her phone from the pocket of her wide-legged black trousers and slowly followed Fred into the room.

The bedroom was dimly lit, illuminated only by a floor lamp hidden behind a glass coffee table with two leather tub chairs facing each other on either side of it, as well as by a small lamp on the nearside bedside table. However, a bright light shone from the open door in the right-hand corner. She edged her way past a table containing a half-full decanter and an empty glass. She followed Fred around the end of the bed as they crept nervously towards the bathroom. Her legs were wobbly as they drew closer to the door. She wanted to flee, but after a glance at Fred's pale face, she gave him a reassuring smile, then hurried past him as she braced herself.

The bathroom was an L-shape. *These must be the rooms*

that were reconfigured a few years ago, she thought as she slipped into the room. Ahead of her, she caught her pale face reflected in the mirror on the wall above a large white double vanity unit. The bath was tucked just around the corner on the right. All she could see was the end with the taps and the shower head suspended above it. Two knees poked out from the water. Looking down there was a puddle on the floor around the end of the bath. A shudder ran down her spine that almost took her breath away. *Pull yourself together, Bea; he's dead. He can't hurt you.* So why did she have a feeling that, like a bad horror movie, he was suddenly going to spring up out of the water, his arms in front of him like a wet zombie? She took a deep breath. *You're spending too much time watching Sam play on his apocalyptic games.* Finally, she peered around the corner; there wasn't much to see. Ben's upper body was fully submerged in the bath, his outline clearly visible underwater, and there were further patches of water on the floor surrounding the bathtub.

Fred's head poked around the wall, and he gasped. She pivoted around to face him. "There's no question he's dead. There's nothing we can do. We need to leave everything as it is and wait for the police." Fred nodded. "And be careful not to touch anything as you leave."

Her brother reversed out of the space, and she turned to follow him, looking down at the tiled floor to make sure she didn't tread in any of the water that had been displaced. *Can they work out anything from the volume of water on the floor?* Suddenly, her eye caught something black just visible from under the bath. She bent down, careful not to touch the bath or the wall. It was a mobile phone. It must have slipped out of Ben's hand while he'd been in the bath. She straightened up, then hesitated. *What would Perry do?* She looked down at the phone in her hand. Perry would take pictures. She raised her phone and tapped the camera app…

———

"What were you doing?" Fred asked, scanning the corridor outside Ben's bedroom as they heard voices coming from just outside the hallway door.

"Nothing," Bea answered, slipping her phone into her trouser pocket. "Are you okay?"

Fred nodded, giving her a grim smile. "You?"

She let out a sigh. "I feel numb. I guess it's the shock. It's so sad. And of course dreadful for his family. But also scary."

He frowned. "Why scary?"

"Because this wasn't an accident, Fred. Someone here at the castle is a murderer…"

12

MID-AFTERNOON, SUNDAY 10 JANUARY

"So what's happening now?" Perry asked, his voice tinged with excitement.

Lady Beatrice moved the phone to her other ear and wandered over to the large bay window in the sitting room of her apartment. "There was a uniformed police officer at the estate's security booth doing a routine check, so he was brought up by the head of security, and together they secured the scene. Fred has been on the phone to PaIRS, but because of the snow, they can't get anyone from there or CID to us right now. That's as much as I know."

On the plus side, if no one from PaIRS could get here, then there was no risk of her having to see Detective Chief Inspector Richard Fitzwilliam. She really couldn't face him again so soon after the last case.

"Are you okay?" Perry said, concern lacing his voice.

"I suppose so, although I'll feel much better when you and Simon get here." If she squinted, she could just about see the snowy outline of a row of cottages in the distance on the left. *How long will it take them to get from there to here?*

"Simon's just getting changed, then we'll get into those

ugly snow suits we found in the boot room and make our way over."

She smiled. *I must go down and get a picture of Perry when he arrives.* "Just be careful; it's still snowing hard."

"I know. It's crazy, isn't it? I've never seen snow this thick before. It's like it's being poured out of the sky from some huge bucket. I found some spiky overshoe things that fit onto the boots we have here, so I'm hoping they'll help."

"There should be some poles there too."

"Oh my giddy aunt, I'll look like Sir Edmund Hillary getting ready to climb Mount Everest."

She laughed. "Don't worry; it's all flat. Don't even try to find the path; just make a beeline for the house."

"Will do. So how's everyone there taking it?"

"Most of them don't know yet. We arranged for them to have lunch as planned, and as far as I know, they're still there." She glanced at her watch. But not for much longer. She'd best go down soon. "I'm not sure if we should keep them all together or suggest they go to their rooms."

"Simon will know."

"Fred has gone to tell Grandmama. She has her maid and butler with her, so she'll be fine. The maids have been told not to touch anyone's rooms yet. I wonder if the bedrooms will need to be searched or something. But maybe you need a warrant for that?" She really had no idea what the procedure was. "And Max and Clive are still in the Blue Salon. Brock is keeping an eye on them. I'm not sure what else we should be doing. Oh, did you show Simon the photos I sent?"

"I tried, but he said he'd look later when we're there. I think he just wants to get to you as soon as possible."

Bea let out a deep sigh. Thank goodness her best friends would be here soon. With no one from CID or PaIRS likely to get to them today, maybe not even for a few days, she would feel safer with them here with her, especially with Simon's experience as an ex-CID police officer. After all, there was no getting away from the fact they were snowed in with a killer among them.

"Right, he's ready, so we're going to get kitted out, then we'll leave. We'll see you soon."

"Indeed. I'll see you soon. Please be careful."

She cut the call and stared out the window. *How long before I'll be able to see them?* Her phone vibrated in her hand.

Fred: *QM is fine. On my way down to see what our guests are up to. I have Daisy with me. Where are you? x*

It was no good. She couldn't hide in her room any longer. They would have to deal with the situation until someone in authority arrived.

Bea: *On my way down now x*

————

Daisy ran up the last few stairs to greet Lady Beatrice. She bent down to scoop up the little terrier. "Hello, Daisy-doo," she said, giving her a kiss on the head. Was it her imagination, or did Daisy feel heavier? Spotting Fred talking to Brock just by the closed door to the Blue Saloon, Bea skipped down the final few stairs and made her way over to them.

"Everything okay?" she asked as she put Daisy on the floor.

"Yes. Max is now in the library making some calls, and Clive has joined the others for coffee and tea in the Drawing Room," Fred replied.

Brock cleared his throat. "If you'll excuse me, sir. I'll check they have everything they need."

"Yes, thank you, Brock."

After watching the butler disappear down the corridor, she whispered, "Do they know yet?"

Fred shook his head. "Not unless Clive told them, and I don't think he would have."

"Well, Simon and Perry are on their way. Simon will know what to do."

"Oh, I have news on that front. I had a message from PaIRS to say they've found someone who is close by and can get to us in the next hour or so. They'll be able to take charge."

"Local CID?"

"I don't know. They didn't say, but I guess so. It's unlikely they'd have someone from PaIRS in the area."

Bea's muscles tensed. *Knowing my luck, Fitzwilliam is on holiday just around the corner!* Then she checked herself. *Even I'm not that unlucky...* "That's great news. Why don't we—"

The main doorbell clanged. Could that be Perry and Simon already? She'd expected it to take them longer. *Rats! I'll be too late to take a photo of them before they start to take all their gear off.* Brock appeared from nowhere, and she rushed forward, beating him to the glass door leading to the small foyer in front of the main door. She took her phone out of her pocket as she turned the handle and then threw open the heavy wooden door. She jumped back in surprise. Standing in the stone portico was a yeti.

The tall man (she assumed it was a man) was wearing a

navy-blue woollen balaclava topped with a Davy Crockett fur hat and ski goggles. A massive fur coat hung from his body, and his ski boots and skis peeked out from underneath it. *It has to be Perry.* Grinning, she raised her phone and took a couple of photos.

There was a muffled sound as a woollen-mitten hand rose up and peeled the balaclava away from his mouth, revealing the lower part of his face.

It wasn't Perry. *Oh, no. No. This isn't possible.* Daisy gave a bark of excitement and ran to greet the man, who was now pushing the woollen mask up over his eyes.

As he freed himself from his face covering, Detective Chief Inspector Richard Fitzwilliam took in a deep breath. "Lady Beatrice, I wasn't expecting to see you again so soon."

13

A FEW MINUTES LATER, SUNDAY 10 JANUARY

Stunned, Lady Beatrice stared at the man before her as he bent down to say hello to Daisy, who was jumping up at him. Brock manoeuvred around her and approached DCI Fitzwilliam. "May I help you with those, sir?" he asked, holding out this hand to take the ski poles from Fitzwilliam.

What on earth is he doing here? He caught her eye, and she looked down at the stone floor. *Of all the people who could have been close by, why him?* She cursed whatever it was that made the one thing you didn't want to happen, happen.

Fred appeared at her side and nudged her. "Is that who I think it is under there?" he whispered in her ear. She nodded as her brother gave a low chuckle.

"Thank you," Fitzwilliam said, handing over the poles. He bent down to unclip the skis from his boots, fending off Daisy's pink tongue as it tried to make contact with his face.

"Daisy," Bea barked. "Come here and let the poor man undress." Daisy stopped and ran back to her mistress. *Did I just say undress?* She stifled a groan.

Propping up the skis on the side of the portico, he pulled

off his mittens, then the balaclava and hat and handed them to the butler. He rubbed his hand over his forehead, then through his short brown hair. "Phew, it was getting hot in there," he said, lowering his arm.

Fred moved forward, holding out his hand. "Detective Chief Inspector Fitzwilliam, this is an unexpected pleasure. I assume you're here in an official capacity?"

Unbuttoning his coat with one hand, Fitzwilliam took Fred's in his other and shook it. "As luck would have it, I was on the estate visiting a friend. They tracked me down, and here I am."

A friend on the estate? Did he know someone who worked here? She racked her brain, thinking of the staff who lived in the cottages but couldn't for the life of her think who that could be. Maybe it was someone who had retired here or was ill. Long-serving ex-staff or those who had been injured during their employment sometimes received accommodation on one of the royal family's estates. *But who?*

"Well," said Fred, holding out his arm to lead Fitzwilliam inside. "That's lucky for us." He looked at his sister and winked. "Please come inside, chief inspector, and warm up." Fitzwilliam, who had now undone his ski boots, slipped them off and followed Fred into the foyer.

Daisy leapt forward and trotted after them, leaving Bea remaining where she was, looking out into the snowy landscape. *Help!* Where were Perry and Simon when she needed them? Her phone vibrated in her hand.

Perry: *Sorry, we had to go back. These spiky things are no good. We kept sinking in the snow. Simon says there are some skis we can use. That should be fun! xx*

. . .

Bea: *Hurry! You'll never guess who just turned up xx*

Perry: *Tell me. Tell me! xx*

Bea: *No. Get skiing and come and find out for yourself xx*

———

"They've gone to the Rose Parlour, my lady," the butler, his arms full of fur, said as she entered the hall.

"Thank you, Brock. Can you organise some coffee to be brought in, please?" She swept through the atrium and turned right.

Right, Bea, pull yourself together. You may not want him here, but at least there's now someone to take charge of the investigation. She passed the door leading down to the basement on her left. After the last investigation they'd both been involved in, she'd speculated about what it would be like if they ever worked together rather than against each other. *Well, this is a good time to find out.* She would not rise to his boorish comments, and she wouldn't start investigating by herself just to prove him wrong. She would listen and help. *I can do that.* So, resolved, she hurried into the open door on her right.

"Fitzwilliam," she said as she strolled into the room. "Sorry. It took me by surprise to see you, but we're glad you're here." *That sounded welcoming, didn't it?*

Fitzwilliam, who was perched on the edge of a large mustard-coloured Chesterfield sofa, stroked Daisy, who was lying on the couch, her head resting on his thigh. "Thank you, my lady. I was just saying to your brother, I have limited resources while we're snowed in, so I would appreciate your help."

He wants my help? Now that's a step forward. He'd never asked for her help before even though she'd been very helpful when it had come to solving previous crimes.

"I don't suppose I'm lucky enough that Simon Lattimore is staying here, am I?"

Her stomach dropped. *So he wants Simon, not me. Of course he does, you dingbat! Simon's ex-CID.*

"He's staying on the estate," Fred informed him. "And he's due over soon, isn't he, sis?"

Bea pouted. "He and Perry will be here later."

Fine, well, he can wait for Simon's 'expertise', and I will study the photos I took earlier and—

"Good. So, Lady Beatrice, will you show me the crime scene, please? And, Lord Fred, if you could find me a room I can use as an office and a separate room to interview your guests and staff, that would be great."

Bea's heart skipped a beat. *So he* does *want my help…*

"Yes, of course, chief inspector. I'm on it." Fred headed towards the door. "Come on, Daisy; you're with me." Daisy jumped down and followed Fred out while Fitzwilliam rose and moved to where Bea was standing.

"Shall we?" He held his arm out towards the door.

"Indeed," she said as they walked out of the room.

———

Ascending the stone staircase, Lady Beatrice and Fitzwilliam bumped into Mrs Kettley, who was carrying a stack of linen.

"Ah, Mrs Kettley, this is Detective Chief Inspector

Richard Fitzwilliam. He's here to investigate Mr Rhodes's death." The head housekeeper nodded at Fitzwilliam. "Fitzwilliam, this is Mrs Kettley, the head housekeeper."

"Mrs Kettley." Fitzwilliam nodded.

"Do you have any idea when we'll be able to get into the guest rooms, my lady? Most of them had baths or showers when they returned after this morning's shoot, and there will be wet towels to be changed," the housekeeper said.

"We stopped the maids cleaning the guest rooms as soon as we found the body just in case you needed to see them as they are," Bea explained to Fitzwilliam. *Have I done the right thing?* His face was expressionless.

"Apart from the bedroom of the deceased, which is now a crime scene, you can carry on as normal, Mrs Kettley," he told her.

Bea twisted the rings on her right hand. *Rats! I did the wrong thing.*

"Thank you. And will you be staying overnight while you're here, Chief Inspector?"

Blast! I didn't think of that either.

"If it's not too much trouble, Mrs Kettley. It took me an hour to get here in the snow, most of which was spent getting all the right clothes and equipment on. I don't fancy going through that palaver again today if I can help it." He gave her a warm smile.

He can be quite charming when he wants to…

Mrs Kettley smiled back. "Of course, it's no trouble at all. I'll get a room sorted for you now. And will Mr Juke be coming back here now, my lady? It's got much worse since he left. He really would be much better off here." She blushed. "I mean, both him and Mr Lattimore would be."

"Oh, yes, sorry. I haven't told you yet, but they're on their way now, so we'll need a room for them too, please."

"Of course, my lady." She swivelled around and hurried back up the stairs.

Looking ahead, Bea followed her slowly up.

"Lady Beatrice," Fitzwilliam said, walking beside her. "That was a good idea not to disturb the rooms until we got here." He sighed. "Unfortunately, with things the way they are these days, it wouldn't be appropriate for us to search people's rooms without their permission. Also, from a purely practical point of view, I don't have sufficient resources to conduct a search even if I wanted to. But thank you anyway."

"Indeed," she said, a warmth slowly spreading through her body as she continued up the stairs.

"So do we know when Ben Rhodes was last seen?" he asked as they reached the first floor landing area.

Bea shook her head. "Not exactly. The shooting party got back about eleven. The snow had got really heavy just before then, so I'd sent Perry and Simon back to their cottage before it got any worse. I was busy organising getting my grandmother and her staff here from Foxhall."

"Yes, I understand The Queen Mother is here. When did she arrive?"

"About the same time as the shooting party. It was chaos for about fifteen minutes while we got everyone in. Her staff took Grandmama up to her suite and settled her there, and most of the guests went to their rooms to get changed. They were due to reconvene in the Drawing Room at twelve-thirty for pre-lunch drinks. My grandmother remained in her apartment and had lunch taken up. Fred and I went to check she was all right just before we came down for drinks."

Fitzwilliam opened the door leading to the west wing bedrooms and waited for her to go ahead of him. "And they found him about twelve forty-five, is that right?"

She nodded. "His brother Max and his bodyguard Clive Tozzi went to find him when he didn't turn up for drinks."

Further along the corridor on the right, a uniformed police officer sat on a wooden chair, looking at his mobile phone.

"Is there still CCTV within the house?"

"Yes. The inside of all the entrances and the main foyer and hall."

"Good. If I remember correctly, it also shows the lower half of the main staircase. That should be helpful."

Of course! Why didn't I think of that? They could see what time Ben had gone up to his room. The royal residences had a more thorough CCTV surveillance system than they had at home in Francis Court. Her father didn't like "being spied on in my own house", as he put it, so there, it was restricted to the entrances to the estate only. But the need to protect the monarch and his family was of national importance, so coverage was wider ranging at the castle. It would be a tremendous help in establishing the guests' movements today.

The constable jumped up as they approached. "Sir. My lady." He handed Fitzwilliam gloves, tongs, and evidence bags.

"Thank you, constable." Fitzwilliam put on the gloves and stuffed the tongs and bags in the back pocket of his dark-grey jeans.

Bea hesitated. *Does he want me to wait outside now I've brought him to the crime scene?* She caught his eye and raised an eyebrow.

"Come on, Lady Beatrice. Don't be shy. I'm sure you've already been in to have a good look anyway." He smirked and opened the door.

Busted! Heat rose up her neck as she took the nitrate

gloves offered to her by the constable, and thrusting her hands into them, she followed Fitzwilliam in.

The room was exactly as it had been earlier. The light from the bathroom shone out like a beacon of doom. Fitzwilliam veered around the end of the bed and made a beeline for the bathroom.

Entering the brightly lit room, Bea glanced over at the mirror dominating the wall opposite. *At least I don't look so washed out this time.* She tucked a thick strand of long red hair behind her ear and inched towards Fitzwilliam's back. There wasn't enough room for two people in the space occupied by the bath, so she poked her head around the edge of the wall. Fitzwilliam was peering into the water, mumbling into his phone.

Is he talking to someone? If so, it appeared to be a one-way conversation.

"There's a phone on the floor just under the bath," she pointed out when he stopped talking and straightened up. He bent down and looked closely at the black phone lying in a puddle of water. Again, he said something into his mobile, then careful not to touch anything else, he picked the wet phone up with the tongs and slid it into an evidence bag.

"Can you keep hold of this for me?" he said, handing it to her.

Her mouth fell open slightly as she took it from him. She peered at the phone through the bag, then holding it up, she pulled it closer to her eyeline. The screen was off. She gently tapped it with her gloved finger, and it came to life, displaying the date and time over a photo of Ben in the middle of a bunch of football players in some sort of semi-official team photo. *It must be the football club he purchased recently.* He was smiling, and her heart shuddered. He looked so happy and proud. And now he was gone... Death was brutal. An unopened notification flashed up. It was a text message from Max.

"Where are you bro? Everyone is here having drinks and—"

She couldn't see the rest of the message, so she swiped up. The PIN code entry screen appeared. She sighed. That was as far as she could go for the moment. She turned the bag over. Droplets of water clung to the plastic, and part of the bag was stuck to the back of the phone. The back didn't appear to be cracked. She looked down at where the phone had been lying. It had been in that puddle, hadn't it? He must have dropped it when someone attacked him. She glanced up at Fitzwilliam, who was taking photos of a drinking glass standing on a shelf in the corner of the alcove. She hadn't noticed that earlier, but then she'd had her back to that end of the bath. The glass looked empty. Fitzwilliam smelled it. *Did someone drug Ben before they held him under the water?* She strained to hear what Fitzwilliam was now saying into his phone.

"... smells like whisky. There are the remains of a brown liquid at the bottom of the glass. No lipstick marks. Glass is intact. Tag as bathroom evidence number two." He lowered his phone and looked up at her. Spots of red appeared on his cheeks. "It's a new method of recording evidence they want us to use. I talk into an app on my phone, and it goes off somewhere into the ether and ends up in the case file." He shrugged. "Spicer loves it and has been on and on at me to use it, but I like my pen and pocketbook." He grimaced. "But, of course, I was supposed to be on leave, so I don't have them with me. I guess now is as good a time as any to give this thing a go."

Bea stifled a giggle. She could imagine Detective Sergeant Tina Spicer nagging her boss to use the new, more efficient method of making case notes, and him refusing, insisting he wanted to stick to his old 'pen and paper' method. *I bet he used the word 'newfangled' somewhere in those conversations with her.* She'd have to ask Spicer the next time she saw her. They would probably laugh about it together.

"So anything on the phone?"

"Just an unread text message from Max asking where he is. The phone screen is locked, so without the pin code, I can't get access."

He nodded.

"Do you think someone drugged him first?" she asked.

He glanced over at the glass. "I'm fairly sure it's only whisky in there. But it's possible. I'm not sure how I can get it tested right now, but that and the autopsy will eventually tell us. In the meantime, I would say the way the water is splashed over the floor and wall behind the bath that, even if someone drugged him, he still put up a fierce fight." He scanned the bath area one last time. "I think I'm done in here. Let's go into the bedroom."

Bedroom? Her ears felt impossibly hot. *Pull yourself together, Bea; you're not a teenager!*

Following the mumbling sound of Fitzwilliam talking into his phone again, she found him wandering around a table.

"…only one glass and a half full decanter. Glass looks used, residual brown liquid. Smells like whisky. Tag as bedroom evidence number one." He looked up and caught her eye. "So either he had a visitor at some stage, or he used both glasses himself."

"Will you be able to get fingerprints?"

"I'm hoping the local chap has access to a basic investigation kit. If not, we'll have to do it the old-fashioned way with cornflour and clear tape."

Bea studied him as he continued to scan the room, stopping every now and again and dictating the details into his phone. At well over six foot, he wasn't exactly lean but neither was he overweight. She knew he ran regularly as she'd been horrified during a previous case when DS Spicer had suggested she and Fitzwilliam run together.

His short brown hair was greying at the temples. *It suits him,* she thought. His slightly sallow complexion was one of a man who didn't get enough sleep. He stood up, wincing as he straightened, then twisted around, and their eyes locked. His brown eyes searched hers for a second, then he smiled. A smile that transformed his previously solemn face. She couldn't help but smile back. Perry had described him in the past as ruggedly handsome, but she'd rarely been able to see what he saw, probably because Fitzwilliam was normally scowling at her. But now, with his white teeth showing through thinly parted lips and his sparkling eyes surrounded by crinkles, he looked like he'd been lit up from inside, and she could see what Perry meant. Suddenly aware she was staring, she broke eye contact with him and diverted her attention to her phone. Still no message from Perry. *I hope they've left. It'll get dark soon.*

"I think I'm done in here now," Fitzwilliam said, returning his phone to his back pocket. "Shall we go?"

She nodded and handed Ben's bagged mobile to him. He opened the door for her, and they stepped into the corridor.

As Fitzwilliam gave instructions to the police constable outside the door, Bea's phone vibrated.

. . .

Perry: *Talk about an epic journey, but we're finally here. Where are you? xx*

Tears welled up in the back of her eyes, and the tension left her body. Her best friends were here now. *Thank goodness!*

14

LATE AFTERNOON, SUNDAY 10
JANUARY

Skipping down the stairs, Lady Beatrice slowed down as she reached the last few steps and saw the butler once again with a pile of fur coats, hats, and scarves in his arms staggering towards the cloakroom.

"Where are they, Brock?" she cried out as he disappeared down the left-hand corridor.

As she landed at the bottom, he stopped and slowly rotated, peering over the mound of outerwear. "They've gone to the Card Room with his lordship, my lady."

She suppressed a smile as the butler tried to bow and balance his load at the same time. "Thank you, Brock," she said as footsteps above her alerted her to DCI Fitzwilliam's impending presence.

"Perry and Simon are here," she told him as she waited for him at the bottom of the stairs.

He nodded, and she led him down the corridor on their right.

Dropping her head, she studied the tartan carpet runner, its areas of leaf-green, salmon-pink, and sky-blue broken by the dark-grey straight lines running vertically and horizontally across them. Her heart dropped. *Now Simon's here, Fitzwilliam won't need me to help anymore.* She stopped at a vast ornately-carved wooden door with a card marked PRIVATE in the brass name holder in the middle and paused. *Oh well, at least I have Perry here now.* They could look at the photos she'd taken earlier together. Perry may spot something she'd missed. That wasn't interfering, was it? She pushed open the door, and they walked in.

Like a bolt of white lightning, Daisy made a beeline for them. *Aw, my girl.* Bea bent her knees, ready to crouch down and greet her little terrier, when Daisy veered off to the side and ran to Fitzwilliam. *What?* Bea bounced back up, stunned by her dog's betrayal, when a strangled sound came from her left.

"Oh my giddy aunt!" Perry Juke, standing with his back to the roaring fire, raised his hand to his mouth, his eyes wide as he stared at Fitzwilliam.

Bea looked over at her brother, who was standing by the side of a table laid out with cups and saucers, a handful of spoons, a large coffee pot, two milk jugs, and a teapot. *Why didn't he tell them Fitzwilliam was here?* Fred smirked at her, then raised his cup of coffee in a salute. He got pleasure from seeing people in situations he knew made them uncomfortable, so knowing about their various run-ins with the detective chief inspector over the last nine months, he must have done it deliberately to see their reactions. *Cheeky!* However, what Fred didn't know was at the end of the last case, after they had agreed to cooperate with Fitzwilliam in keeping some speculative information out of the public arena, they had all parted on good terms. It was only because she'd made such a fool of herself during the investigation that had led her to never want to face him again. In fact, he'd been kind to her. Which had only made the whole situation even more intolerable.

Simon Lattimore, a smile breaking over his face, marched forward, his hand held out in front of him. "Fitzwilliam, this is unexpected. How on earth did you get here so quickly?"

Fitzwilliam grabbed Simon's hand and shook it. "I'm visiting with a friend who's recuperating from an accident. She's staying here in one of the estate cottages to convalesce."

She? Bea blinked. Had Fitzwilliam gained a girlfriend since they'd last seen him? She glanced over at Perry, who, his mouth now closed, raised an eyebrow in her direction.

"Well, that's handy." Simon chortled. "Did you have to trek through the snow to get here like we did?"

Fitzwilliam nodded. "It felt like I completed an expedition to the North Pole by the time I arrived." He and Simon laughed, then Fitzwilliam's smile disappeared. "CID can't get here because of the snow and neither can DS Spicer. There's one PC from the local station who was here when it started snowing and that's it. I could really do with your help, Lattimore."

"Of course." Simon patted Fitzwilliam's shoulder. "Anything you need."

"Great, thank you." Fitzwilliam turned and nodded to Perry. "Mr Juke, good to see you too."

Bea watched Perry's face to see if he was disappointed not to be asked to help as well, but Perry smiled at Fitzwilliam, apparently unconcerned. "I hope your friend is okay?"

She stifled a smile. Perry, always interested in a bit of gossip, was clearly digging to find out more about Fitzwilliam's 'friend'.

"She'll be fine as long as she follows the doctor's orders and rests up…"

Well, that wasn't helpful.

"…but you know what women are like."

Bea scowled. *What's that supposed to mean?* It was normally men who ignored doctors' advice and carried on regardless. She huffed under her breath.

Fred stepped towards them. "Help yourself to tea and coffee, everyone. Chief inspector, you can use this room as your base, and there's an adjoining door there" —he pointed to a smaller door built into a panelled wall— "that leads into the anteroom I think will work as an interview room."

Fitzwilliam strolled over and opened the door, then peeked around the frame into the room. "Perfect," he said, leaving the door open as he walked back to the table and helped himself to a coffee. "Right, so here's what needs to be done." He took a sip of black coffee and turned to Simon. "The crime scene needs processing and all the evidence logged with videos and photos of the room sent to DS Spicer. Lattimore, can you help with that? I suggest you call her via video link. She can then talk you through it."

Simon nodded. "Sure."

"We also need to get everyone's fingerprints. I'm hoping the PC upstairs has a basic fingerprint kit with him. Once I have a list of everyone who's on-site, can you work with him to get that done?"

Simon nodded again.

Bea stifled a sigh. She knew it made sense for Simon to be Fitzwilliam's sidekick in all of this, but it was still disappointing not to be involved at all.

Fitzwilliam addressed her brother. "Lord Fred, I need a list of all the guests and staff on-site today between eleven and twelve forty-five. Then can you talk to security and see what they have in terms of CCTV footage from outside and inside the house? I need to know the movements of all the staff and guests, and in particular, I'm interested in establishing what time Ben Rhodes went up to his room. Can we get a couple of security guards up here as well? One to stand at the bottom of the stairs to stop guests from going upstairs until I give the all clear and one to sit outside Mr Rhodes's bedroom to stop anyone going in and interfering with the crime scene. That should release the PC to help Lattimore."

So Fred also had an important job to do. *I could have done that...*

"Also, my lord, do you know of anywhere we can store the body once we've finished until someone can get here to pick it up for the postmortem?"

"I believe there's a room off the chapel that was used years ago to lay out the dead when it was a local custom for the body to be displayed prior to burial. Leave it with me. I'll sort it out."

"Great." He turned to Perry, who was looking at something on his phone. "Mr Juke?"

Perry started. "Yes?"

"I need to talk to the guests, who I believe are still in the Drawing Room?" He looked at Fred, who nodded. "After I tell them what's happening, I will ask them to stay put until we secure the scene upstairs. I'll interview all of them at some stage today and then they'll be free to return to their rooms or remain downstairs, whichever they prefer. Can I take you with me and then put you in charge of liaising with the guests, please?"

Perry seemed at a loss for words. Eventually, he raised his hand to his chest and whispered, "Really? Me?"

"I just need you to keep an eye on them and make yourself available if they have any concerns. I'll be interested in your observations of how they act over the next few hours. Can you do that, do you think?"

It's the perfect job for Perry. He was observant and good at getting people to relax around him. But then, so was she. *And* she knew them better than Perry did. *He could've asked me to do that.*

Perry's hand dropped to his side, and looking flustered, he nodded. "Yes, of course."

"Thank you. After I've spoken to the guests, the first people I want to interview are the ones who discovered the body." Again, he referred to Fred. "I believed that's the victim's brother and his bodyguard?"

Fred nodded. "Max Rhodes, Ben's twin brother, and Clive Tozzi, who Ben hired as his personal security."

So all the *men* had jobs. Bea could feel her throat constricting. *If he asks me to arrange for food or drinks, then I'm going to tell him to—*

"Lady Beatrice, I don't want the guests leaving this floor, so is there a bathroom we can make available for them down here? I noticed there's a keyhole for Mr Rhodes's bedroom. Could you find me the key, please? I want to lock it securely once we finish processing the crime scene."

Bea's stomach clenched. *Great! I just knew it!* He was treating her like a glorified housekeeper. *He'll be asking me to arrange refreshments next...*

"Oh, and Lady Beatrice?"

She scowled at him. *Go on, ask...*

"Will you sit in on the interviews with me, please?"

She suddenly felt slightly light-headed. *He wants me to be there when he questions the suspects?* She could hardly believe it... *Oh hold on...* "Do you mean to take notes?" she asked tentatively.

He put down his coffee cup, a smile tugging at the corners

of his mouth. "Not unless you want to, my lady. I'll record everything on the app so we have a transcript of each interview. I know people trust you and are more likely to talk freely with your encouragement."

She raised her chin. In past cases, that had been one reason she'd been able to find out information more quickly than him. People talked to her. She smiled and happily replied, "Indeed. I'll also arrange refreshments and a buffet dinner for later."

"That's great, thank you." He clapped his hands together, and Daisy, still standing by his side, gave a short bark. "Oh hold on, Daisy. I nearly forgot you," he said, addressing the little dog. "Your job is to find some clues to prove who did it. Can you do that for me?" Daisy tilted her head to one side, then sat down and offered him her paw. He turned to Bea, his eyes dancing mischievously, and raised an eyebrow. "Does that mean yes?"

Fighting the urge to laugh, she gave him a pitying look, then walked over to the table and poured herself a coffee. Who was this man, and what had he done with the boorish and dismissive Detective Chief Inspector Richard Fitzwilliam she'd known and loathed for so long?

15

FIVE MINUTES LATER, SUNDAY 10 JANUARY

A hush descended on the Drawing Room as Perry Juke followed Detective Chief Inspector Richard Fitzwilliam into the large south-facing room. As Fitzwilliam strode into the centre of the cluster of sofas and armchairs, Perry made his way over to the wall next to the large bay windows where he had a good view of the entire room. Fitzwilliam had asked him to watch and see how the guests reacted to the news of Ben Rhodes's death, and this seemed the perfect place to observe them all.

Sitting in an armchair diagonally facing one of the bay windows, a man with a shaved head swirled an amber liquid around a cut-glass tumbler. He hadn't reacted to their entrance into the room. *He must be Clive Tozzi, Ben Rhodes's personal security.* Bea had done her best to give him a brief rundown of the shooting party guests, and he was the only person in the room who fitted her description of "he looks like a heavy from a gangster movie". So he was the only person in the room who already knew about Ben's death given Max was still in the library. Perry dismissed him and moved on to a cluster of four sitting on two sofas opposite each other in front of the central bay. "A grey-haired man in his early sixties", "a petite woman with blonde hair", next to "her husband with big glasses who looks like a games nerd", and "a hipster-looking young guy with a beard and pale skin". Bea's descriptions fitted the group perfectly. So this must be the McLean family. Bea had told him to scrutinise them the most, as it was the woman and the cool-looking dude who she'd overheard on the stairs the other evening. He'd come back to them.

Fitzwilliam cleared his throat. "Ladies and gentlemen, can I have your attention for a minute, please?"

Perry hurriedly glanced at the two other people in the room. He recognised the woman with very short hair from breakfast. She sat opposite a clean-shaven man with coffee-coloured skin who, according to Bea, "has a nice smile". He must be Fred's other work contact. They both had laptops open on the tall coffee table and looked up reluctantly.

"I'm Detective Chief Inspector Richard Fitzwilliam." Perry darted his gaze to the gang of four (as Perry had now named them) by the window. They looked at each other, frowning, then gave their attention back to Fitzwilliam. Fred's spies (as Perry had christened them) didn't refer to each other, both continuing to focus on the chief inspector.

"I'm sorry to tell you, but there was an incident earlier this afternoon that resulted in the death of Ben Rhodes."

Rose McLean let out a strangled wail. Perry quickly rotated his head. She had her hand over her mouth and was staring, her eyes wide, at her brother opposite her, whose mouth was open in shock. Her husband grabbed her other hand and patted it reassuringly while her father coughed and took a sip of water. Perry swivelled around to observe Fred's spies, who were now looking at each other. They seemed more curious than surprised. *I suppose it takes a lot to shock spies.*

"I can imagine this has come as a bit of a shock to you all."

Clive Tozzi remained still in his chair, staring out into the darkness where a grey carpet of snow was still falling while the elder McLean rose. "Hector McLean," he said, holding out his hand to Fitzwilliam. "This is my daughter Rose, her husband Ed, and my son Fergus." He waved his other hand at the others in the gang of four. "I'm sorry to hear about Mr Rhodes's death, chief inspector. Exactly what happened?"

Perry stifled a gasp. *Wow, he's bold.* Maybe when you ran a successful company like McLean and Co, you had the confidence to demand answers when others didn't.

Fitzwilliam took the extended hand and shook it briefly before dropping it as he said, "I'm afraid I can't go into details at this stage, Mr McLean. I'd be grateful if everyone in the room could keep this information to themselves until we have time to inform Mr Rhodes's family." Perry followed Fitzwilliam's gaze as the chief inspector made eye contact with everyone in the room. Clive Tozzi remained mesmerised by the snow falling outside.

"In order to establish the events leading up to Mr Rhodes's death, I will need to speak to all of you about your movements today."

Hector McLean opened his mouth, but Fitzwilliam ignored him and continued. "In the meantime, I'd be grateful if you would stay here until you're—"

"You mean we can't go up to our rooms?" Hector interrupted.

Fitzwilliam's face hardened as he turned to the man still standing close to him. *He's got on Fitzwilliam's bad side already*, Perry thought.

"Not at the moment, I'm afraid. We're processing the crime scene. Until we've completed that, there's no access to the first floor."

The blonde woman from the gang of four jumped up. "But I need to go to the bathroom."

"There are bathrooms downstairs you can use. Further refreshments are also being arranged."

His face flushed and his eyes wide, Hector McLean spluttered, "But—"

Fitzwilliam raised his hand. "Everyone, I appreciate this is inconvenient for you, but a man is dead. This is a serious situation. I'm asking for your co-operation while we establish what's happened."

Perry suppressed a grin as Hector McLean fought with himself, clearly wanting to say more, but aware to do so would make him sound petty in the circumstances. In the end, he huffed, then slouched back to his family. His daughter patted his arm as they both sat down again.

"Thank you. I'll try not to keep you any longer than I have to. This" —he twisted around and indicated Perry— "is Mr Juke. He'll be looking after you in my absence. If you have any pressing questions, then please ask him. He will do his best to answer them, although, of course, he won't be able to discuss the case with you."

At that moment, the door opened and a footman entered, pushing a trolley ladened with small cakes, scones, sandwiches, and fruit.

That looks yummy, Perry thought, watching Owen empty the goodies onto the table next to the coffee and tea.

"Mr Juke?" Fitzwilliam was now standing beside him. He said in a voice low, "I'll let you know when I need the first interviewee. Just keep an eye on them, will you?"

Perry nodded, and Fitzwilliam left. Perry scanned the

room and was relieved to see the occupants were more focussed on the food being laid out than they were on him. *Hopefully, they'll just ignore me if I remain here out of the way and don't make eye contact.* As he glanced up at the ornately-crafted white plastered ceiling high above him, Perry's stomach rumbled. *Will it be okay for me to grab a plateful of food while I'm here?*

16

5 PM, SUNDAY 10 JANUARY

"I'm so sorry for your loss, Mr Rhodes." DCI Fitzwilliam ushered a subdued Max Rhodes into the anteroom attached to the Card Room and gestured for him to take a seat in a dark-green armchair in the middle of the room.

Lady Beatrice, sitting in a substantial brown leather tub chair by the window, Daisy squashed against her side, rested her hand gently on her dog's back to stop her from jumping up to greet the newcomer. "Good girl, Daisy," Bea whispered as the terrier relaxed beside her.

Max, clutching his phone tight in his left hand, slumped down into the chair.

Bea wasn't sure if he'd even noticed her presence. If he had, then he'd not acknowledged it. Sagging in the chair, his shoulders hunched around his neck and his eyes focussed on his knees, he looked a long way from the overly confident man she'd had dinner with on Friday night. Although she'd known the loss of a loved one only too well after the death of her husband fifteen years ago, she couldn't imagine how awful it must be to lose your twin. *Like losing a part of yourself, I imagine.*

Fitzwilliam perched on the edge of the two-seater sofa opposite Max and retrieved his phone from his back pocket. He tapped the screen. "I'd like to ask you a few questions, if I may?" He leaned over and rested the phone on the low coffee table between them.

Max raised his head to look at Fitzwilliam and nodded. "Of course, chief inspector. Anything I can do to help."

"When did you last see your brother, Mr Rhodes?"

Max sighed. "Just before eleven-thirty, I think. I left him in the library down here and went up to my room."

"And was that the last contact you had with him?"

Max shook his head and opened up the hand holding his phone. Staring down at it, he said, "I had a text message from him at ten past twelve saying he was going to have a quick bath and would see me downstairs for drinks at twelve-thirty."

"And did you respond?"

"Yes, I texted back to say be quick and reminded him not to be late." He shifted in his seat and crossed his legs.

"Was your brother often late?"

"Time got away from him sometimes." His voice quivered, and he slowly shook his head.

Bea recalled what she'd heard about them. Max was the oldest twin. Did that mean he was the responsible one? If the papers were anything to go by, Ben was the charming risk taker and Max the quiet and steady businessman. But then the papers liked to stereotype people. Last night at dinner, she certainly hadn't found Max to be shy and retiring. She suppressed a smile. Max had worked very hard to flirt with her. Ben, on the other hand, had certainly been charming over breakfast this morning, but he hadn't come across as so sure of himself as his elder brother. But then could she really make a sound judgement on the twins from two brief encounters with them? She'd ask her cousin Caroline. Lady Caroline Clifford was the 'it' girl in the family and knew everyone in London who was worth knowing. In fact, it had been at a dinner party at her cousin's when she'd met Max Rhodes previously. She returned her attention back to the conversation between the two men.

"I understand your brother brought his own personal security with him. Why was that?"

"Yes, Clive Tozzi." Max hesitated, then glancing down at his phone, continued, "Ben purchased a London football club, Urshall United, recently, and it wasn't a popular move. The club was in trouble, but the fans didn't want the club to be sold. When the share price crashed, the consortium that owned it had no choice, and Ben stepped in. The press have vilified him ever since, and the fans have convinced themselves he will sell off the assets and destroy the club."

"And was that his plan?" Fitzwilliam asked.

"Not that I know of. I think he just wanted to try something different. He's not a big football fan, but thought if he had a club that was his, then he would become one."

"So the security was because he was being hounded by the press?"

Max hesitated, then shook his head. "He was getting death threats. They were just online at first, and he reported them to the police. Then recently, someone targeted his house. They sprayed a message in red paint across the doors of his garage."

"And?"

"It said, 'Get out of our club or die!'"

Oh gosh! She'd known about the online abuse, but when it got that close to home… No wonder he'd arranged his own security.

"Did he report it?"

"I don't know. He showed me the photos, but he was so worried the press would find out and splash it all over the papers, that he got a specialist cleaning company in to get rid of it. It was gone within an hour of being discovered."

"So that's why he got his own security?"

Max nodded. "It totally freaked his wife out. She was at home that night on her own." His face clouded over. "Gemma!" Wide-eyed, he looked over at Fitzwilliam. "Someone needs to tell Gemma."

"Don't worry, Mr Rhodes. We'll get her details from you, and one of my team will go to see her. So your brother employed a security company?"

"Initially, it was just to patrol the property twenty-four hours and upgrade the CCTV, but then he got some letters sent to the house..." Max trailed off. Daisy jumped off the seat she was sharing with Bea and landed on the floor with a thud. Max spun around. "Lady Beatrice!"

The look of confusion confirmed her earlier assumption he hadn't seen her here. He stared at her for a few seconds, frowning, then shifted his gaze back to Fitzwilliam.

Fitzwilliam lifted his chin slightly and met his eyes. "Lady Beatrice has kindly offered to sit in on the interviews with me. It's always preferable to have another person to act as a witness to safeguard both parties. She will, of course, not divulge anything you say in this room to anyone outside of the investigation."

Will Max protest? She held her breath as he looked down at his phone. Was Fitzwilliam on dodgy ground by allowing her to attend the interviews? But then they were just informal at this stage. Unless he had something to hide, it shouldn't be a problem, should it? *Is Max hiding something?* He raised his head and gave a small shrug.

"You were saying your brother had received death threats

in the post," Fitzwilliam continued as Bea breathed a sigh of relief. Daisy, now lying on the floor, gave a huff and, turning onto her side, closed her eyes.

"Yes. They began arriving a few days after someone vandalised the garage. They threatened to kill him if he didn't withdraw his interest from the club. I didn't see them, but Ben told me he'd reported it to the local police. He then employed someone as personal protection when he was away from home."

"Mr Clive Tozzi?"

"No. Not initially. He got a guy through an agency." He closed his eyes and rubbed his brow. "I think his name was Brian someone or other. Anyway, he was with him until Friday. Then he was sick or unavailable to come to Scotland. I can't remember which. So the agency sent Clive as a replacement."

"Thank you, Mr Rhodes. So back to today. When your brother didn't arrive for drinks on time, what did you do?"

"At first, I just thought he was late. Then I thought maybe he'd fallen asleep in the bath. So I texted him to chase him up."

Bea recalled the half-displayed text she'd seen on Ben's phone from Max. That must be the one he was referring to.

"And when he still didn't show?" Fitzwilliam prompted.

"I spoke to Clive about my concerns and suggested we go to check he was okay."

Why didn't he go on his own? It was his brother…

"Why did you want Mr Tozzi to go with you?" Fitzwilliam asked.

"Well, he was Ben's security, after all. I told him I would've thought he should be with him or at least waiting at his door."

"And did he say why he wasn't?"

"He was quite defensive. Ben told him he would meet him downstairs, he said. He wasn't keen to go up, so I told him to forget it and I'd go on my own."

"But you didn't?"

Max shook his head as he scooted forward in his seat. "I was halfway up the stairs when he came charging up behind me. He'd obviously changed his mind."

"Did you notice anything unusual when you went into your brother's room?"

"No. It was quiet. I immediately thought I was right, and he must have fallen asleep in the bath. I shouted but got no reply, so we went into the bathroom." There was a hitch in Max's voice, and he tried to cover it up with a cough. "And that's when I saw Ben under the water." He rubbed the hand holding his phone with his thumb. "I froze. Clive went past me, then said Ben was dead and we needed to leave everything as it was and tell someone, so we left." He fell back in the chair and let out a deep breath. Shaking his head, he said, "I still can't take it in. Did he fall asleep and drown?"

Bea frowned. *Surely he doesn't really believe that?* Then she remembered when her mother had told her the news of her husband James's death, how she'd argued with her it wasn't possible. James couldn't be gone just like that, in the blink of an eye. Someone had made a mistake. Maybe Max wanted to believe that was what had happened rather than face the truth that Ben was not only dead, but someone had killed him. But why had they? Was it something to do with the threats he'd received? But then how did one of those murderous fans get into Drew Castle? Did Max recognise anyone here? Someone who could be a fan in disguise? She looked at Fitzwilliam. Would he ask that? If not, maybe he would give her a chance to ask as she was now part of the investigation team…

"I think that's highly unlikely, Mr Rhodes. There was clearly a struggle."

Max slumped forward and rested his elbows on his knees. Staring down at the floor, he said, "So you think someone killed him?"

"We'll need confirmation from the doctor, but yes, that's what I think."

He looked up at Fitzwilliam. "Because of the football club?" he asked solemnly. "Did someone follow through on their threat?"

Ask him if he recognises anyone! She stared at Fitzwilliam, willing the words to come out of his mouth.

"I think it's too early to speculate at the moment." Fitzwilliam rose. "Thank you for your time, Mr Rhodes. I may need to talk to you again later, but for the moment, you can return to the library or join the others in the Drawing Room if you'd prefer."

As they watched a slightly hunched Max Rhodes walk out of the room, Bea rose and rocked on her hips, stretching her stiff muscles. "You didn't ask him if he recognised anyone here who knew Ben," she said to Fitzwilliam. He turned and raised an eyebrow. "Er, I mean, if it was a football fan who killed Ben Rhodes, then it would have to be someone here, so he might have recognised…" In the face of Fitzwilliam's cold stare, she stopped, not wanting to be asked to leave so soon.

"All in good time, my lady."

She nodded. "Sorry."

17

5:45 PM, SUNDAY 10 JANUARY

Clive Tozzi rubbed his hand over his shaven head as he sat in the same green chair Max Rhodes had vacated only a few minutes before. DCI Richard Fitzwilliam was in his familiar position perched on the arm of the facing sofa. Daisy was curled up on the couch within touching distance of him, gently snoring.

Unlike Max, Clive had noticed Lady Beatrice as soon as he'd walked into the room. When Fitzwilliam had explained her presence, he'd grumbled about privacy, but when she'd reiterated that nothing he said would go outside of the investigation team, he'd reluctantly accepted the situation with a scowl.

"Mr Tozzi, can you tell us about how you came to be in Ben Rhodes's employment, please?"

Clive settled back in the chair and crossed his arms and legs. "A security agency I often work with asked me if I could come to Scotland for a few days to do an assignment."

"And presumably you said yes. Did they tell you who the client was?"

Clive nodded. "They gave me his name and some background."

"And what did that background include?"

Clive shrugged. "That he had a lot of negative press after he bought a London football club. He had his house targeted by angry football fans. And he'd had some threatening mail."

"So, just to be clear, you knew about the death threats?"

Clive uncrossed his arms and shifted in his seat. "I saw none of them, but the agency told me he'd had some."

"And when you met Ben Rhodes, did he seem concerned about it?"

Clive leaned back into the chair and shook his head. "Not really. In fact, he didn't want me here at all. I think it was his brother who insisted I come."

"Why do you say that, Mr Tozzi?"

"Well, for a start, when I arrived at the airport, it was Max who asked me to check the interior of the plane before we left. Then I heard them talking when we were in the air. I was sitting behind them, but I could hear some of what they were saying. Ben asked Max if he really needed me here. He said something about a royal palace ought to be able to keep a bunch of football hooligans out."

What Clive was saying was consistent with Bea's observations over the last few days. Ben Rhodes hadn't seemed like a man who'd been worried about his safety. But had that been just a front? Or was the security man right, and it had been Max who'd been uneasy about the situation?

"He didn't think his life was in danger then?" Fitzwilliam asked.

Again Clive Tozzi shrugged. "I know it seems strange saying it now, especially with him being dead and all, but no, I don't think so."

Fitzwilliam shifted his weight. "Okay, so let's talk about

this evening. Why did you go downstairs without your client?"

Clive Tozzi shuffled forward to the edge of the chair and fixed his stare on Fitzwilliam. "I know what you're thinking. What everyone is thinking. How did this happen when I was supposed to be protecting him?"

Fitzwilliam cocked his head to one side and said, "Well, it's a fair point, Mr Tozzi."

Why didn't Clive wait for Ben outside his door? Wouldn't that be the normal procedure?

A thin mist of sweat was now visible on the man's forehead as he shook his head and said, "I wish I hadn't agreed now."

Bea inched forward in her chair. *Agreed to what?*

"What did you agree to, Mr Tozzi?"

"Look, I also have to respect my client's wishes, right? Ben was uncomfortable about me being around him right from the start. When he came out of his room that first evening to go to dinner, I was standing outside, and he nearly jumped out of his skin. Then he told me he'd had enough and I didn't need to follow him around while we were indoors. He was nice about it. He didn't shout, but he was clearly unhappy with me being there. I told him it was my job to make sure he was safe, and he said there was CCTV everywhere, so he would be fine as long as he was inside the castle. I was getting a bit frustrated, so I asked him why he'd bothered to engage my services, and he sort of relaxed and suggested we find a solution that worked for both of us. In the end, we agreed I wouldn't wait outside his room, but I would accompany him when he was downstairs and mixing with others."

He shrugged. "Look, I got he wanted his privacy when he was in his bedroom, and anyway, I had a room in the same wing as him. I would hear if there was any big commotion." He twisted his head and caught Bea's eye. "It seemed fair to me, you know?"

Bea stared back. What did she do now? On one hand, she sympathised with him, but on the other, it had been his job to protect Ben and he hadn't. Ben hadn't been much older than her. He'd had years ahead of him. Now he was dead. A slight shiver made her wriggle in her chair, and she dropped Clive's gaze.

"When did you last see Ben Rhodes?" She looked up at Fitzwilliam's question and was grateful Clive was now slumped back in the chair, his eyes on the floor.

"Just after we got back from the shoot this morning," he mumbled at the blue tartan rug in front of him.

Fitzwilliam cleared his throat. Clive raised his head. "I got soaked helping push the vehicles out of a snowdrift, so Ben told me to go up and get changed. He said he'd see me down here at twelve-thirty for drinks."

"Did he go up with you?"

Clive shook his head. "No, he followed Max into the library."

"So you went to your room. What next?"

Clive shrugged. "I had a shower, took a quick nap, then went downstairs for drinks."

"And what time was that?"

"About twenty-five past twelve, I guess."

"Then what?"

"I stood and waited for Ben."

His face flushed, and he rubbed the back of his neck. Bea glanced at her watch. Five past six. It felt later.

"When Mr Rhodes failed to show up on time, were you concerned at all?"

Clive cleared his throat. "No, not really. He was only ten minutes late."

"I understand Max Rhodes then suggested you accompany him upstairs to see if everything was all right."

"Yes. He said he'd texted Ben but had not had a reply, and he was worried he'd fallen asleep in the bath."

"But you refused to go with him. Why was that?"

Clive raised his chin. "We had an agreement, remember? I would respect his privacy when he was in his room. I didn't think he'd take kindly to having me there when he woke up in the bath!"

He has a point. Ben would have been embarrassed and would probably have also been angry at his bodyguard for having not respected their agreement.

"But then you changed your mind?"

He made an odd noise in his throat, then sighed. "Max pointed out I was supposed to be Ben's protection. If anything had happened…" He looked down at the floor.

Well, it did! Bea suppressed a sigh. It seemed like Clive was feeling sorry for himself. Maybe he was worried about his reputation at work… *I don't suppose it's a good recommendation when a client dies on your watch.* Bea caught Fitzwilliam's eye, and he raised an eyebrow. *Is he getting fed up with this witness too?*

Fitzwilliam cleared his throat. "So you went to Ben's room with his brother. Talk me through what happened."

Clive shifted to the edge of the chair again and rested his elbows on his knees. "Max knocked on the door, but there was no reply, so he opened it and shouted for Ben. The bathroom door was open, and the light was on, so we went straight there. Max stopped partway in and just froze, so I pushed past him. As soon as I saw Ben, I knew he was dead, but I checked for a pulse anyway." He shook his head. "But there was nothing we could do."

"Was the water hot, warm, or cold when you put your hand in?"

"Er, cold."

"Thank you. So what did you do next?"

"I told Max we needed to leave and call the police, so we left."

"And did you see anything in the bathroom while you were in there?"

Clive shot Fitzwilliam a look, his brow wrinkled. "Apart from the dead body, do you mean?"

"Yes. Did you notice anything unusual or out of place?"

He pressed his lips together. "I don't think so. I was only in there for a few minutes. As soon as I saw he was dead, I knew we needed to tell someone quick."

Fitzwilliam shifted in his seat. "Did you see anyone acting suspiciously around Ben Rhodes?"

Clive shook his head. "No."

Fitzwilliam stood up, waking Daisy, who jumped down from the sofa. "Well, thank you Mr Tozzi. That will be all for now. Can I ask you to return to the Drawing Room and wait with the others until we've finished upstairs, please?"

Clive Tozzi closed his eyes briefly, then heaved his hefty frame out of the armchair, and with a quick glance in Bea's direction, he hurried out of the room.

Fitzwilliam let out a deep breath and, leaning forward, tapped his phone to switch off the recording. "That was like pulling teeth!" he said, stretching his neck from side to side. He walked towards her, Daisy by his side. "What do you think of our friend Mr Tozzi?"

Bea tilted her head to one side. "He was very agitated,

wasn't he? I can't work out if he has something to hide or if he's just worried about his professional reputation."

Fitzwilliam nodded. "Yes. He was defensive, which is understandable in the circumstances, but you're right, there was something else. Like he was frightened I was going to ask him about something in particular he was dreading." He huffed. "I didn't find out what it was, but I will." He glanced at his watch. "Shall we take a—"

There was a knock on the connecting door.

Fitzwilliam turned and shouted, "Come in."

Simon's head poked around the door. "I've finished upstairs. They've just brought us some food and hot drinks, if you're ready to take a break. The guests are eating now too."

Bea rose. "Perfect. I'm peckish. Chief inspector?"

He nodded. "Let's grab some food and have a catchup. Can you text Mr Juke and ask him to join us?"

She took out her phone as she followed him and Daisy towards the Card Room next door.

18

──────────

6:15 PM, SUNDAY 10 JANUARY

"So, Mr Juke, any observations to make about the guests?" DCI Fitzwilliam asked just before popping a small cheese sandwich into his mouth.

Perry, next to Simon on a two-seater navy sofa opposite the chief inspector, shifted forward to reach for another ham roll. "They've all been pretty subdued, to be honest. The McLean family whispered to each other occasionally, but I couldn't hear what they were saying. The daughter seemed skittish and kept glancing at her brother, and he looked like he was deliberately avoiding engaging with her. So something's going on there, but I don't know... Hold on! Bea, do you think it's something to do with the conversation you overheard? Could they have been referring to Ben?"

Fitzwilliam paused in the middle of grabbing another sandwich and eyed Lady Beatrice, raising an eyebrow.

Heat rose up her neck. *He's looking at me like I was deliberately keeping something from him.* "Er, sorry. I forgot about that."

She cleared her throat and turned to face Fitzwilliam, but before she could say anything, he spoke. "You overheard a conversation, did you, Lady Beatrice? Now why doesn't that surprise me?"

Her hackles rose instantly, and she looked down at her lap. *What's that supposed to mean?* Was it her fault she was often present yet not visible when people were having private conversations? She tucked a loose strand of hair behind her ear, then, about to open her mouth, she raised her head and caught Simon's eye. He subtly tilted his head towards Fitzwilliam. Following his direction, she closed it again. A wide grin had split Fitzwilliam's face, and his eyes shone as he winked at her. The tension left her shoulders, and she smiled. *He's teasing me!* Making a mental note to not be so quick to react in the future, she told Fitzwilliam about the conversation Fergus and Rose had had on the stairs the night before.

"Interesting," he said when she'd finished. "It's certainly something I can explore when I interview them."

Oh no! She didn't want them to know it was her who'd overheard them. Eavesdropping wasn't an attractive pastime in most people's book.

Fitzwilliam held up his hand. "Don't worry, my lady. I won't tell them at this stage someone overheard them. I will just ask if they knew Ben well. We'll then see how they react and if they lie about it or not."

"Of course, it's always possible they were talking about someone else," Simon pointed out.

"Indeed," Bea added. She rather hoped they had. She didn't want to think of the McLean siblings as killers.

Fitzwilliam inclined his head. "Yes, that's possible. Let's see what we can find out." He swivelled around to Perry. "Good job, Mr Juke. How about the others?" He took a sip of his coffee.

"Who? The spies?" Perry asked.

Fitzwilliam spat out his drink. He grabbed a napkin, wiping his face and then down his blue striped shirt. "The *what*?" he cried.

Bea stifled a giggle as Perry shrugged. "The man and woman who work with Fred."

Fitzwilliam opened up his arms and shrugged his shoulders. "So…"

"Well, if Fred's a spy, then the chances are they are too, don't you think?"

While Fitzwilliam looked incredulously at Perry, it was Bea's turn to grin at him. "Perry is convinced my brother's a spy, Fitzwilliam."

His mouth fell open, then he checked himself and rubbed his hand over his chin. "And is he?"

Bea shrugged, the smile still lingering on her face. "I've no idea. He says he isn't, but then if he was, he would say that, wouldn't he?" She was enjoying this. She glanced over at Perry, and he winked at her.

"Fitzwilliam, they're both taking two and two and making eight," Simon, the voice of reason, interrupted their fun. "Fred works for the Home Office, and admittedly, he's cagey about exactly what he does, but it's something diplomatic to do with international trade agreements from what I can establish. We like to joke he's a spy, but I think it's unlikely."

"When I asked Brett Goodman about what he and Fred did, he said if he told me, he'd have to kill me," Bea jumped in, not wanting to give up the joy of winding Fitzwilliam up just yet. "*And* when I asked Eve Morrison over breakfast this morning, she denied Fred was a spy—"

Perry sagged against the back of the sofa and whispered, "No," shaking his head.

"—then admitted she'd have to say that even if he was!"

Perry bounced up, a grin pasted on his face, and gave her

a thumbs up. Next to him, Simon gently grabbed his partner and pulled him back down, mumbling, "You're not helping, Perry."

Fitzwilliam, confusion marring his face, drank his remaining coffee and refilled it from the pot on the table.

Bea started. *Does he know? Is his reaction because we've found out, and now he doesn't know what to say. Oh my goodness, is Fred* really *a spy?*

With perfect timing, her brother entered the room, carrying a stack of paper in one hand. "Oh good, food. I'm starving. It's…" He trailed off as all eyes were on him. "What?" he asked, a look of bewilderment on his face.

Simon jumped up from the sofa. "Nothing, Lord Fred." He scowled at the others. "Coffee or tea?"

As Fred walked across the room to join them, Bea studied Fitzwilliam. A frown of puzzlement still marred his slightly crinkled brow as his gaze followed her brother. *Does he know anything, or is he genuinely considering the possibility?* She suppressed a sigh. Either way, it would have to wait until they were alone. She'd ask him then.

Holding out the papers he was carrying to Fitzwilliam, Fred said, "This is the list of the guests and staff here at the moment, along with a list of movements as logged by the security guys from the CCTV footage."

Seeming to recover his composure, Fitzwilliam put down his cup and said, "Thank you, my lord." Fitzwilliam leaned back in his chair and studied the papers. "All right, so according to this, all the guests went up to their rooms between five past eleven and eleven-fifteen, except for the Rhodes twins. Max told us just now they were in the library, then he left his brother in there and went up. So, let's have a look. Okay, yes. One of the Rhodes brothers went up the main stairs at eleven twenty-five and the other, five minutes later, at eleven-thirty. Max Rhodes told us he went up before his brother, so if that's true, then Ben went up at eleven-thirty." He shuffled the papers and pulled one to the top. "A Rhodes brother came down at twelve-ten." He looked up at Bea. "That seems a bit early. Do you recall if Max told us what time he came down?"

Bea raked through her mind. "No, I don't think so. But he did say he'd had a text from Ben at about that time to tell him he was having a quick bath. I remember thinking Ben was cutting it fine if they were due down in twenty minutes, but then I suppose you can have a quick bath, can't you?" She looked at Perry, the only person she knew who preferred a bath to a shower, and he nodded.

"So there's a gap of about ten minutes, then the four McLeans came down together, followed a minute later by Eve Morrison, and two minutes after that was Brett Goodman. Clive Tozzi was the last to descend the stairs at twelve twenty-nine. We know Ben Rhodes was alive at eleven-thirty and dead at twelve forty-five, give or take a few minutes. His brother Max received a text message from him at twelve-ten, so once we can verify that by checking Ben's phone, then we can conclude someone killed him between then and twelve forty-five."

Bea frowned. "Can't we limit it to just the nineteen minutes since we can account for all the guests from twelve twenty-nine onwards?"

"If it was a guest who killed him," Fitzwilliam pointed out. "We cannot rule out any of the staff yet until we have established alibis."

"But Fitzwilliam." Fred put down his plate and rose. "I find it highly unlikely any of the staff are involved. They're all trusted members of the household and most have been here for years. Why would they want to kill a guest?"

Fitzwilliam waved him back down again. "I'm not suggesting they did, but nevertheless, we still need to check their alibis. Lattimore." He turned to Simon. "Can you ask the PC to interview each of them, and will you sit in with him?" Simon nodded. "You can use these" —he handed him the remaining papers— "to corroborate their movements." He looked at Fred next. "Lord Fred, is there any other way up to the floors above, apart from the main staircase?"

Fred shook his head. "Not for guests."

"But what about staff?"

"Well, yes, of course, there are the backstairs that run from the basement all the way to the top floor of the castle."

"Is the only way to access them through the basement?"

"No. Each floor has a staff exit that leads to the stairs, where they can go up or down."

"And are those doors covered by CCTV?"

"The camera angles on the ones that cover this floor pick up the staff access door to the basement; they're included in the security report you just gave Simon but not on other floors."

Fitzwilliam nodded. "Good. So no one can get from here to the first floor without either going up the main staircase or using the staff door, both of which are covered by CCTV. That's good to know. Thank you." He rose. "Right, I need to speak with DS Spicer and have her conduct some research on our suspects. She can also contact the police who were looking into the threats Ben Rhodes was receiving to find out if they made any progress. Mr Juke, would you mind returning to the Drawing Room and keeping an eye on our guests, please?" Perry nodded and rose. "Lady Beatrice, we'll carry on interviewing as soon as I'm done with Spicer. I think we'll talk to the McLeans next."

Bea stood. "Yes, no problem. I'll see if any of them have

finished eating and bring them next door, shall I?"
Fitzwilliam nodded. She joined Perry as he walked towards
the door. *Where's Daisy?* She spun round to spy her little
terrier curled up next to Fitzwilliam, who was talking to Fred.

I've lost her, haven't I? she thought as she sighed and left
the room.

19

7 PM, SUNDAY 10 JANUARY

In the annex room connected to the Card Room, Lady Beatrice grabbed the final set of thick-lined curtains. A fluttering across the windows confirmed it was still snowing heavily outside as she pulled them closed. Walking over to a table along the far side, she picked up the coffee pot. It was empty. *Rats!* She sighed as she grabbed the water jug instead and poured herself a glass of ice water. Sauntering to the back of the room where she'd been earlier, she settled herself into the armchair to wait for Fitzwilliam. The door between the two rooms was open slightly, and the faint rumble of a man's voice confirmed he was still on the phone to DS Tina Spicer. *Is he telling her how hard it is to investigate with only amateurs to help him?* Was he complaining he'd had to ask for Bea's help when, in previous cases, she'd been the last person he'd wanted to talk to, let alone discuss the case with? Was he begging Spicer to get on a plane in a snowsuit with a set of skis and get here as soon as possible so he could tell Bea to butt out and let them get on with their job as he had done so many times before?

Bea smiled. *It must be killing him to need us.* She

sighed. If she was honest, sitting in on the interviews wasn't as exciting as she'd hoped. She'd imagined Fitzwilliam would do more to discover who had a reason to dislike Ben Rhodes enough to kill him, but he was more focused on finding out what had happened around the time of the murder. She knew alibis were important, but without a motive, they meant nothing. *And he hasn't once asked me if I have questions...*

The noise stopped next door, and Daisy was the first to trot into the room, heading for her mistress. *If only Daisy could talk...* "Oh, so you remember me, do you?" Bea whispered to the little terrier as she jumped onto her lap. Daisy raised her head and licked her face. "Yuck!" Bea said as she wiped the back of her hand over her cheek. Daisy jumped down and met Fitzwilliam as he entered the room. He looked around and frowned.

Bea rose. "They're just finishing eating. Hector McLean will join us any minute—" There was a brisk knock on the door. She shouted, "Come in, please."

Fitzwilliam moved over and perched on the arm of the sofa. Daisy jumped up and settled next to him.

The main door opened, and a stocky grey-haired man entered. "Lady Beatrice, chief inspector." He nodded at them as he made his way across the room towards Fitzwilliam.

"Mr McLean, please take a seat." Fitzwilliam indicated the armchair opposite him as he placed his phone on the table.

Bea sat down at the same time as Hector McLean. He crossed his legs, his face relaxed as he prepared to answer Fitzwilliam's questions. *He doesn't look upset or agitated, like both Max and Clive did.* Did that mean he had nothing to hide?

"Thank you for your time, Mr McLean. I just need to ask

you a few questions that hopefully won't take too long. Did you know the deceased, Ben Rhodes?"

Hector gave a half-shrug. "Like most people, I knew of him, of course, but I'd never met him before Friday."

"And did you spend much time with him since then?"

"Not really, chief inspector. I chatted briefly with him and his brother after dinner that night, but that was all."

His lip curled slightly, and there was an edge to his voice. *I don't think he liked Ben*, Bea thought.

"But you didn't like him much, did you?"

Bea gulped.

"I really didn't know him, chief inspector." Hector McLean gave a hard smile and leaned back in his chair.

That's not really an answer! She glanced over at Fitzwilliam, who hesitated for a moment, then said, "Thank you, Mr McLean. Now can you go through your movements from when you returned from the shoot until you found out about Mr Rhodes's death."

Bea frowned. Why hadn't Fitzwilliam pursued the man's obvious dislike for Ben? It could be relevant. Maybe Ben had done something to him or one of the family? She stifled a gasp. Does he know about whatever Rose and Fergus had been discussing and had it been about Ben? She straightened up. *Should I ask?*

But it was too late. Hector McLean opened his mouth. "We got back about eleven, I believe. We were all cold and wet from the snow, so we dumped our boots and coats in the boot room, then I went up to my room and had a shower. My son Fergus knocked on the door at about twelve, and we sat and had a whisky in my room. We talked about the impact of the weather on our chances of getting home tomorrow as planned. Then we collected my daughter Rose and her husband and went downstairs. We were in the Drawing Room from then until you came in and told us of Mr Rhodes's death."

"And your bedroom is in the west wing, I understand?"

Hector nodded.

"Did you see or hear anything in the corridor as you were opening the door to your son or leaving to go downstairs?"

"No, chief inspector."

Mrs Kettley had put the McLeans in the three rooms on the other side of the west wing to Ben Rhodes. They would have no reason to go past anyone else's rooms on their way out onto the first floor landing. She would explain the layout to Fitzwilliam when they finished here. Fitzwilliam rose. *That was quick!*

"Well, thank you for your time, Mr McLean. That's all for now."

Hector uncrossed his legs and rose from the armchair. "When will we be able to go up to our rooms, chief inspector?"

"Very soon, sir. We'll let you know."

Hector opened his mouth, then closed it again. He glanced at Bea, gave a small nod, then left the room.

Fitzwilliam sighed as he picked up his phone and returned to his perch. Patting a dozing Daisy on the head, he pocketed the mobile.

Bea rose. "Why didn't you push him a bit more about his dislike of Ben Rhodes?" she asked as she moved towards him.

"I know his type. They will only give the minimum amount of information possible, and if you push them, they demand lawyers and stuff. Yes, it's clear he didn't like Ben Rhodes, but it's unlikely that if he'd never met him before, that he would kill him—"

"But he could know about Fergus's dealings with Ben and

whatever Ben did to upset his son even if he never met him," she cut in.

Fitzwilliam nodded. "I agree. But for the moment, I just want to establish if he has an alibi or not, which it seems he does if his son corroborates his story. Let's see what Fergus has to say next, shall we?"

She shrugged, then picked up her phone and texted Perry.

While they waited, she told Fitzwilliam about how the west wing corridor followed a horseshoe shape, coming out through a door on the left of the landing, opposite the door to the entrance where the Rhodes brothers' rooms were. "So the McLeans would come and go through that door as their rooms are at the end, not the door I took you through."

"Ah." Fitzwilliam nodded. "I see now. So they wouldn't need to go past—"

Fergus McLean's head peeked around the open door. "Hi, you wanted to see me?" His soft Scottish accent had a hitch in it as he stared at Fitzwilliam, who rose and walked towards him.

"Yes, please come in, Mr McLean." Fitzwilliam gestured with his arm to the armchair recently vacated by the man's father.

As Fergus made his way to take a seat, Bea moved back to her original position. He caught her eye and smiled nervously. Giving him a reassuring smile in return, she hoped he would be honest with them. She didn't want to see him get in trouble.

Fitzwilliam pushed record on his phone. "Thank you for your time, Mr McLean—"

"Please, please, er, call me Fergus. My father is, er, Mr McLean," the bearded man stuttered as he fell into the chair and scraped his hand through his reddish-brown hair.

Bea wanted to get up, squeeze his hand, and tell him not

to be so worried. She hated to see him in such a nervous state. When she'd encountered him in the past, he'd been calm... Unless, of course, he had something to hide? She studied him as he pulled at his shirt collar, his chin slightly quivering. Surely Fergus wasn't involved in Ben's death? Although she only knew him socially, she had him down as a gentle soul. She couldn't imagine Fergus holding someone's head underwater while they fought for breath. But then, she'd not been able to imagine *any* of the killers she'd unintentionally come across over the last nine months brutally ending someone's life...

"So, Fergus. Did you know Ben Rhodes well?"

Fergus flinched slightly, then stopping to take a breath, he lifted his chin. "We met several times in London. We run... sorry, we ran... with the same social group, so I'd see him around, you know?"

"And how did you get on?"

Fergus shrugged. "Fine."

Fitzwilliam frowned. "When did you last see him before this visit?"

Fergus became unnaturally still. He said nothing.

"Fergus?" Fitzwilliam prompted after a few seconds.

"Er, sorry, I was just trying to remember. Um, it was sometime last summer, I think. I'm sorry; I can't recall the details."

He looked wildly around and met Bea's gaze, then looked away instantly. *He's lying. It's clear he knows Ben better than he's admitting.* She was now, more than ever, convinced it had been Ben, Fergus and Rose had been talking about. Bea was desperate to ask some questions. She glared at Fitzwilliam, willing him to push Fergus for answers.

"So, Fergus, just to get things straight, you're saying you

knew Ben Rhodes as he was part of your social circle, but you hadn't seen him since last summer?"

Fergus narrowed his eyes. "Yes," he replied tentatively.

"And when you last saw Ben Rhodes, did you part on good terms, would you say?"

Noticing a bead of sweat appearing on Fergus's forehead, Bea waited. *Please, Fergus, tell the truth…*

He leaned forward and held Fitzwilliam's gaze. "Yes, chief inspector. Why are you asking?"

Fitzwilliam stared back at him for a few seconds.

Is he going to tell him what I overheard?

Fitzwilliam broke eye contact and, ignoring the question, asked, "Did you and Ben Rhodes spend much time together over these last few days?"

Again? Why did Fitzwilliam back off?

Fergus leaned back and crossed his legs. He suddenly looked just like his father — feigning indifference with a confidence that suggested he felt the danger was now over. "No, chief inspector. It's been busy. I've been with my family."

"Can you talk me through your movements since you returned from the shoot, please?"

Fergus tilted his head back. "Um. So we got back about eleven, I think. We got rid of our wet coats and boots, then I went up to my room. I had a quick shower, then knocked on my father's door to see if he was ready. That was about twelve. He let me in, we had a drink, then went and picked up my sister and Ed, and we went down together. We got to the Drawing Room a bit early and made ourselves at home."

"Was anyone else in the Drawing Room when you arrived?"

"Yes, one of the Rhodes twins. Oh, I guess it must have been Max." His face clouded over for a moment. "Yes. Max.

Then shortly after us, the woman with the really short hair arrived, and not long after that, the American chap."

"And neither you nor any of the other guests left the room before Lord Fred and Lady Beatrice arrived?"

He shook his head.

"And did you see or hear anything unusual when you were in your room or in the corridor outside your father's or sister's room?"

Bea suppressed a sigh of frustration. Had he forgotten already they were nowhere near Ben Rhodes's bedroom?

Fergus McLean shook his head again. "No."

Fitzwilliam stood. "Well, thank you, Fergus. That will be all." Fergus heaved himself out of the chair. Fitzwilliam leaned towards him and smiled slyly. "For now, at least."

Fergus's head flinched back slightly as Fitzwilliam continued to stare at him.

"Um, thanks." He darted a look at Bea, his eyes wide, his earlier confidence seeming to drain out of him. *Oh, Fergus, why aren't you telling us the truth?*

20

8 PM, SUNDAY 10 JANUARY

"Well, clearly he's lying about his relationship with Ben Rhodes," DCI Fitzwilliam said to Lady Beatrice as the door closed behind Fergus McLean.

Bea stood and stretched her back. "So why didn't you call him out?"

A smile tugged at the corners of Fitzwilliam's mouth. "Patience, my lady. He knows we know he's lying. That's now going to play on his mind overnight. I bet you Fergus McLean will come clean tomorrow, and confess all."

Confess? Bea felt a little breathless. He didn't think Fergus was the killer, did he? "You think he did it?"

Fitzwilliam strode over to the table and poured himself a glass of water. "I don't know. He doesn't seem the type, and he has an alibi, albeit from his father, who is also holding out on us. But he definitely knows something, and that might help us find out who the killer is." He looked pensive as he returned to the sofa. "Often the key to finding the killer is in knowing the victim."

She moved to the sofa and sat next to Daisy, stroking the

terrier's wiry head as she asked, "So you think Fergus may know something about Ben that Max doesn't?"

He shrugged. "Or maybe something he doesn't want us to know." He raised an eyebrow.

"Indeed. Max offered little in terms of what his brother was like, other than to say he was sometimes a bit late."

"Again, in my experience, people are more guarded the first time you talk to them. We may have more luck tomorrow." He looked at his watch. "Right, it's getting late. Let's have Rose and her husband in together."

She tilted her head to one side as she tapped the screen to open her phone. "Don't you normally interview people separately as a sort of test for consistency?" She texted Perry.

"If these were formal interviews, then yes. But let's be fair, they've had plenty of time to get their stories straight if they needed to, and sometimes I like to see the interaction between two suspects. What they don't say sometimes is more interesting than what they do say. And" —he heaved a heavy sigh— "it's getting late, and we still have two more after this."

———

Thirty minutes, later Bea sighed as Eve Morrison left the room. Just one more to go and then Fitzwilliam had promised they would stop for the day. She hadn't realised how much concentration was required just to listen to someone talk. Stretching her legs in front of her, she wiggled her toes inside her suede boots. She glanced up at Fitzwilliam, who was mumbling something to Daisy next to him. He looked up and caught her eye. A smile slowly spread across his face. She smiled back. He wasn't quite growing on her yet, but Bea had to admit the compulsion she'd felt in the past to slap

Fitzwilliam's face was dissipating. Mainly, she thought, because he hadn't been rude to her or dismissive of their help like he had in previous cases. His need for her help had over-ridden his previously boorish behaviour. *Long may it last...* She didn't understand why he wasn't pushing for more answers, but she didn't want to upset him by bringing it up again now. She'd try later when they were done.

Her phone buzzed.

Perry: *Sending Brett Goodman now. The natives are getting restless and asking when they can go to their rooms. xx*

"Fitzwilliam. Perry says the guests are asking when they can go to their rooms."

Fitzwilliam looked up from his phone. "Good timing. Spicer has just confirmed they have all the photos, videos, and evidence from Ben Rhodes's room, so although it will be sealed off and locked, they're done there now." He rose from the arm of the sofa. "You can tell Mr Juke he can thank them for their cooperation and let them go."

As Bea typed a message to Perry, the door swung open, and the slim frame of Brett Goodman entered the room. Pressing send, she rose and watched him walk confidently up to Fitzwilliam and introduce himself. Daisy, previously out for the count (how she slept so much was beyond Bea), jumped off the sofa and went to sniff the newcomer. He patted her head, then looking up, he met her gaze. There was a fleeting glimpse of a cheeky grin. Then he winked and immediately returned his attention to Daisy. Heat rose up Bea's neck. She slid back into her chair and arranged her long charcoal-grey jumper over her knees.

Fitzwilliam, having pressed record on his phone, placed it on the table and leaned back onto the arm of the sofa, placing his hands in his lap. "Sorry to have kept you so long, Mr Goodman. I've just got a few questions, if that's okay?"

Brett smiled and nodded. "Sure."

Bea watched Daisy as she climbed back onto the sofa and spun slowly in a circle before settling down on the couch, her head gently resting on a tartan pillow in the corner.

Would they get anything out of Brett? The last two interviews had been brief. Rose and Edward Berry had had little to add to what her father and brother had said. They had told them they had both had showers and had stayed together in their room in-between coming back from shooting and coming down for drinks. Bea had thought Rose looked uncomfortable, frequently glancing at her husband sitting next to her on the couch (Daisy and Fitzwilliam had moved to the armchair opposite) and resting her hands on her legs, which bounced up and down like she had puppet knees. When Fitzwilliam had asked Rose if she had known Ben Rhodes, she'd told them no and had said here was the first time she'd met him. It had seemed to Bea she was telling the truth. But when Fitzwilliam had asked her if she'd known her brother Fergus knew Ben socially, she had tried (unsuccessfully) to disguise the guilty blush spreading over her face as she'd looked down and mumbled that he might have mentioned it, but she wasn't sure. It had been clear she had known more than she had been prepared to say. Bea was now more convinced than ever it had been Ben Rhodes that Rose and Fergus had been talking about on the stairs. However, Rose wouldn't say anything more, and Fitzwilliam had let them go with the ominous parting shot of, "That will be all... for now."

"Had you met Ben Rhodes prior to this weekend, Mr Goodman?" Fitzwilliam asked.

Brett shook his head. "No, chief inspector. I'm just over here on vacation at the moment."

"I understand you're here as a guest of Lord Frederick Astley's. Is that correct?"

Fitzwilliam was asking Brett exactly the same questions he had asked Eve Morrison a few minutes before. She too had denied knowing Ben before this weekend.

"That's correct. He heard from a mutual friend I was in the UK for a few weeks and asked me if I'd like to join him. I've never been to this part of Scotland before, so I said yes." He glanced over at Bea. "I'd no idea it would be so beautiful here," he said, holding her stare.

Bea's face, neck, and ears were impossibly hot. Fitzwilliam cleared his throat, and she looked away. *Goodness, this is so embarrassing…*

"Did you have much contact with Ben Rhodes since you got here?" Fitzwilliam asked abruptly.

Bea didn't dare look at Brett. While he told them how he'd only spoken to the twins twice, Bea snuck a glance at Fitzwilliam who was listening intently to Brett. *Did he see me blush like a young girl on a first date?* She hoped not. She wanted him to take her and her views seriously, especially after she'd messed up on their last case, her woman's intuition having let her down badly until it had almost been too late. If he saw Brett flirting with her so openly, would he decide she was a liability to this investigation and cut her out? Her heart felt like it was shrinking. She didn't want to go back to being on the outside anymore. She started. *I enjoy working with Fitzwilliam.*

"… had a shower, answered a few emails, and then came down for drinks." Brett looked relaxed and comfortable, as if being interviewed by police about murder was something that happened to him all the time.

The tension left her shoulders, and she stifled a giggle. *Maybe when you're a spy and you're used to being interrogated, this all seems a bit tame?*

"And did you notice anything odd or unusual when you left your room or made your way downstairs?"

Brett shook his head slowly. "No. Sorry."

Fitzwilliam pressed his lips together tightly, then stood. "Well, thank you, Mr Goodman. You're free to go up to your room now if you wish."

Brett jumped up and smiled. "Great. There's only so much tea I can drink." He turned to Bea. But seeing the twinkle in his eyes and fearful of what he might say or do, she quickly averted her gaze and remained seated.

Hearing the door close, she let out a sigh of relief and got up out of the chair. It was a shame that, like Eve Morrison, Brett Goodman hadn't seen or heard anything. It was getting late now, and she was grateful they'd finished.

"Let's go next door and catch-up with the others, shall we?" Without waiting for her reply, Fitzwilliam moved towards the connecting door, Daisy trotting faithfully by his side.

———

Perry Juke inched forward in the seat of a large brown leather upright chair in the Card Room and let out a deep sigh as he reached over and grabbed the glass of red wine Simon had just poured for him. "Thanks, love. I need this," he said, taking a sip.

Opposite him in a tartan-patterned armchair, Simon Lattimore placed a half empty bottle of wine on a table between him and Perry. "Cheers," he said, picking up his glass and raising it to his partner.

Lady Beatrice, standing over by the main door, closed it behind Brock as he left, then went back to the group sitting by the fireplace. Simon handed her a glass of wine, and she sat on one end of the sofa next to a snoozing Daisy. She looked towards Fitzwilliam, who was perched on the arm at the other end. *Surely it can't be comfortable to sit like that all the time; it must hurt his—*

"So what do we know?" Fitzwilliam said, a coffee cup halfway to his mouth. "Mr Juke?"

Perry raised an eyebrow. "I really think it's time you call me Perry, don't you, Fitzwilliam?"

Fitzwilliam nodded and raised his cup.

"Well," Perry began. "The McLeans are up to something. They're *terrible* at whispering quietly, and I distinctly heard Rose say to Fergus as she and her husband were on their way out, 'You didn't tell him, did you?' and he shook his head. After that, he just slumped into the chair and didn't speak for the rest of the time they were gone even though Hector McLean was obviously getting impatient and was belly aching about them not being allowed to go upstairs. When Rose and Ed came back in, I swear I saw her shake her head at her brother."

"Well, that would make sense," Bea said. "She and Ed barely said anything other than they were together the whole time."

"So whatever this secret is, and even if we assume it's to do with what you overheard, Bea, and they knew and hated someone, maybe Ben, they all have alibis from what you've been saying," Simon said. "Unless they're all in on it together."

Hold on, could they all be in it together? A knot formed

in her belly. Could that explain the comment Rose had made to Fergus when she'd said, "After all he's done to us?"

"In fact," Bea added, leaning forward. "It wouldn't have to be all of them. It could just be Hector and Fergus McLean working together or Rose and Ed Berry. Both couples had time for one of them to go to Ben's room and kill him, while the other acted as a lookout. They could have been back in their room before they all came down together at twelve-twenty."

Oh my goodness! Had they cracked it already? In past cases, it had taken them days, if not weeks, to find the killer, but now—

Fitzwilliam raised his hand. "Before we get carried away, if they stick with their stories that they were together, then we'll need evidence to show they were lying. And" —he shifted on the arm of the sofa— "we mustn't forget we have other suspects that could also have strong motives who don't have alibis. So we can't get too carried away along one path."

Bea nodded.

Fitzwilliam turned to Simon. "How about the staff? Are they all accounted for?"

"All but the footman, Owen Buckey, and Libby Carpenter, the head maid. The CCTV cameras show the butler, Brock, moving backwards and forwards between various rooms with drinks and food, and likewise with the head footman, William Featherstone. After we interviewed them, Fred and I looked at the CCTV footage, and it supports what they said. There wouldn't have been time for either of them to get up to the first floor. I'm confident we can rule them out."

Fitzwilliam nodded.

"Mrs Kettley, the head housekeeper, was settling in The Queen Mother and her staff until about eleven forty-five, then she was in the kitchen having a break until twelve thirty-five, when she went up to the second floor to check on the maids. We have confirmed her movements with The Queen Mother's butler and the cook. Talking of the cook — Mrs Wilton and Maddie Preston, the kitchen maid, were together from ten-thirty this morning until two this afternoon preparing lunch and dinner. Maddie Preston then went to her room, as did Mrs Wilton, who is staying here temporarily until the snow clears. They both came back down at five to finish getting dinner ready. Brock and Featherstone also confirmed their presence in the kitchen as they went back and forth, as did Mrs Kettley, and vice versa; Mrs Wilton and Mrs Kettley confirmed Brock and Featherstone were in and out of the kitchen and the butler's pantry too."

Perry fidgeted in his seat. "So what about Buckey and the maid?"

"Well, Libby Carpenter was on her break in her room on the fourth floor until twelve, then she claims she went straight down to the second floor via the back stairs and was in the housekeeping room in the east wing sorting out clean towels and linen ready for when the guests left their rooms to go to drinks at twelve-thirty. She says she heard you, Bea, and Lord Fred heading down the corridor from your grandmother's apartment, so she then took her housekeeping trolley and started making up your rooms first, intending to move down to the first floor to do the guest rooms after. Mrs Kettley came up and joined her at twelve thirty-five. At about one Brock found them both still on the second floor and told them what had happened."

"So she has no alibi from twelve until twelve thirty-five?" Perry asked.

Simon shook his head. "No one saw her, and she didn't talk to anyone during the critical time."

"And what about the footman?" Fitzwilliam asked, a handful of salted peanuts in his hand.

"That's more difficult," Simon told them. "Buckey says he was also backwards and forward during the time in question. He was gathering all the wet coats and boots and taking them to the laundry room in the basement to get them dry. The CCTV recorded him moving between the ground floor and the basement up to eleven-forty, when he went into the basement and didn't emerge again until twelve forty-five. He says he was in the laundry room the whole time, but no one can confirm that. Those in the kitchen say they didn't see him, so he has no alibi and could easily have slipped upstairs."

"Thank you, Lattimore. So we have two members of staff with no alibis and—"

The door opened, and Lord Frederick Astley strolled in. "Sorry, I was just catching up with the security team to make sure they're all being extra vigilant tonight. They've pulled a couple of extra guys who live on-site in for the night." He stopped at the bar in the corner of the room and pulled a bottle of whisky out from a cupboard. "Anyone want to join me?" he shouted across the room.

Simon, Perry, and Bea shook their heads, but Fitzwilliam nodded. Fred gathered two glasses and made his way back to them. He put the bottle and the glasses on the table. "So I heard you say you have two members of staff without alibis?" he said as he picked up the bottle and poured two generous measures of whisky.

Fitzwilliam nodded. "The footman, Owen Buckey, and the head maid Libby Carpenter." He took the glass Fred held out.

Fred shook his head as he took a sip of the amber liquid. "I still don't think any of the staff are credible suspects."

Bea agreed. She couldn't imagine why either of them would want to kill a guest.

"Anyone who doesn't have an alibi has to be investigated further to see if there is any link between them and the victim. If there isn't, then I agree they are unlikely to have a motive. My DS will do some background checks on them, but if you have any personnel files or anything, that would be helpful."

Bea nodded. *This is more like it.* Fitzwilliam was looking at motives now. "I'll talk to Mrs Kettley tomorrow. She'll have access to their files," she said.

"Thank you, Lady Beatrice."

"And in terms of the guests?" Fred asked.

"It's early days yet, my lord. I need to go through the recordings of the interviews and look at the CCTV reports so I can confirm people were where they say they were and at what time."

"Well, I don't know about you, but I'm bushed," Simon said, rising from his chair and looking at his partner. "Come on, Perry. The sooner we go to bed, the sooner it will be breakfast time."

Bea smiled. Simon knew how to motivate his other half. Perry sprung up and rubbed his hands together.

Glancing over at Fitzwilliam, who had his head bent looking at the papers in his hand, Bea rose. "Fred, you and I need to say goodnight to Grandmama." Fred nodded and necked his drink. "Come on, Daisy." Her little dog scrambled off the couch and joined them. She turned to Fitzwilliam, who had put down the papers and his glass of whisky, now rose from the arm of the sofa. "You're on the second floor in the east wing, Fitzwilliam. Third room on the right-hand side. I've arranged breakfast for us in here from eight tomorrow morning."

"Thank you, my lady. I'm just going to stay in here and make a few calls, if that's okay?"

She nodded. "Ring for Brock if you need anything."

Fitzwilliam turned to face the group. "Thank you all for your help today. I'll see you in the morning."

21

BREAKFAST, MONDAY 11 JANUARY

The delicious smell of bacon greeted Lady Beatrice as she walked into the Card Room, Daisy by her side. The heavy curtains had been pulled back to reveal a murky grey land-scape with few distinct features on show, the snow having smothered everything. *It will look beautiful once the sun rises.* She checked herself. *Poor Max.* He was waking up to a new life this morning — one without his brother in it. She knew just how shocking that was. The hope that the previous day had been just a bad dream, then the moment of crushing realisation that it hadn't been, and the person was really gone and never coming back. She sighed. They must find out who killed Ben, for Max's sake.

Would CID be able to get to them today? It had only stopped snowing a short while ago. No, it would still be too difficult for them to get through. *Well, at least, I hope so.* She didn't want them to arrive now and shut her out, relegating her to watch from the sidelines. If they did, how could she prove to Fitzwilliam she was a valuable asset to him?

Reaching out, she felt for Daisy. She wasn't there. She stood and scanned the room, finding her little dog sitting in front of the table along the wall where the footman had laid out breakfast. *Cheeky!* As well as bread rolls, toasting bread, fruit, and pastries, the bain-maries would be full of crispy bacon, sausages, and eggs. Not being a breakfast person, Bea ignored the food and headed to the end of the table, where a large steaming pot of coffee stood.

She poured herself a large black coffee. "Come on, Daisy." She walked to the table in front of the far window. She pulled out one of the six chairs and sat down. Daisy, who had stopped before she'd reached Bea, sat with her back to her mistress, staring with pleading eyes at the breakfast table. *Woof!* Suddenly she redirected her attention to the door.

A wagging bundle of white fur greeted Detective Chief Inspector Richard Fitzwilliam when he entered the room. Bea, averting her eyes from the commotion by the door, took a sip of her black coffee. *She never greets me like that!*

"Good morning, Lady Beatrice," Fitzwilliam called over as he headed for the breakfast table.

"Morning." Bea moved her head and watched him through the corner of her eye as he grabbed a plate and a couple of rolls before taking the steel cover off one container and, using the tongs that were lying on a plate in front of it, grasped a pile of bacon rashers and deposited them on his plate. Daisy, sitting by his side, looked longingly up at him and licked her lips.

Fitzwilliam cleared his throat as he sat down. "It seems to have finally stopped snowing then," he said, leaning over for the butter dish.

"Indeed." She took another sip of the hot black liquid to moisten her dry mouth. *Why do I feel like I want to get up and flee the room?* She slipped her hand under the table to steady her right leg, which was bouncing and hitting the underside of the wood, causing the silverware in front of her to vibrate gently. She was aware of the proximity of the man sitting opposite her and slowly leaned back in her chair. *Get a grip, Bea!* She put down her coffee cup, and creeping her hand under the table, she pinched the inside of the lower part of her other arm. *Ouch!* The shock of the sharp pain immediately stopped her leg moving, and the butterflies in her tummy fluttered away. *That's better.* She quietly breathed out, then bringing both her hands back up, she reached again for her coffee cup. "I hope you slept well, Fitzwilliam?"

He nodded. "Very, thank you. You?"

"Yes. I always sleep well here. I think it's all the fresh air." *Oh my goodness, I sound like a cliche!* She had, in fact, slept badly, visions of Ben's face submerged under water never far from her mind. But she wasn't going to tell him that. *Well, that was the weather and how well we slept covered.* What was next in the 'awkward conversations and how to get through them' manual? "How's your food?" *Oh, just shoot me now!*

He grinned. "Good, thank you."

Is he laughing at me? She pinched her mouth indignantly. *If he's going to—*

Daisy, who had been waiting patiently by Fitzwilliam's feet, let out a short bark and ran towards the door. Perry Juke and Simon Lattimore appeared around the frame. The little dog launched herself at them, her tail wagging nine to the dozen. The tightness in Bea's muscles unwound, and she stifled a sigh of relief as they shouted, "Good morning," and waved. She smiled and waved back. *Thank goodness they're here…*

Having gathered food and drinks, her friends joined her and Fitzwilliam by the window, Perry sitting next to Bea and Simon taking the chair opposite him.

"All right, Bea?" Simon asked, his slightly tanned face creased with a smile.

She nodded as a movement to her left made her glance at Perry. "Perry!" she cried, and he stopped, his hand midway under the table, a rasher of crispy bacon dangling from it.

"It's just one small piece, Bea," he replied, fixing her with a stare. "She was such a good girl yesterday…"

"Okay, I give up," Bea said, waving her hand at him. "But you can take her to her next vet checkup and get scolded for allowing her to get too podgy."

A snort came from across the table, and she whipped her head around to see Fitzwilliam covering his mouth. He coughed, then cleared his throat. "Now we're all here, I can tell you the latest from Spicer."

"What about Lord Fred?" Simon asked.

"He's having breakfast with the guests," Bea informed him. She'd questioned her brother about if it was the right thing to do, bearing in mind one of them was most likely a murderer, but he'd replied that it would be rude for the host not to be there, and unless she wanted to volunteer, then he would have to step up.

"Well, then let me start with his colleagues, Eve Morrison and Brett Goodman. Neither of them have alibis as we found out yesterday, and now Spicer's struggling to find any background on either of them, so—"

"Well, if they're spies, isn't that what—" Perry jumped in.

Fitzwilliam held up his hand. "Mr Juke… Perry… I appreciate you have your own opinion of who they are, but I'm more interested in why they're here. Even if their jobs are, shall we say, 'classified', then I don't think they're here for the sport, do you? According to Lord Fred, Eve Morrison didn't attend either of the shooting days due to work commitments, and Brett Goodman was only ever an observer. Lord

Fred told me Brett enjoyed the sport but not the shooting. I find it all odd, and I intend to tackle them about it later today."

He took a mouthful of coffee and carried on. "Spicer didn't have much luck with the local police investigating the threats against Ben Rhodes. Her view is they didn't really take it that seriously, so it was still on their 'to do' list." He shook his head. "As you can imagine, they were worried when they heard he'd been killed. It's likely there will be an investigation into their handling of the matter. But anyway, that won't help us." He took another sip of coffee, then continued, "I looked at all the CCTV, and as you told us last night, Lattimore, it confirms everyone's movements as you logged them. We sent photos of all fingerprints that were taken from the guests and the crime scene to Forensics. They confirmed it was Ben's finger prints on the glass in the bathroom. Someone wiped the glass and the bottle in the bedroom clean."

"So the person who killed him had a drink with him first?" Simon asked.

"I can't think of any other reason they would've removed them, so it would appear so."

Bea wrinkled her nose. So it was someone who he'd been happy to have a drink with then? Had they put something in it to make him less likely to struggle? "Was he drugged?"

Fitzwilliam shrugged. "We don't know for sure, but the basic tests the PC did on the liquid left in the glass found in the bathroom suggest it was just whisky. He couldn't lift any useful fingerprints from the door handle because of the large number of smudged prints there."

Simon nodded. "He did what he could with his basic kit, but I don't expect we'll get anything from it. The photos have been sent on though."

"Thanks. We got the passcode from Mrs Rhodes for Ben's phone, but that didn't work. He must have changed it recently and not told her. However, the tech bods at PaIRS got me in." He paused and touched his throat. "I'm shocked at how easy it is with the right software." He shook his head and continued, "Anyway, I can confirm Ben's last text was to Max at eleven minutes past twelve to say he was having a bath, and Max replied a minute later, telling him to hurry. Also on his phone, I found copies of threatening emails saying, in a variety of ways, to cease his involvement with Urshall United or face the consequences. Two text messages, one sent on Friday and another sent yesterday morning, both said he'd be sorry if he didn't do as he was told."

"So they were threatening him to get out of the football club?" Perry asked, putting down his napkin and pushing his empty plate away.

"I assume so, but all the messages came from different numbers, so it's hard to say. I'll check with Max Rhodes just to make sure no one else was threatening Ben. I've sent copies to the IT chaps at PaIRS, and they're seeing if they can trace the numbers and email addresses the threats came from, but these people are clever. Apparently, they use software to generate masking phone numbers and email addresses to use that can't be traced, so I doubt that will come up with anything useful soon. Apart from that, the phone was surprisingly empty. The tech guys will see if there are any deleted items once I can get Ben's mobile to them."

Bea leaned back in her chair. Was there a way to truly delete all your information? She'd ask Fred later...

"So the good news is we have confirmation Ben Rhodes was alive at eleven minutes past twelve. Clive Tozzi told us the water was cold when he felt for the victim's pulse at twelve forty-five. It takes about ten minutes for a bath of water to go cold, so unless he chose to sit in cold water, then I think we can safely assume he died before twelve thirty-five. So we only have a window of up to twenty-five minutes, during which someone killed him."

They sat in silence for a few minutes, letting what Fitzwilliam had told them sink in.

"Spicer is still doing background checks on our other suspects, including the two members of staff without alibis. In the meantime, I'd like to—" The phone in front of him rang. He picked it up immediately. "Fitzwilliam?" He listened to the caller for a few seconds, then putting his hand over the microphone, he stood. "Sorry, will you all excuse me for a moment, please? I'll just take this call in the other room." He moved around Simon's chair and headed off towards the connecting door. He opened it and disappeared into the ante-room attached, closing the door behind him.

22

MEANWHILE, MONDAY 11 JANUARY

Lady Beatrice watched DCI Fitzwilliam close the door to the anteroom, then turned to her breakfast companions. "What is that all about, do you think?"

Simon Lattimore, who had been gazing out of the window, shrugged. "Probably DS Spicer with more information for him."

She huffed. "But then why not take it in here? We're involved in the investigation too, aren't we?" Did Fitzwilliam not need them anymore now that they had processed the crime scene and had interviewed everyone? A wave of nausea hit her. *Will he carry on without us now? Or maybe it's just his new girlfriend?* That would explain why he was taking the call in the other room.

"Perhaps he doesn't need our help anymore," Perry Juke said, taking a sip of tea. *Thanks, Perry!* "The heavy lifting has been done. He has all the statements and the CCTV video. Him and Spicer can probably manage on their own now." He raised his hand to his chest. "And I won't be disappointed if that's the case. It was so boring sitting in that room last night. I'm happy to let him get on with it without me."

What? Perry had been the most enthusiastic participant in their previous investigations. Why was he backing out of this one so easily? "I know it's slower than we're used to, but you loved investigating previous cases…"

"I know, but they were people we knew, or we were helping people we knew. I didn't know Ben Rhodes, and to be honest, from what I read about him, he wasn't the sort of person I would want to know. His acquisition of Urshall United was dodgy if you believe what the papers say—"

"But, Perry, we know the papers aren't always a reliable source of fact," she pointed out. Even though her own mother was involved in the news arena, Bea still recalled how the press had treated her when her husband had died. When it came to light that Gill Sterling, the estate manager's wife, had been found in the car with him when it had crashed, the news had prompted relentless and brutal speculation about her and James's relationship. And even last year, when her and Seb's relationship had been in its fledgeling stages, the coverage in the media had been ridiculous. When they'd only been together for a few weeks, some newspapers had reported that marriage between them was on the cards.

Simon grabbed a pastry from his plate. "Actually, Bea, I'd normally agree with you. But it's not just the popular press who thinks Ben Rhodes's involvement with the Urshall United deal was suspect. The business press is reporting accusations of insider information forcing a fire sale of the club."

She shuffled her feet under the table. "Er, what's a fire sale?"

"When they sell the shares at a price that's well below market value. The rumour is Ben Rhodes got his shares at fire-sale prices because the company was in deep water financially."

"But it wasn't?"

"Well, this is the thing. The reports say it had some debt that needed repaying, but it was within terms, as in it wasn't due yet. Then rumours started that they wouldn't be able to meet their commitments. The creditors got nervous despite reassurances from the consortium that owned the club, and they demanded their money back. The club couldn't pay, the share price dropped, and it forced them to sell out to avoid the club going bankrupt."

"I get Ben may have taken advantage of their situation, but doesn't that just make him a good businessman?"

"Not if he was in someway involved in starting the rumours in the first place…"

"Oh, I see."

Simon put his hands up. "I'm not saying he was, but that's what is being bandied about in the newspapers."

"Would that give someone a motive to kill him?" she asked.

"Maybe if they lost a lot of money in the process?" Perry answered.

She narrowed her eyes. "I thought you weren't interested in who killed him?"

He shrugged. "I suppose I don't care that much."

She gasped. "Doesn't it bother you there's a murderer staying here at the moment?"

He pulled his fingers through his short spiky blond hair. "Yes, of course. But I'm happy to let Fitzwilliam deal with it."

She shook her head in disbelief. "But what if he needs our help?"

He sighed and leaned back in his chair. "Then I suppose I'll do what I can, but I'm telling you now, I'm not sitting in a room with a bunch of strangers spying on them again."

She smiled. "Okay, point taken."

Simon rose. "Well, while I'm happy to help if I'm needed, I also have a book deadline. I'm off to write. If you need me, you know where I am. See you later." He grabbed his coffee cup and strolled out.

Perry also rose. "Another coffee?" She nodded, and he walked over to the table, Daisy trailing behind him.

There was a knock on the door, and the butler entered with a coffee pot in one hand. "My lady, I thought you might be in need of a refill."

"Perfect timing!" Perry cried out from the other side of the room, shaking the empty pot.

Brock glided over and placed the full one on the table, then he moved towards Bea. "Lady Rossex," he said as he stopped by her side. "Can I have a word, please?"

She looked up at the butler, his face giving nothing away about what he wanted to talk to her about. "Yes, of course, Brock."

The tall pristinely-dressed man glanced over at Perry, who was filling two cups with coffee. "It's, er, confidential, my lady. It's information about Mr Ben Rhodes."

"Don't worry about Mr Juke, Brock. He's completely in my confidence." She frantically waved Perry over.

"What?" Perry asked as he arrived, two cups of coffee in his hands and Daisy by his feet.

"Brock here wants to talk to us about something... confidential." She raised an eyebrow at him. Perry hurriedly put down the coffee cups and sat. She turned back to the butler. "Go ahead, Brock."

"Well, my lady, yesterday after most of the guests went up to get changed and I was clearing up in the Drawing Room ready for drinks later, I heard an argument going on in the library next door. The connecting door was slightly ajar, it would seem." He cleared his throat. "I didn't like to close it and announce my presence…" He trailed off and waited.

"Of course, Brock. I understand. Did you inadvertently hear what was being said?"

He coughed. "Well, my lady. The two men who were arguing sounded agitated. One asked the other, 'What are you going to do about it?' and the other replied, 'I don't know. I thought it would go away if I were here.' Then the first one said, 'It's serious, Ben. You can't just keep ignoring it. Deal with it.'"

"So the two men were the Rhodes brothers?" Perry asked, wide-eyed.

Brock gave a brief bow. "I surmised so, Mr Juke."

"Did they say anything else?" Bea asked.

"A lot of what they said was muffled, my lady. I think they were moving around. Just before they left the room, one asked the other, 'Will you help me out then?' And the other replied, 'I'll have to think about it.' And that was all, my lady." The man looked down at his shoes. "You know I make it a rule never to repeat what I hear when I'm performing my duties, Lady Rossex. That's why I said nothing to Mr Lattimore and the police constable yesterday." He looked up, his Adam's apple bobbing up and down like it was dancing a jig. "But after careful consideration overnight, I thought I should say something to you or his lordship in case it's pertinent to Mr Rhodes's death, my lady."

"Of course, and you did the right thing. What time was this, Brock?"

"About twenty past eleven, my lady."

"And are you sure it was Max Rhodes who was talking to his brother?"

Brock swallowed. "As I left the Drawing Room not long after, I saw one of the Rhodes gentlemen leave the room and go upstairs. I then headed to the staff door to go down to the kitchen, and as I turned to pull the door handle, I observed the gentleman's brother walking down the corridor from the library towards the stairs."

"Well, thank you, Brock. That was very useful."

The butler bowed, then walked to the breakfast table, retrieved the empty coffee pot, and left the room. A few seconds later, the door to the anteroom opened and Fitzwilliam walked in. "Sorry about that," he said as he headed towards them. Daisy jumped up from under the table and ran to meet him.

"There's fresh coffee in the pot, if you want some," Bea shouted across the room. He nodded, then pivoted on his feet, and Daisy followed him to the breakfast table.

Perry leaned in. "Are you going to tell him?" he whispered.

"Yes, of course," she whispered back. "We're helping him, remember?"

Perry looked down at his coffee cup and mumbled, "Yeah, but it's not as much fun."

She cocked her head to one side. *So that's the issue.* She suppressed a smile. Only Perry could think investigating a murder on their own was 'fun'. She hesitated. Although she had to admit being up against Fitzwilliam and trying to prove they could do as good a job as him *was* more exciting than cooperating with him. But then, as Simon would no doubt point out to them, it was also a lot more dangerous! She raised her hand to her throat, remembering their previous cases. A lot more…

"Where's Lattimore?" Fitzwilliam asked. He sat down next to her and patted Daisy on the head as she curled up by his feet.

"He's gone to do some writing," Perry replied. "He said we're to let him know if he's needed."

Fitzwilliam nodded. "Of course, I—"

The door opened, and Lord Frederick Astley strolled in. "Sorry I'm late. I had to show my face to our guests." He walked over to the breakfast table and helped himself to tea, then picking up a pain au chocolat, he joined them at the table, a delighted look on his face.

Bea frowned. *What's he up to?*

"I have news," he declared, taking a bite of his pastry.

Aw, so that's why he looks like the cat who's got the cream.

"Your digging was fruitful then, I gather?" Fitzwilliam asked.

What digging?

Fred nodded, his mouth still full.

"I asked Lord Fred to use his contacts to see if he could find out anything about the McLeans' business dealings," Fitzwilliam explained.

Bea nodded. Fred had been helpful to her during previous cases when they'd not had access to the same background information the police had.

Fred wiped his mouth with a napkin. "Yes, very. The McLeans may have been telling the truth when they said they'd not met Ben Rhodes before, but they certainly know him much better than they made out. McLean and Co were part of the consortium who owned Urshall United, and rumour has it, they lost a fortune when the share price dropped and they had to sell their almost worthless shares to Ben Rhodes. Now *that* sounds like a motive to me!"

23

9 AM, MONDAY 11 JANUARY

"Oh my giddy aunt!" Perry Juke raised his hand to his mouth.

"Indeed." Lady Beatrice raised an eyebrow.

"Interesting." Detective Chief Inspector Richard Fitzwilliam nodded.

Lord Frederick Astley smiled smugly. "No one is absolutely sure how much they lost as they'd also sold some shares earlier in the trading period, and those haven't been reported yet, but they had a five percent share when the club was worth around eight hundred and fifty million."

Bea was desperately trying to work out the maths in her head. *One percent will be eight point five million, so five percent is… a lot.*

"Forty-two point five million. Wow!" Perry said, wide-eyed.

Bea suppressed a grin. *Thank goodness Perry does all the ordering for our business, not me.*

"Exactly. So when the rumours they couldn't pay their debts hit the share price, it tanked. The club's value hit rock bottom at just over two hundred million."

"So they could have lost as much as thirty-two and a half million?" Fitzwilliam asked.

How did he work that out so quickly?

Fred nodded. "Seems to me you'd be pretty hacked off at someone who cost you that much."

"But would they blame Ben? After all, he just took an opportunity that was there. If he hadn't bought the club, then someone else would have," Perry pointed out.

"Ah, but here is where it gets *really* interesting." Fred paused and took a gulp of tea.

Bea gave him a look. *Stop over-dramatising this, and get on with it!*

He gave her a cheeky grin, then continued, "The 'rumour'" —he air-quoted the word— "the business could not meet its deadlines to repay its debts came from *inside* the company. Now bear with me because this is where it gets complicated. The club had a new junior administrator who had started the week before. They allegedly found him digging into some confidential files on day two of his employment and sacked him. He then went to the fans' website and posted on there that the club had mistreated him. Fans started asking what had happened, and eventually, he claimed he'd found out the club was in financial difficulty and management was keeping it secret. The whole thing blew up, and the national papers got hold of the story. That's when the actual damage was done. Even though the board of the club denied it was true, it was too late." He looked around at the three of them expectantly, a knowing smile on his face.

"Fred…" Bea said in a low warning voice.

"Okay! Guess who the junior administrator was?"

"Fred!"

He laughed. "Turns out he's the son of Ben Rhodes's former chief finance officer, a guy called Nathan Ferris.

Nathan left Ben's company six months ago because of health issues, but it's rumoured the two were still close."

"So you think Nathan's son was a deliberate plant to get the share price down and allow Ben to buy the club for a steal?" Perry asked.

Fred shrugged. "I don't know. But if the McLeans knew about the connection, then they'd be pretty mad, I would think."

Bea frowned. "But surely Ben wouldn't get away with it once the connection became public?"

Fred shook his head. "It would be hard to prove. There's a Financial Conduct Authority investigation going on after the consortium, which of course includes the McLeans, made an allegation of insider dealing. However, my contacts say it's currently stalled because Nathan's son, who is only nineteen years old, claims they sacked him because he'd accidentally come across a memo that said the board was concerned it would struggle to meet its obligations in the future if season ticket sales didn't increase. He said he hadn't originally intended to tell anyone. He simply went onto the site to whine about being mistreated by the club. It was only when someone from the club's management replied to the post saying that they had sacked him for being dishonest, that he retaliated, claiming it was the club who had been dishonest and then shared the information he'd found." Fred sighed. "It's hard to prove he could have known how it would have escalated and ultimately what the financial impact it would have had on the club. The FCA will probably say there's insufficient proof it was a deliberate act of insider dealing as the outcome couldn't have been predicted."

Fred smirked and looked at Fitzwilliam. "Well, what do you think?"

"I think it's a plausible motive. You've done well, Lord

Fred. I'm very grateful. It would have taken us days, if not weeks, to find out that level of detail."

Bea shuffled her feet under the table.

Fitzwilliam leaned forward. "But Lord Fred, unfortunately, neither of your colleagues have alibis. My sergeant is doing some background on them, but it would be helpful if you could—"

"But I can vouch for them, Fitzwilliam," Fred interrupted. "They have no connection to Ben Rhodes, and—"

"As far as you know, my lord," Fitzwilliam interrupted back. "Of course I value your opinion, but even you can't be sure they don't have a past with him. Neither is being forthcoming, and I want to know what they're doing here because they're clearly not here for the sport." He held Fred's gaze. Silence descended on the room.

Bea looked at Perry. He pulled a face that said he had no clue what was going on either.

Fred pressed his lips together, then rose. "All right, Fitzwilliam. Leave it with me. I'll have a word with them."

Fitzwilliam stood. "Thank you, my lord. I appreciate your support."

Fred gave Bea a dry smile and headed for the door. *What just happened?*

Still standing, Fitzwilliam said, "I think it's time to tackle Hector McLean again, don't you?"

24

9:45 AM, MONDAY 11 JANUARY

"Thank you for coming, Mr McLean. I have a couple of follow-up questions after our interview yesterday." DCI Richard Fitzwilliam ushered the grey-haired man towards an armchair in the middle of the anteroom. "Please take a seat."

Hector McLean sighed and leaned back into the chair so heavily, Lady Beatrice, who was sitting by the window, thought it would tip back. He picked at his trousers, straightening the seams so they lay neatly over his shoes, and huffed. "I'm not sure there's much I can add."

Fitzwilliam pressed record on his phone and leaned back, propping himself up with the arm of the sofa. It was strange not to see Daisy by his side.

Bea had now resigned herself to the fact her little dog preferred Fitzwilliam's company to her own these days. When she'd moaned about it to Fred last night on their way up to see their grandmother, he'd pointed out it was the novelty of having someone new around rather than a shift of affection away from Bea, but she wasn't so sure. Whenever Fitzwilliam was in the room, Daisy mooched around after him like a love-struck teenager. *Do dogs fall in love?* She'd been pleased when Perry had offered to take the little terrier with him on the 'special assignment' Fitzwilliam had given him. Daisy was a good icebreaker.

"When we spoke yesterday, Mr McLean, you said you didn't know Ben Rhodes well."

"That's correct." He sounded less confident now. Was he worried they had found him out?

"But you're actually familiar with him, aren't you, Mr McLean? After all, it was Ben Rhodes who purchased your company's shares in Urshall United at a knock-down price, wasn't it?"

This is more like it! This was what she'd been waiting for.

Hector McLean's face turned puce, and a purple vein pulsed on his forehead. "I don't know what that's got to do with anything," he snapped.

"Don't you? By our estimates, you lost over thirty million when you sold your shares. You must have been angry at the man who caused you to take such an enormous loss."

Hector glared at Fitzwilliam. "Thirty million! That's ridiculous. It was nothing like as much as that."

Hadn't Fred said something about the company having sold some of their shares just before the trouble had all started?

"How much *did* you lose then, Mr McLean?"

The man stilled and narrowed his eyes. "I'm sorry, but I'm not in a position to divulge that information. All I can tell you is that it was a *lot* less than your estimate."

"We can find out, Mr McLean," Fitzwilliam informed him.

Go, Fitzwilliam! Don't let him push you around. Hector McLean was clearly trying to downplay the impact so it looked like he had no reason to have killed Ben. She inched forward in her seat.

"Not without due cause, chief inspector. I'll give you my corporate lawyer's number. You can have that conversation with him!" He catapulted out of his seat. "Now, if that's all, please excuse me." He glanced at Bea, raised his chin, then returned his stare to Fitzwilliam. "And I can tell you now, chief inspector, unless you intend to arrest me or one of my family, then we won't be answering any more of your absurd questions. As soon as I get upstairs, I'll be ringing my solicitor!" He stomped across the room and disappeared through the doorway.

Wow! Bea closed her mouth as the rushing in her ears disappeared. That had taken a turn. *Is Fitzwilliam in trouble?* She caught his eye, and he grinned as he stood and turned off the recording app. "There's nothing like an outraged suspect, my lady. All that blast and bluster is something to behold."

"Aren't you worried he'll make a complaint, and you'll be in trouble?"

He shook his head, a smile still playing on his lips. "No. I doubt he'll do anything. I think that show was all for you. But even if he does, my questions are legitimate. This is a murder inquiry, and he's a suspect. If he wants to make it formal, then he can. It won't stop me pursuing him if I think he's a killer." His smile vanished, and his brows pulled in.

"But you don't think he is?"

Fitzwilliam opened, then closed his mouth. He shrugged. "Sometimes the sort of behaviour Hector McLean just displayed is to disguise guilt. But I think that was more about him not wanting me, and in particular you, knowing his business. He didn't seem so much guilty as indignant I had mentioned money in front of royalty."

Her head was fuzzy. *So does he think the McLeans could have done it or not?*

"I'm going to leave the McLean family to calm down a

bit and focus on our suspects without alibis." He looked at his watch. "I'm hoping Spicer will have some background on our two members of staff soon, then we can see if that leads us anywhere. And who knows, Perry might have some luck with Mrs Kettley."

Bea smiled. Fitzwilliam's idea of Perry going to collect the personnel files on Owen Buckey and Libby Carpenter from the head housekeeper had been a stroke of genius. Mrs Kettley had a soft spot for Perry, so if anyone could get her to open up about the staff, it would be him. Throw Daisy into the mix as well, and she should be putty in his hands.

"Hello?" Fred's head appeared around the door. "Have you got five minutes, Fitzwilliam?"

Fitzwilliam nodded. "Yes, of course."

Fred walked in, stopping as he reached them in the centre of the room. He gave Bea a tentative smile, then said. "Sis, I'm sorry, but I need to talk to Fitzwilliam alone."

Her chest tightened. *What's going on?* She narrowed her eyes. *What could he have to say that he can't say in front of me?* She opened her mouth to ask, but Fitzwilliam beat her to it.

"With all due respect, my lord, Lady Beatrice is helping me with this investigation, and I would prefer not to keep things from her. She's tenacious in her pursuit of the truth, and I know she will badger you and me to find out what it is we're keeping from her until we capitulate. It would save us all a lot of pain if you don't exclude her now." He held up his hand as Fred went to respond. "I might also add that she, Perry, and Lattimore think you're a spy, so keeping things from them will only perpetuate that myth, I'm afraid."

Fred shot Bea a look, his eyebrows raised high on his forehead. "Oh, blast!" he cried as he flung himself onto the sofa and held his palms up and out. "I surrender!" he mumbled as he sagged into the plush blue velvet.

Bea slowly walked over to the table that was laid out with biscuits, coffee, and tea and poured a glass of water. In what appeared to be a full one-eighty from previous cases, Fitzwilliam was now insisting they included her in everything. She looked down as she picked up another glass. *There's definitely something in the water here*. She filled the second glass up and took them over to the men.

"Cheer up, Fred," she said, handing him a glass of water. "Your secrets are safe with me, I promise." He leaned forward, and taking the glass, he necked half of its contents in one go.

"Fitzwilliam," she said, turning and holding out the other glass. He smiled and said, "Thank you." She hurried back to the table and poured one for herself.

"Come on then, bro," she said as she walked back towards them. "Spill the beans."

Fred glugged back the rest of his water and scooted to the edge of the sofa. Inhaling deeply through his nose, he then blew the air out through his mouth. "The truth is, Bea, you're not far wrong. I kind of am a spy."

25

10 AM, MONDAY 11 JANUARY

The Society Page online article:

BREAKING NEWS _Wife Announces the Sudden Death of_ _Ben Rhodes at the Age of 38_

Gemma Rhodes (35), the wife of the new owner of Urshall United, has confirmed in a statement released via her lawyers a short while ago that her husband Ben Rhodes has died aged 38.

Ben Rhodes, twin brother of multi-millionaire business tycoon, Max Rhodes, recently purchased the London football club in a controversial deal that saw seventy-five percent of the value of the club wiped out in the three days before Mr Rhodes stepped in and bought it. Fans have been up in arms ever since, accusing the Greek-born businessman of wanting to sell off the land owned by the club in Hackney and move it to a cheaper base on the outskirts of the city. Angry fans have been making verbal threats to Mr Rhodes, vandalising his home and allegedly sending him death threats.

No further details are known about the cause of Mr

Rhodes's death, However, Mrs Rhodes posted an emotional TikTok video this morning before the formal announcement of her husband's death was made, where she claimed, 'our lives have been a living hell these last few weeks' and shared clips of recent damage done to their twelve-million-pound house in Surrey and what appeared to be copies of 'death threats' sent to the couple. Mrs Rhodes finished by saying, 'The fans have finally got him.' The post was taken down an hour later, and an official statement was made by the Rhodes's lawyer confirming his death.

Urshall United fans were quick to take to social media to comment on the news. One fan wrote, 'We shouldn't be blamed for his death. He was the one who wanted to destroy our club. Karma is a b**ch.' Another said, 'At least we can now find someone who appreciates how great this club is. RIP Ben Rhodes.'

Both Ben and his brother Max Rhodes were last reported to be staying in Drew Castle, the royal family's private estate in Scotland, as guests of Lord Frederick Astley, the King's nephew. It is not known if Ben Rhodes died there or else-where. No statement has been made yet by Max Rhodes or other members of the Rhodes family.

26

MEANWHILE, MONDAY 11 JANUARY

Lady Beatrice, the Countess of Rossex, cocked her head to one side and stared at her older brother. *Is he being serious?* It was hard to tell as Lord Frederick Astley was staring at his feet, not meeting her gaze. She looked over at Detective Chief Inspector Richard Fitzwilliam. Scratching his jaw, he too stared openly at her brother. She'd suspected Fitzwilliam had known more about what her brother did than her, but she now revised that view. *He looks as shocked as me...*

Fred raised his head, a wry smile on his face. "It's complicated, but I'll try to explain. Can you both sit down, please?"

Nodding, Bea put her glass of water down and sat next to him on the sofa, turning to face him. Fitzwilliam took the chair opposite, took a sip of water, then placed his glass on the table in front of him.

Fred took a deep breath. "Okay. So as you both know, I was in intelligence in the Army before I left. When I came out and was unsure of what to do next, Uncle James was keen for me to become a working member of the royal family, but I didn't fancy that while I was still single. Of course, I agreed to take on some roles related to the military, but apart from that, I needed something else to do. I was approached by the Foreign Office to take on a diplomatic role.

"I was told I could make it my own, but basically, it involved being a figurehead when it came to official trade talks and the like, adding a bit of royal kudos to the proceedings. Uncle approved, and I was all set. It was fine for a few years. I didn't get involved in the nitty-gritty or anything political, but I got to travel and learn a lot about other nations. It was a good life. But I was a bit bored, if I'm honest." He took a sip of water, then continued, "Then I met Eve Morrison. She was part of the same delegation to China as I was. She was about the same age as me, and we ended up spending a lot of time together. We talked a bit about our experiences in other countries, and I made some observations about our hosts that she found amusing. We just hit it off."

Oh my goodness, is Fred in a relationship with Eve Morrison? Bea fiddled with the rings on her right hand. She'd liked the short-haired woman when they'd spoken over breakfast yesterday, but she couldn't imagine her and Fred together…

"Anyway, when we got back, she said she had someone she wanted me to meet. That's when I met her boss. He worked for MI6 and asked if I'd like to use my intelligence skills to help them."

Bea took a sharp intake of breath. "So you really *are* a spy?" she whispered.

Fred shook his head. "No. I'm not employed by MI6, so it's nothing official. I just help them by feeding back my observations about heads of state and governments I come across in my role at the FO." He smiled. "An extra pair of eyes for them, if you will. And because of my position, I get to see and hear things others don't. You know what it's like, Bea; people talk around royalty in a way they don't around other people. I don't know if they think we're not listening, or they think we're too inbred to understand." He laughed and shifted backwards on the sofa, crossing his legs. He no longer looked like a panther ready to pounce.

"So Eve Morrison works for MI6?" Fitzwilliam asked.

Bea started. For a moment, she'd forgotten he was there. She studied his face —his head tilted to one side, a wry smile having replaced his frown. A knowing smile. *He knew!*

"You knew!" she said, turning to Fitzwilliam.

He frowned. "That Eve Morrison was MI6?" He shook his head. "I didn't, but it would explain why Spicer is struggling to get any background on her."

Is he deliberately being obtuse?

"You knew about Fred!"

"No, I didn't"

"No, he didn't!" Fred cried. "It's supposed to be an enormous secret." He shook his head. "I still can't believe I just told you both."

She ignored Fred, keeping her eyes fixed on Fitzwilliam. "But you didn't seem surprised when Fred mentioned his relationship with MI6."

He sighed. "I've heard of this before. Not Lord Fred specifically but other prominent people, who in their day job mix with international governments and head of states, and at 'night' feedback any concerns or particular observations to MI6 through a contact."

Fred uncrossed his legs and scooted forward on his seat. "You know about this?"

Fitzwilliam rubbed the back of his neck, then shrugged. "I came across it during another case." He coloured slightly and stared back at Fred.

"Oh." Fred slumped back in his seat and glanced at Bea. "Of course."

What? She looked from one man to another. An understanding had passed between them. *What aren't they telling me?*

"Anyway," Fred said in an upbeat tone. "So now you know. You need to keep it to yourselves. I could be seriously compromising my position if this gets out. Do you both understand?"

Bea hesitated. Still focused on what it was they both knew and weren't telling her, it took a few moments for what Fred had said to sink it. "Do Ma and Pa know? Sarah?"

He shook his head.

"Er, can I tell Perry and Simon?"

Fred shook his head again. "No, Bea. You can't tell anyone. I need you to promise."

She slowly nodded. She hated keeping anything from her best friends, but then, she didn't want to do something that would put her beloved brother in danger. "All right."

Fred turned to the chief inspector. "Fitzwilliam?"

"Of course, my lord."

"Okay. Thank you both. So yes, to answer your question, Eve Morrison is MI6. I can vouch for her one hundred percent."

"And Brett Goodman?"

Fred glanced at Bea, a smile creeping across his face. "CIA."

"Oh my goodness," Bea exclaimed. She hadn't been expecting that. Brett looked a bit of a nerd, albeit a charming one with an enticing smile. Could he really be part of the Central Intelligence Agency? Was he a spy too? She rubbed her forehead. *This is madness!*

"He really is on holiday. But when I heard he was in the country, I asked him here to help Eve and I out."

"So, as I suspected, they're not here for the shoot?" Fitzwilliam asked, a wry smile on his face.

Fred grinned. "No. Shooting for fun is not their thing." His grin disappeared. "We're all here to observe Max Rhodes."

Bea frowned. "Observe him? What for?" Were they spying on him? *Is he a baddie?*

"To assess his suitability to be a MI6 Special Observer. That's what we call ourselves, SO for short. He's a respectable businessperson with contacts all over the world, so he fits the initial criteria for selection. Eve, who is the SO recruiter for MI6, wanted to spend some time observing him before she approached him to start the selection process. Brett and I are here to give her our two pennies' worth."

"So the entire shooting party was a cover?" Fitzwilliam asked.

"Yes. I asked the McLeans so it wasn't too obvious we were only interested in Max."

"And you didn't know about their relationship with Ben Rhodes?"

"No. Not that it should have mattered because I didn't invite Ben Rhodes."

Fitzwilliam raised an eyebrow. "Oh?"

"No. I invited Max and the McLeans. Then at the last minute, Max asked if he could bring his brother. I didn't feel I could say no, and Eve thought it could be interesting." He smiled. "She got a bit carried away with the possibility of having twins as SOs." He shook his head. "Not that it's a possibility now."

"So you can vouch for Eve Morrison and Brett Good-man?" Fitzwilliam asked in a business-like voice.

Fred nodded. "Absolutely. I've told you why they're here.

I can confirm neither of them knew Ben Rhodes before this weekend."

"And do either of them have an alibi?"

Fred crossed his arms and glared at Fitzwilliam. "I believe they were both working in their rooms. Isn't my word good enough, chief inspector?"

Bea held her breath. Fred looked pretty angry.

"It's not that, Lord Fred. I believe you, and your word is good enough for me. But this is a murder investigation. If I'm to officially take them off my suspects list, and I'm not permitted to explain their presence here, then…" He shrugged.

Fred uncrossed his arms and relaxed back into his seat. He raised one hand to his chin. "I see what you mean. Let me see if I can confirm it for you. If they were on their laptops or phones, there will be time-stamped records, won't there?"

Fitzwilliam nodded. "Yes. Anything like that will be sufficient. In the meantime, I'll just tell Spicer they have alibis, and we're getting the evidence to prove it."

Fred jumped up from the sofa and held his hand out to the chief inspector, who also rose. "Thanks for your understanding and discretion, Fitzwilliam."

Bea scrambled up. Her mind was awash with questions to ask her brother.

He turned and grinned. "I know you have questions, sis. Save them until this is over, and I promise I'll tell you all about my adventures…" He leaned in and whispered, "As a spy…" He winked at her wide-eyed stare, then strolled out of the room before she had time to respond.

27

11 AM, MONDAY 11 JANUARY

Lady Beatrice turned to DCI Richard Fitzwilliam. "I think my head's going to explode. Shall we go next door and find some coffee?"

He smiled and nodded, then followed her through the connecting door into the larger and brighter Card Room. A cough made them both start as Brock moved towards them from the breakfast table, which was now cleared of pastries and hot food containers and instead laid out with biscuits, fruit, cake, and fresh hot drinks.

"I thought you might require more coffee by now, my lady," the butler said.

She smiled at him. "That's exactly what we need, Brock. Thank you."

A glimpse of a smile crossed his face fleetingly, then he gave a quick bow and left the room. *Brock!* Bea suddenly remembered what the butler had told her and Perry after breakfast. She peered at her watch. Had it only been an hour and a half ago? It seemed like forever with everything that had happened since. *Focus, Bea!* She'd told Perry she wouldn't keep anything from Fitzwilliam this time, and she'd meant it.

"Oh, Fitzwilliam. Seeing Brock has reminded me that while you were on your call earlier, he asked to talk to me." She moved towards the table by the wall. Grabbing the coffee pot in one hand and a large cup in the other, she told him about the conversation Brock had heard between the Rhodes twins.

She passed him a black coffee. "Do you think it helps?"

He took it with one hand and picked up a biscuit with the other. "It sounds like it could have been a conversation about threats from the football fans, but I'm interested in the part when he, presumably Ben, asked Max for help." He moved across the room, heading for the table by the window, now clear of their breakfast debris.

Bea followed. "But Clive Tozzi gave us the impression Ben was unconcerned by the threats being made against him. So why was he asking Max to help him? With what? And why would Max need to think about it if earlier he told Ben to sort it, and he was the one who pushed him to bring along his bodyguard?"

Fitzwilliam sat down on the seat nearest the window. "I'll have another chat with Max Rhodes." He took a bite from his biscuit and turned to stare out over the white landscape.

Drawn by the breathtaking snowy picture-perfect view before them, Bea walked around the table and took the seat opposite him. She took a sip of coffee, hoping it would help to unscramble her brain. The reality of what Fred had told them needed time to seep in and settle. *I shouldn't be that surprised. We've all speculated for years he did something hush-hush for the government.* But it had all been tongue-in-cheek. An ongoing family joke everyone kept going. But, of course, it had just been a joke. Except now it wasn't.

Fitzwilliam was still staring out of the window, his chin resting on one hand, his other grasping his coffee cup. She scanned his profile for signs of what he was thinking. Should she believe him about not knowing about Fred's extra job with MI6? And what was all that about knowing MI6 had SOs? Something had passed between him and her brother, but what?

There was a scuffle at the main door, then it opened and Daisy ran in, her tail wagging as she headed towards them at full speed. Slowing down as she got to within a few metres of the table, she shook her head from side to side, clearly not sure who to greet first. *If you go to him before me...* Bea held her breath, then let it out with a whoosh as Daisy took a leap towards her and landed on her lap. *Ah, my girl...* Bea hugged the squirming bundle of fur, then let her go as she jumped down and ran around to greet Fitzwilliam.

Perry had hurriedly made his way to the food table, gripping two manilla folders in his hand. He turned and waved them enthusiastically at her.

He must have had a fruitful morning, Bea thought as she watched him pour himself a large coffee. Leaving it on the table, he picked up a dinner plate and added a slice of cake, a scone, and two small dishes — one of butter and one of jam. Then, balancing the plate in one hand, he tucked the folders under his arm, picked up his cup and scurried over to join them.

He slipped into the chair across from Bea, bursting with excitement. "You'll never believe what I found out!"

Bea couldn't help but smile, "What is it?"

"It's Owen Buckey. He's a huge football fan according to Mrs Kettley. And guess who his team is?" Perry said, picking up a knife and cutting the scone in two.

Bea had butterflies in her tummy, already knowing what he was going to say. "Urshall United!"

"Exactly!" Perry cried, adding a generous layer of jam on top of the now buttered scone. "Apparently you can see the way he lights up when he talks about them. He follows every match and knows all their stats and records by heart. He rarely misses a game."

"Indeed."

Perry, scone half-way to his mouth, stopped. "He could be our murderer," he murmured, then he took a bite.

Owen Buckey? Really? Could they have found their murderer that easily? Perry seemed to think so. *But he's leaping to conclusions, isn't he?* Admittedly, that gave Owen a link to Ben Rhodes, but just because he was a fan of the team owned by Ben, it didn't really make him anything more than another suspect. After all, he may have been pleased to have Ben as the new owner. She trawled through her memory to see if she'd observed Owen interacting with either of the Rhodes's brothers, but couldn't recall him paying particular attention to either of them. He'd been his usual professional self.

Fitzwilliam, who until now had not reacted at all to what Perry had said, nodded at the manilla files still by Perry's side. "It seems you have the personnel files then?"

Perry nodded, his mouth full, and handed them to Fitzwilliam.

"What else did Mrs Kettley have to say about Owen Buckey?" Bea asked.

Perry placed what was left of his scone on the plate before him and wiped his mouth. "I think her words were, 'He thinks a lot of himself, does that one.'" Perry grinned. "I don't think she approves of him. She also said he's obsessed with some famous Portuguese footballer whose name she doesn't know—"

"Does Urshall United have any Portuguese footballers?"

Perry shrugged. "You're asking the wrong person."

It was the blind leading the blind with her, Perry, and football. She'd ask Simon.

"Oh, there was one other thing. She said Mr Brock, the butler, had to have words with Owen, the other footman William, and Libby Carpenter, when he caught them in the housekeeping storage room on the second floor watching football on an iPad when the two footmen should have been back on shift five minutes before."

I bet Mrs Kettley wasn't happy about that.

Fitzwilliam, who had been flicking through Owen's file, closed it and picked up the other one. "Not much to go on in here. Owen was born in Hackney, and he's been here for six months. He's here on a royal palace training scheme." He sounded bored. "We'll have to wait and see if Spicer can come up with anything else." He picked up his coffee.

"Isn't Hackney where Urshall United is based?" Bea asked excitedly. *So he's more than just a fan of the club; they're his local team!* Hadn't Simon always said that what he referred to as 'home-grown fans' could be extremely loyal and sometimes fanatical?

"Yes. See, I told you," Perry said, then looked at the door and lowered his voice. "He could be our murderer."

28

Lady Beatrice, taking a sip of her coffee, looked over at DCI Richard Fitzwilliam, expecting a reaction from him about Owen Buckey being Ben Rhodes's killer. Shouldn't they be going to interview Owen straight away? But Fitzwilliam, who was silently perusing Libby's personnel file, merely looked up but said nothing. *Is he even listening?* "So are we going to interview Owen now, Fitzwilliam?"

He shook his head. "As I said, I want to wait and see what Spicer can dig up first." A touch of impatience laced his voice.

But why wait? Surely they could find out so much more by talking to him now? She stifled a sigh. *He must know what he's doing, but it's so slow… How about Libby Carpenter then?* "What did Mrs Kettley have to say about Libby?" she asked Perry.

"Well, overall, she seems to rate her from a work point of view, saying she's very conscientious and works hard. She's not been here that long. But this is interesting — she came from the McLeans' place, Invergate House, where she was a maid. Mrs Kettley says Mrs McLean's death affected her badly, and Libby left there a few weeks after she died. Hector McLean arranged it all. He asked The Queen Mother if they had any vacancies here for a hard worker looking for promotion, and as luck would have it, a maid had handed her notice in on that day."

"Is she still on good terms with the McLeans, do you know?" Bea asked.

Perry shrugged. "Mrs Kettley didn't mention it."

A flutter in Bea's tummy made her pause. Had Hector McLean deliberately got rid of Libby, setting her up with a new job so she wouldn't rage her grievances like Nathan had with Urshall United? Or had she wanted to leave? Something about it seemed a bit off, but she couldn't make sense of it at the moment with all the other things going on in her head.

"Mrs Kettley said Libby liked to get dressed up for her days off. I don't know why she mentioned it, but I got the impression she didn't approve."

Bea nodded, then glanced at Fitzwilliam, who had now closed the file on Libby and was scrolling on his phone. "Don't you think it's interesting that Libby used to work for the McLeans?" she asked him.

He stopped and looked up. "I would think that if you're in service in this area, it would be a natural progression to come here."

She pinched her lips together. *Is he being deliberately irritating?* "But we should at least ask her about it, shouldn't we?"

Fitzwilliam gave a heavy sigh. "Lady Beatrice, we have to be smart about how we do this. I have very limited resources and interviewing suspects takes up a lot of time. At this stage, gathering evidence is the key. Once we have more information, then we will narrow down who we need to talk to and what we need to ask them about."

Smart? Was he implying that her and Perry's investigative method of talking to people wasn't smart? She crossed her arms. *What a cheek!* They'd passed on information to him during previous cases that his 'smart' methods would never have found out.

Fitzwilliam stood. "I understand you're keen to move this along, my lady, but we just need to be patient and wait until we have more information to go on." He reached down, and picking up his coffee, he drained it in one go. "And on that note, I'm off to call Spicer."

Scowling as she watched him walk across the room and out through the door, she then turned to Perry. "Well, that's us told!"

Perry, who was staring out of the window, turned towards her and shrugged. "I told you. Being Fitzwilliam's lackey isn't anywhere near as much fun as doing it on our own."

"You're right. Surely if we're part of his team investigating this murder, we should be off doing stuff, not waiting around for him while he makes calls. He says he's pushed for resources, and yet we're here doing nothing!"

"DS Tina Spicer wouldn't be sitting around drinking coffee; she'd be off finding out things," Perry agreed.

"Indeed!" Bea glanced at her watch, then took a last sip of her coffee. "Well, so am I. I promised Grandmama I would pop in and let her know what was happening." She rose as Daisy jumped up from under the chair. "And I'm sure I'll be able to find Libby Carpenter upstairs somewhere while I'm in the vicinity and have a quick chat, don't you?" She smiled wryly.

"I think it would be almost impossible for you not to bump into her," Perry said with a grin.

———

Lady Beatrice closed the door of her grandmother's apartment in the west wing on the second floor of Drew Castle and looked at her watch. It was nearly lunchtime. *Rats!* She hadn't meant to stay with her grandmother long, but once Queen Mary started talking, it was hard to break away. She had to hunt down Libby now. *The maid should be around here somewhere…*

She headed towards the door at the end of the corridor when a door to her right bounced open.

Woof! Daisy headed towards a woman with shoulder-length thick brown hair pushing a laundry basket on wheels. She halted when she saw Daisy and stopped to bend down and fussed over the small terrier. She looked up and gave a short curtsy. "My lady," she said as Bea approached.

"Hello, Libby. How are you getting on?"

The woman straightened up and smiled. "It's busy, Lady Rossex, but we're managing."

Bea nodded. "Well, you're all doing an amazing job. And it must be nice to see Fergus and the rest of the McLean family again."

Libby hesitated and swallowed. She looked down at the floor, shifting her weight as she held on to the basket.

Why's she so uncomfortable? Is it something to do with her leaving Invergate House? "You used to work for them, didn't you?"

Libby's eyes sprang open. "Er, yes, my lady. My mother is still a cook there."

I guess there's no harm in asking… "So what made you leave?"

Libby sighed. "When Mrs McLean died, the life went out of the place, and when Mr Fergus and Miss Rose went back to their own lives, there wasn't much to do." She lifted her chin. "I want to be a housekeeper one day, my lady, and it wasn't going to happen there with just Mr McLean on his own. He was good about it. He said he'd see if there was anything coming up here, and the next thing I knew, I had an interview with Mrs Kettley, and she offered me the job."

It was clear from the way she talked, Libby had a good relationship with Hector McLean. So why had she been so jittery when she'd first mentioned them? *I mentioned Fergus!* Could Fergus have been the problem... Surely not. Fergus wasn't the sort to harass a maid, was he?

"Well, that worked out well then. But you seemed a bit worried when I mentioned Fergus McLean. You didn't have a problem with Fergus, did you?"

Libby gasped. "Oh no, my lady. Mr Fergus is lovely and always a gentleman. Although I don't think he'd be interested in me, anyway." She smirked, then continued, "It's just that, well, I don't like to repeat things out of turn, but I overheard him and his sister talking a little while ago, and I'm a bit worried, what with the murder of Mr Rhodes and all. I don't know if I should tell anyone."

Bea raised an eyebrow. "Well, why don't you tell me? I've been working with the police on Mr Rhodes' murder, so..." She trailed off. *Well, it's true. I am working with Fitzwilliam on the case...*

Libby's eyes narrowed, then her face relaxed. "Yes, my lady. Mrs Kettley said you're helping the tall police officer, but I don't want to get anyone in trouble."

"Tell me what you heard, and we'll see if we can work out what to do..."

Libby looked up the corridor towards the door, then continued, "I just went into Mr Goodman's room. He's in the room across the corridor to Miss Rose and her husband. I hadn't closed the door yet when I heard someone knocking on the room opposite. I didn't want to close the door then, my lady, and draw attention to myself, so I left it open and carried on. Miss Rose opened the door and greeted Mr Fergus. He said the police had interviewed their father again and knew about the money. He told her their father said they weren't to talk to the police now until their lawyer got here. Fergus said he was just glad they all had alibis, or else they'd be in serious trouble, and Miss Rose burst into tears. I heard her say she'd lied to the police, and her husband didn't have an alibi. Mr Fergus sounded confused and said he thought Mr Berry had been with her in their room. She told him her husband had gone out to vape and had been gone for twenty minutes. She sounded upset, my lady, saying how she'd lied to the police and now she'd be in trouble. Mr Fergus told her not to worry, and he would talk to her husband and figure it out."

Libby looked down into the basket. "I don't want Miss Rose getting into trouble if she lied to the police and they find out. But then what if her husband is a murderer and I say nothing? What should I do?"

Bea patted the woman's arm. "You've told me about it now, so don't worry."

"Are you going to tell anyone I told you, my lady?"

"No, of course not. I'll keep you out of it."

Libby Carpenter took in a deep breath and let it out slowly. "Thank you, Lady Rossex. I feel better for telling you. I'll get back to the laundry now."

Watching her walk away to the other end of the corridor, Bea grinned. So Rose had lied to the police, and Ed Berry didn't have an alibi. Now they had every reason to bump him to the top of their list of suspects. She opened the door that led into the landing, and letting Daisy go ahead, she started down the stairs.

29

12:15 PM, MONDAY 11 JANUARY

Daisy darted ahead of Lady Beatrice as she entered the anteroom and hurtled towards Detective Chief Inspector Richard Fitzwilliam, who was sitting in a chair by the window reading something on his phone. He rose and greeted Daisy, then turned to Bea. "I was wondering where you'd got to."

"Sorry," she said, walking over. "I was talking to Libby Carpenter. Turns out—"

"What?" he asked sharply. "I thought I'd made it clear we needed to wait before we talked to any more suspects."

Rats! She was in trouble now… "I know, but I bumped into her as I left my grandmother's rooms, so I thought as I was there I'd ask her about why she left the McLeans…" She trailed off as she saw a look of thunder cross his face.

"Did it occur to you at any point that she could be the killer?" he asked in a clipped voice. "And if she was, you asking questions could make her view you as a loose end that needs dealing with!" He huffed and threw his arms up in the air. "Why am I the only one who takes your safety seriously?

You just seem determined to put yourself in harm's way. She could have hurt you, my lady."

Surely he's exaggerating for effect. And anyway, she'd found out about Ed Berry not having an alibi. *I bet he doesn't know that yet! I've a good mind not to tell him now...* She took a deep breath. They were supposed to be a team. She should tell him even if he was being grouchy about it all. "I found out that Ed Berry doesn't have an alibi."

Fitzwilliam lowered his arms and sighed. "Go on then, tell me," he said, wearily shaking his head as he sat back down.

Daisy jumped up onto his lap and curled up as Bea took the chair opposite. She filled him in on her conversation with Libby Carpenter. "So shall we interview Ed Berry now and find out why he lied to us?" she asked him when she finished.

Fitzwilliam shook his head. "We can only deal with one lead at a time, and right now I want to—"

"But we know he was lying. He could be our killer. Why don't you let me and Perry talk to him while you—"

"No, my lady!" he barked, shaking his head. Red spots appeared in his cheeks. "That might be how you and Mr Juke did things in the past, but going after suspects alone like some demented Holmes and Watson is not how we do things when we're investigating *properly*."

His emphasis on the word made Bea flinch. Her head pounded. *Demented Holmes and Watson? How dare he!* She was just trying to help. She jumped up. "But you—"

"Lady Rossex!" he shouted as he too got up, expelling Daisy from his lap. The familiar sneer she'd known in the past was back on his lips. "I've been doing this for fifteen years. Please give me the professional curtesy of believing I know what I'm doing." He ran his fingers through his short brown hair and let out another heavy sigh. His eyes were no longer flashing, but his face was set hard. "Please, my lady. Just stop."

She lifted her chin. Boorish Fitzwilliam was back. *We were just trying to speed things up a bit. Well, if he wants to go at a snail's pace, then...*

"This isn't going to work, Lady Beatrice."

Her eyes shot open. *He's breaking up with me?* She checked herself. *I mean, he's throwing me off the case?*

"I really appreciate the help you and Mr Juke have given me so far, but I think I can manage on my own from now on." He coloured slightly and looked over her shoulder at the connecting door.

Bea clenched her jaw. *Well, we'll see about that!* He might want her off the case now, but she wasn't going to stop investigating. *Stuff him!* She'd done it before, and she would do it again. She'd find the killer, and he would be made to look like a fool. *And serve him right!*

About to open her mouth and tell him what he could do with her help, she hesitated. *No, Bea. No more arguing with him. Actions speak louder than words.* Taking a deep calming breath, she mumbled, "Very well, chief inspector." She pivoted around and headed towards the connecting door. "Daisy, come!" she barked over her shoulder. *Please, Daisy, show your loyalty to me, little girl.* A smile split her face when she heard the *tip tap* of paws on the wooden floor as her little terrier followed her out of the room.

———

Slamming the connecting door to the anteroom shut, Bea stormed across the Card Room, Daisy just ahead of her, to where Perry sat munching on a biscuit and scrolling through his phone. He looked up, his eyes wide as she cried, "That man!"

Expecting a look of concern on his face, she was startled to see a huge grin spreading.

"What?" she demanded as she threw herself into the chair opposite him.

His face straightened, and he reached over, resting his hand on her arm. "Coffee?"

She nodded. He got up and walked over to the coffee pot on the table by the wall, Daisy on his heels. Bea rubbed at her itching eyelid. *He's got a cheek to throw me off the case just like that after all the help we've given him. And to call us demented! How rude!* She moved her hand up to her forehead where the beginning of a headache was threatening. She stretched out her neck. *Breathe, Bea. Don't let him get to you.* She rubbed her forehead. *I'll show him. That's the best revenge.*

Perry sat down and slid a large cup of black coffee towards her. "What happened?"

She took a deep breath. "Well—"

The main door opened, and Simon Lattimore strolled in. Perry jumped up and hurried to the coffee pot and poured his partner a generous cup of coffee, adding a large splash of milk.

"Bea and Fitzwilliam have fallen out," he shouted to Simon as they convened at the table.

"Oh dear," Simon said as he sat down next to her and wrapped his arm around her shoulders. "What happened?" he asked, giving her a squeeze.

She enjoyed the hug for a moment, then as Simon dropped his arm and picked up his coffee, she said, "Mr I-have-it-from-here-know-it-all Fitzwilliam no longer requires our services. He'd rather carry on alone. Perry and I are, and I quote, a 'demented Holmes and Watson'!" She air quoted furiously.

A snort came from opposite her as Perry whipped up his napkin and held it in front of his mouth.

She rested her arms on the table and turned to Simon. "He's back to his usual rude and dismissive self, and after all the help we've given him…" She exhaled loudly.

Perry sniffed and, moving the cloth away from his mouth, wiped his eyes. "Sorry," he muttered as he composed himself.

Simon, struggling to not smile, took a slow sip of his latte, then shook his head. "What did you do?"

"What?" She leaned back. "I didn't do anything other than ask Libby some questions."

"And did you ask her with Fitzwilliam present, recording?" Simon asked.

"Well, no. But no one is talking that way. It made sense to talk to her outside of a formal setting so she would relax." Which was what she should have been doing all along. Then they might have already cracked this case wide open!

"I know that look." Simon sighed. "Don't tell me you want to investigate this on your own now?"

"Not on my own!" she replied indignantly. "But with you and Perry."

"I'm up for it!" Perry cut in, rubbing his hands together.

Simon raised his hand. "Whoa, slow down, you two." He turned to Bea. "I know you're pretty mad at Fitzwilliam at the moment—"

"Simon, he called us demented! Yes, I'm furious. But it's not just that. We're all stuck here with a murderer. I don't know about you, but I'd like to find out who it is and hand them over before they turn on one of us."

Perry gasped. "They won't, will they?"

"No. It's very unlikely," Simon said slowly, looking deliberately at Bea. "Unless, of course, someone who isn't the police starts asking questions and becomes a threat." ·

Bea blushed. *Oh come on, Simon!* He was just saying that to put them off. Wasn't he? "But what happens when the snow melts? Everyone will go home, and we might never know who killed him."

Simon held his palms out. "Murderers are caught all the time, even when they're not trapped in the snow." He rubbed his palm across his chin. "If you go around sticking your finger in a pond of piranhas to test the water, then you may just get your hand ripped off."

Bea flinched. Perry leaned over and grabbed Simon's arm. "You will help us, won't you?"

Simon hesitated, then stared at his partner. "I really think we should leave it to Fitzwilliam."

"But—" Perry began.

"Plus I have a book to write—"

Bea jumped in, "Perry and I will do all the leg-work. Please, Simon."

"We can't do it without you, love," Perry said, turning large eyes towards his other-half.

Simon sighed, then shrugged. "I'll do what I can, but I'm up against a deadline, remember? But I suppose if you two do all the work, then we can talk it through when you think you have something, okay?"

They both nodded enthusiastically.

"And you remember the rules?"

They nodded again.

"Okay, then let's quickly run through what we know."

"Well," Perry said. "The McLeans have weak alibis, and we think they have a motive because of the money they lost."

"Actually Ed Berry doesn't have an alibi any more," Bea

informed them, then told them about her conversation with Libby Carpenter.

"So that means Rose doesn't have one either?" Perry said, his eyes glowing.

"Indeed."

"So we should talk to those two first," he said, leaning forward.

Bea raised her hand. "Hector McLean told Fitzwilliam none of the family would talk to him any further without a lawyer, so we need to tread carefully."

Perry slumped back in his chair.

Bea continued, "But I think Fergus will talk to me."

Simon nodded. "Great, see what you can find out from him, but just be careful. You don't want him telling his father. So that leaves Clive Tozzi and Owen Buckey."

"And Libby Carpenter," Bea groaned, realising she hadn't actually asked the woman anything she'd meant to. "I didn't ask her about either knowing Ben or if she was still working for Hector."

They nodded.

Perry raised an eyebrow. "And what about Max Rhodes?"

They both frowned and stared at him. "But he's got an alibi," Bea pointed out.

"We know he came down at ten past twelve, and we know he was in the Drawing Room at twenty past twelve," Perry said.

Bea nodded.

"But what about the ten minutes in between? Could he have got upstairs and—"

"Not without CCTV picking him up," Bea chimed in.

"Unless there is some other way we haven't worked out yet that someone could get upstairs without being seen on CCTV?"

"I really don't think there is—" Bea stopped when Simon coughed.

"I hate to spoil your fun, but when I interviewed Brock, he said he saw Max Rhodes come downstairs, and then he followed him into the Drawing Room and offered him a drink. The butler then made up the drink for him and asked him how the shoot had gone. Once you factor that in, it would have only given him maybe five minutes minimum before the McLeans arrived. I think we can safely write Max Rhodes off as a killer."

Perry slumped back in his chair and mumbled, "Well, I didn't know that, did I?"

Bea coughed. "I think Perry did such a good job with getting Mrs Kettley to talk that he should try Mrs Wilton and Maddie in the kitchen and see what they have to say about Owen and Libby."

Perry pouted. "I don't know. I've not met them before. It might seem odd to them when I turn up asking questions."

"You could say you wanted to tell them how much you're enjoying the food and thank them. They'll love that," Bea said.

Perry sat up straight and bobbed his head up and down. "Okay, that would work. And what about Clive Tozzi?"

"I'm stumped on that one," Bea said. "Not only did he not know Ben Rhodes before he took on this job, but bearing in mind it was his job to keep Ben safe, it seems crazy he'd kill him."

"Yes, it won't look good on his CV," Perry added with a snarky smile.

"The only thing I can think of is there's some connection between them we don't know about. But how do we find it?" Bea turned to Simon. "I guess we don't have CID Steve to call on up here." Detective Inspector Steve Cox was an ex-colleague of Simon's from Fenshire CID who had helped them with previous cases.

Simon tilted his head to one side. "He wouldn't have access to what PaIRS are doing, but he might pull some background on Clive Tozzi for us. Leave it with me and I'll give him a shout." His brow furrowed, and he looked serious. "And if we find out anything, we'll tell Fitzwilliam, all right?"

Bea huffed. "But he doesn't want my and Perry's help…"

"I don't care. If needs be, I'll tell him. We can't keep information from the police. Remember, it's one of the rules."

"Okay," Bea said reluctantly, glancing at Perry, who nodded too.

30

12:45 PM, MONDAY 11 JANUARY

Reaching the first floor, Lady Beatrice was delighted to see Fergus McLean disappearing through the door leading to the west wing bedrooms. As all the guests were coming down for lunch, she'd been hoping to find him around here. *Perfect!* She ran along the landing and wrenched open the door. "Fergus?" she cried as she spotted him halfway down the corridor.

He stopped and turned, then seeing it was her, he walked towards her, smiling. "Beatrice." He held out his hands, and she took them, allowing him to kiss her on both cheeks. "I can't believe this is the first time we've seen each other properly since we got here," he said as he let go of her.

"Yes, I'm sorry. It's all been crazy, you know."

"And you're helping the chief inspector. I imagine that's keeping you busy." He was still smiling at her, but the warmth didn't quite reach his eyes.

If he thought she was working for the police, he probably wouldn't tell her anything. "Oh that? I was only really there to make sure it was all above board. I'm not working with him or anything. Whatever next!" She gave a short laugh and held her hand to her chest in a gesture Perry would be proud of.

Fergus laughed too, his shoulders relaxing as he shifted his weight to one side and put his hands in his trouser pockets. "How's Caroline? I haven't seen her since the drinks party just before Christmas. I hear she spent Christmas and New Year in the Caribbean?"

Bea smiled. Her cousin, Lady Caroline Clifford, was always jetting off somewhere exotic at this time of year. She claimed it was the only way to keep her vitamin D levels up. "Yes, she's still there, in fact, and having a great time. Meantime we're stuck here in four foot of snow. It's all right for some, isn't it?" She laughed, and he laughed with her. *Right, so now how do I try to find out what's going on?*

"Have you had lunch already?" she asked.

"Er, no. I came to find Ed. He's not come down yet."

Interesting. Where is he then?

"Is he not in his room?" She looked at the room Ed and Rose were staying in. Fergus had just passed it.

"Er, no. So I was going to go back downstairs."

What, the long way round? Fergus was as bad at lying now as he had been yesterday. Which gave her an idea...

"Fergus, why did you lie to the chief inspector yesterday about not knowing Ben very well?"

Fergus froze and took a step backwards. "I don't know what you mean," he said in a cracking voice.

Bingo! Her hunch yesterday had been right. He knew Ben beyond running in the same social circle.

"Oh come on, Fergus; it's obvious you were lying yesterday, and now you're lying to me too. Look, I'm not the police. You can tell me. What did Ben do to you that upset you so much?"

She hoped she wouldn't have to confess to overhearing his and Rose's conversation on that first night.

Fergus gave a long, inaudible sigh, then his hands went limp by his sides. His cheeks were red when he spoke. "Look, I was mad at him, Beatrice. I won't deny that to you, but I promise you I didn't kill him. So if I tell you everything, will you promise not to tell the police? If it comes to it, I'll tell them myself. With a lawyer present."

She nodded. *Surely it's worth the trade off? Simon will understand, won't he?* "I won't tell them."

Fergus clutched his arms around his body and swallowed. "Ben Rhodes and I met in London during the summer. A mutual friend introduced us, and we really hit it off. One thing led to another, and we, well, you know…" He hung his head and looked down at the wooden floor.

Ah, so that's what Grandmama meant when she said she'd heard rumours about Fergus! Well, there was nothing wrong with two people who were attracted to each other to enjoy— *Wait! Wasn't there a second whisky tumbler in Ben's room the night he died?* She gasped as she realised she could be staring at his killer. Her eyes widened as she thought of something to say to explain her gasp. "Hold on; he was married!"

Fergus lifted his head. "I know, and I'm not proud of enabling him to cheat on his wife, but he said they had an understanding, and she let him do his own thing as long as he kept paying the bills."

Bea nodded. She needed to keep him talking. "So when did it all go wrong?"

"About three months ago," he said, staring beyond her face at something over her shoulder. "He just had his offer accepted for Urshall United and the deal was going through and then he ghosted me. Just like that. Out of the blue, he stopped calling, texting. Nothing. I tried to get hold of him through mutual friends. I even went to his house, but at the last minute, I couldn't bring myself to cause him and his wife any trouble. Then I got a letter. Can you believe it? Not any email or anything like that. An actual letter. He said he was being threatened and didn't want me to get caught in the crossfire. He said it was to do with the football club purchase, and we needed to keep our connection secret, or it would mean trouble for both of us. Then he begged me to let him go and not to contact him again." He rubbed his hands up and down his arms, still wrapped tightly around his body, as if letting go would break him apart into pieces.

"Oh, Fergus, I'm so sorry. That must have been devastating for you."

He shrugged. "It was only a few months, but I really loved being with him. His energy was invigorating, and we had a lot of fun."

"But weren't you mad at him when you had to sell your family's shares at a rock-bottom price—" She stopped. Had Fergus been in on it all along? Had he enabled Ben to get the shares cheaply? And then killed him when Ben ghosted him? Was he a jilted lover and business partner?

"Don't believe everything you read in the papers. We sold seventy percent of our shares before they took a dive."

"Because you knew the share price was going to plummet?"

He shook his head, his eyes widening. "No, of course not! No one knew it was all going to go belly up. The club was sound financially. We were looking to get out for about seven months. I want to diversify into producing whisky —"

Whisky! Her heart raced.

"— in this area, but it takes years after setting up before you have anything to sell to the public, so we needed the investment to provide the working capital. We were talking to a few investors who were interested in buying a share of the club for ages, I promise."

"But you still lost money on the shares you kept?" She needed to find out as much information as she could before he closed up. She might not get another chance with their lawyer coming.

Fergus shrugged. "We can offset the losses against our tax bill, so the impact has been minimal."

"So how did you feel when you saw him on Friday?"

"At first I was stunned. I'd no idea he was going to be here. And then he completely blanked me. He couldn't even look at me. I was angry. He wouldn't give us a chance to work it out. Then I thought maybe the whole, 'I'm being threatened, and I'm doing this for your own good' line was just an excuse." He shook his head. "But now he's dead, I'm not so sure. Maybe he was ignoring me to keep me safe?"

His shoulders slumped. She could see the lines of his face, the way his brow knit together in concern and the pain he felt in his eyes. *He seems genuinely sad. Maybe I've jumped the gun, and he's not the murderer?*

"Did he say who was threatening him?"

Fergus unwrapped his arms from around his body. "No. It was vague."

"Do you still have the letter?"

He stared down at his hands. "I was so mad, I burnt it. I wish I hadn't now."

Bea leaned forward and patted his arm. "I'm sorry, Fergus." *Just one more question...*

He looked up and smiled. "Thanks, I—"

A door opening just behind Fergus made them both start.

Ed Berry strolled out of a room on the right, then halted when he saw them. Fergus spun round. "Ed, I need to talk to you." The older man looked up and down the corridor, then shrugged and remained where he was.

Fergus smiled at Bea. "Thanks for listening, Beatrice. I'll see you again before we all go, I hope."

"Indeed." *I still have one more question, but it can wait.* She smiled back, then turned and slowly made her way towards the corridor door. As she opened it, she could just hear Fergus saying to Ed, "You'd better tell me what you were up to yesterday before you get us all in trouble."

With the door handle in her hand, she turned and watched them dart back into the room Ed had just vacated. *Whose room is that?* She couldn't recall who occupied it. She hesitated. *Isn't it the room that can be turned into a family room by opening up the connecting doors?* Fergus was clearly going to confront Ed about where he'd been when he'd told the police he'd been with Rose. *Should I go back?* She gazed at the door of the room they had disappeared behind. She had to know. Tiptoeing as fast as she could back down the corridor, she stopped outside the door of the room next to the one they'd gone in. She checked the brass plate on the room. It was empty. She slowly turned the handle and slipped in, closing the door behind her. She smiled when she saw the connecting door. *Bingo!* Hurrying over, she leaned on the crack between the wall and the connecting door and listened.

"… of course I can't promise not to say anything to Rose. She's my sister!"

"But you're my business partner, Fergus. We're setting up the distillery together. If Rose finds out, she might want a divorce. Then what happens to our plans?"

Fergus swore. "Can't you just end it? If I knew it was

over and not going to happen again, then maybe I can convince myself it's best for Rose not to know."

"I don't know, mate. Morag's really keen, and I'm worried if I end it, then she'll tell Rose anyway."

"What were you thinking?" Fergus shouted. "You've got a great wife, two fabulous kids, and a lovely home. Why would you risk throwing it all away on some gold-digging trollop from Accounts!"

"Look, you don't understand. Since the twins were born, Rose has been putting all her energy and attention into them. We do nothing together anymore. She's either too tired or wants to be with them. And since your mother died, she's been even worse. Withdrawn and quiet. She won't talk to me about what's wrong. I know it's not an excuse, but it's hardly been a bed of roses at home, I can tell you."

"So you thought you'd play away from home for a bit, get a bit of excitement in your life, did you?" Fergus asked sarcastically.

"Something like that, yes. You wouldn't understand. You're still young, free, and single. What do you know about being trapped in a marriage that's slowly sucking all the life out of you?"

Bea raised a hand to her chest. *Oh my goodness, I shouldn't be listening to this.* As she was about to move away from the door, she heard Fergus say, "You're right. I don't know. And now isn't the time or place for us to discuss it any further. We need to deal with the immediate problem of you being in this room chatting on the phone to your mistress while my sister told the police you were with her. We need to come up with a plan that will reassure Rose she's not providing an alibi for a murderer."

Bea had heard enough. She knew what Ed had been up to while someone had killed Ben. That was all she needed to know. She rushed back across the room, and checking first to make sure the corridor was clear, she tiptoed back to the hallway door. Yanking it open, she calmly walked out onto the landing and headed for the stairs. She had so much to tell Simon and Perry.

31

MEANWHILE, MONDAY 11 JANUARY

Detective Chief Inspector Richard Fitzwilliam paced back and forth in front of the window of the anteroom. The snow was still thick on the ground, but the dripping of melting ice from the trees and bushes suggested a thaw had begun. Could he get this case wrapped up before the snow was gone, and they were open to the world again? He sighed. *It doesn't feel like it.* And now he'd fallen out with Lady Beatrice. Again. He shook his head.

Why did I call her and Perry Juke a demented Holmes and Watson? And now she was almost certainly off digging up what she could on her own and putting herself in danger. *What is it with that woman?* He was trying to keep her safe, and she seemed to be determined to get into trouble! *Why can't she follow my lead and work with me, not against me?* In the past she, Perry, and Simon had been useful in gathering information, and he'd enjoyed having them around these last twenty-four hours to bounce ideas off… He huffed. It was too late. He'd told Lady Beatrice he didn't need her help anymore. She would be mad at him and want to prove him wrong. He groaned. She'd been the bane of his life for the last nine months. *How can you admire someone and want to throttle them at the same time?*

Someone cleared their throat, and Fitzwilliam looked up. Max Rhodes stood in the open doorway.

Fitzwilliam mentally pulled himself together and strolled across the room."Ah, Mr Rhodes, thank you for coming." Closing the door behind him, he ushered the other man towards the seating area. "Please take a seat. I have a couple of further questions to ask, if you don't mind."

With a glance around the room, Max sat down in the armchair while Fitzwilliam placed his phone on the table in-between them, then leaned back to rest on the arm of the sofa.

"Mr Rhodes, were the only threats your brother received from football fans?"

Max's eyes widened, then he raised his chin. "I don't understand what you mean, chief inspector."

Oh yes, you do! Well, I don't have the patience for games today...

"I believe your brother was receiving threats from another source as well. He asked you to help him, didn't he? What did he need from you, Mr Rhodes? Was it money?"

Max Rhodes crossed his arms, his face pinched. "I don't know what you're talking about."

"You were overheard, Mr Rhodes. Your brother asked for your help after you told him he couldn't ignore things. You told him you would have to think about it. What did you have to think about, Mr Rhodes?"

Max's eyes narrowed, and he glanced around the room.

There's no one here to help you...

After a few seconds, Max slumped back in the chair and let out a heavy sigh. "Okay. I hoped to keep this from getting out. Look, chief inspector, I loved my brother, but we had a different way of doing things. I'm cautious. I decide based on facts and professional advice. Ben was more… impulsive. He was always chasing the next big shiny thing. I tried to help and advise him when I could, but…" He paused and slowly shook his head. "He didn't always listen to me. When he told me he wanted to buy a premier football club, I wasn't keen; they are rarely a solid financial investment. People buy them because they want to show off their wealth or because they have a passion for the game. Ben had neither. When I tried to talk him out of it, pointing out he wouldn't be able to afford enough shares to have any control, he told me he'd heard the share price was about to crash, and he could get them cheap. I absolutely refused to get involved or lend him money. I told him to walk away." He gave a short sharp laugh that had a distinct edge to it. "But he didn't listen, of course."

"So he went ahead without your help?"

Max shrugged. "I knew he must have had to borrow the money from somewhere. I assumed he'd persuaded one of his less circumspect friends to go in with him." He swallowed hard. "When the threats started, I'll be honest, I thought it was all bluster. I know football fans can be fanatical, but I didn't take them too seriously. Then I was with Ben when he took a call. I didn't hear what they said, but my brother promised the caller he would have the money within the fort-night. He looked pretty rattled when he came off the phone. I asked him what was going on. He admitted he'd borrowed money to help fund the share purchase, and now they wanted him to begin the repayments at a higher amount than he thought he'd agreed to because of an extortionate rate of interest they'd added. I told him to sell some of his shares. The price had bounced back after the deal, so he'd make a good return. He said he couldn't sell them for a certain period, that was a condition of the purchase agreement."

"Did he say who it was he'd borrowed the money from?"

Max lowered his gaze and shook his head. "He wouldn't tell me."

I don't believe you... "Come on, Mr Rhodes. Surely you wouldn't have even considered helping him out without knowing who you were dealing with..." Fitzwilliam caught his eye and held his gaze. *Come on, tell me the truth...* Max Rhodes hesitated. *Got you!* "Mr Rhodes, do you think these people will let it go now just because your brother is dead? If they killed him, do you think they'll hesitate to come after you too?"

Max Rhodes sprung up. "It's got nothing to do with me. It was Ben's mess, and it's Gemma's problem now." A bead of sweat trickled down the side of his face. "They have an expensive house; she can sell that!"

Well, that's nice. Leave it for your sister-in-law to deal with it. Max Rhodes was rapidly going down in his estimation. He couldn't imagine why MI6 would consider such a man. Then again, the fear of death often changed people. "Sit down, Mr Rhodes," Fitzwilliam said firmly.

Max threw himself back into the chair, crossed his arms, and glared at him.

"When was your brother due to make his first payment?"

"At the end of December," Max replied quietly.

"And I assume he didn't?"

Max shook his head, his arms still firmly crossed over his chest.

Fitzwilliam stifled a groan. *I'm not going to get much more out of him now.* He rose. "That will be all for now, Mr Rhodes. Please think carefully about what I said."

Max jumped up and scuttled out of the room.

Fitzwilliam turned off the recording app and put his phone in his pocket. It was important they found out who had been threatening Ben Rhodes, but he wasn't convinced whoever it was had killed him. When he'd been in City Intelligence, he'd had some experience with protection rackets and loan shark organisations, and while they were happy to kill each other for power or revenge, they rarely killed people who owed them money. They threatened, they hurt, they even kidnapped relatives, but a dead person couldn't pay, and ultimately it was the money they were after.

Unless the threat had gone wrong? Had someone tried to frighten Ben Rhodes by holding him underwater but had gone too far? It was certainly possible. But who? Clive Tozzi was there to protect him. His brother had a strong alibi. MI6 and the CIA were unlikely to be interested in a domestic issue like this. Libby would probably not be strong enough to hold him under if he'd fought back. So that just left Owen Buckey and the McLeans. Although there was now doubt about Ed Berry and Rose Berry's alibis, he suspected they would stick with their original statements, family normally stuck with family and that was why such witnesses didn't hold up in court. And of course he was unlikely to get anything further from them without their lawyer present. He'd have to park that for the moment. Owen had means and motive, so he would start with him next.

Walking towards the door, he stopped when a head appeared around it. "Fitzwilliam," Lord Frederick Astley said. "Have you got five minutes?"

Fitzwilliam nodded and returned to the centre of the room. Fred marched across to join him and sat down in the chair recently vacated by Max Rhodes. "So Eve Morrison was on FaceTime with her new girlfriend from eleven-fifty until twelve twenty-five. She showed me her phone, and that confirms it. She's prepared, although reluctantly, to give you the woman's name if you deem it absolutely necessary. Brett Goodman was working on his laptop from eleven forty-five until twelve twenty-five. I've seen the timings of the emails he sent and when he saved some documents. I can confirm none of them were over four minutes apart. Again, if you wish to see his laptop, while he can't hand it over to you because of security restrictions, he's happy for you to take photos or for him to provide screenshots." Fred leaned back, a satisfied look on his face, and smiled.

"Thank you, my lord. I don't think it will be necessary to bother Ms Morrison or Mr Goodman again."

Fred nodded and scanned the room. "Where's Bea?"

Heat rose up Fitzwilliam's neck. "Er, your sister and I had a... difference of opinion on how to proceed with the investigation."

Fred smirked. "So she's off doing her own thing now, is she?"

Fitzwilliam let out a deep breath. "I fear so."

Fred got up. "I wouldn't worry too much. People talk to her. She might find out some useful stuff for you."

Fitzwilliam rose too. *But she might also get herself in trouble...* "Thanks," he said instead as he followed him to the door.

Fred halted. "Oh, just one other thing. We decided not to approach Max Rhodes as a potential SO."

That's a wise decision. He remembered how easily Max had been to throw his sister-in-law under the bus. Scared whoever had killed Ben might come after him or not, that wasn't a trait fit for the MI6; he might give them up if he was threatened.

"While Eve was doing her due diligence on Max Rhodes, she also did some digging into Ben Rhodes's situation. Did you know he was nowhere near as financially stable as his brother?"

"Max hinted as much when I spoke to him earlier. I'm

waiting for my DS to come back with a report on his financial situation."

He nodded. "We found Ben had a connection to an organisation called The Hack Crew. Ever heard of them?"

Fitzwilliam shook his head.

"We believe they may be some sort of organised crime outfit. They're too small to be on our radar at MI6, but perhaps the people at City will be familiar with them."

Fitzwilliam's pulse raced. Could these be the people Ben owed money to? "Thanks. I'll get Spicer on it ASAP."

Fred nodded. "If Eve can help, put your DS in touch with her." He walked towards the door. "There's food ready when you want it. I'll catch you later."

Fitzwilliam pulled his phone out of his pocket and dialled Spicer's number.

32

***

1:30 PM, MONDAY 11 JANUARY

"So you think we can rule out the McLeans?" Perry Juke asked as he walked back to the table by the window in the Card Room with a bowl of trifle.

Lady Beatrice, who had just told Perry and Simon Lattimore of her encounter with Fergus McLean, nodded. "I believe Fergus when he says he was with his father. Libby overheard him say that to Rose too. I also think it's likely Rose was in her room waiting for Ed to come back. We now know Ed was on the phone with his mistress in a room down the hall. So that's all of them accounted for. And," she said as she pushed her plate away from her, "if Fergus is telling the truth, then they didn't lose that much money on the deal. Their motive is nowhere near as strong as we thought it was."

Simon nodded. "I'm inclined to agree with you. Although I'm not happy you won't tell Fitzwilliam."

"I can't. I gave Fergus my word. He said he'd be prepared to tell the police himself if it came to it. But he'd want a lawyer there." She picked up her coffee. "Perry, how did you get on?"

Perry, a mouthful of cream and jelly, waved his hand around near his mouth and shook his head.

"While he's devouring dessert, let me tell you what I found out," Simon suggested.

Bea lifted an eyebrow. *That sounds promising.* Simon hadn't looked animated when they'd met for lunch. She'd assumed he'd not got anywhere. Unlike Perry, who'd been buzzing to tell them about his conversation in the kitchens before the range of hot and cold food laid out for them on the table along the wall had distracted him, and he had rushed over to help himself to roasted chicken legs with chips, then dessert soon after, completely forgetting his potentially important news.

"Yes, please."

"Nothing. I found out diddly squat." Simon huffed. "Steve's tied up on a murder case in King's Town. He said he'd ring me later, but I don't hold out much hope." He scratched his beard. "If there's something in our suspect's background that's important, then we're going to struggle without access to Steve or DS Spicer. I really think we need to talk to Fitzwilliam and—"

A burning in Bea's throat made her take a sip of water. "After the way he spoke to me?" she cried indignantly.

Perry let out a squeak and shook his head. Slapping his hand on his partner's arm, he swallowed the mouthful of food. "Wait. I have some background." He put down his spoon and wiped his mouth with a napkin. "Owen Buckey is a massive fan of Urshall United, but not just a regular fan either. He's an active member of their supporters' club too, as are his father and two brothers. Maddie Preston told me he was furious about the takeover of the club and especially over the rumour they are going to sell someone called Santiago Dias, I think she said. He's their best player, apparently, and worth a fortune." He raised an eyebrow at Simon, who sat next to him.

"Yes. He's their striker and by far their best scorer. He's Portuguese."

"Indeed," Bea said, not understanding what Simon was talking about. *Are all the best strikers Portuguese?*

"Anyway, Maddie said he was ranting about it just before Christmas. When it was in the paper that someone had vandalised Ben Rhodes's house, Owen claimed to know who did it. He said Ben Rhodes was lucky it was just his house." Perry nodded knowingly.

"So we're right. Owen had a motive to harm Ben Rhodes," Bea said hesitantly.

Simon leaned towards her. "You don't seem convinced."

She shrugged. "I like Owen. He's really kind to Daisy. I just can't imagine him killing Ben Rhodes over something as silly as a football team."

"You wouldn't believe how obsessive some football fans are. I saw it when I was in uniform and had to deal with the fans at football matches in King's Town and Fenswich. Especially when they're all together. They develop gang-like behaviour, egging each other on and getting more and more violent."

"But that just doesn't seem like Owen. He's trained to be serene. I don't see him suddenly deciding to drown Ben Rhodes…"

"I don't know," Simon said slowly. "Did you find out anything else, Perry?"

"Not much. Mrs Wilton said the same thing about Libby Carpenter as Mrs Kettley did — she liked to dress up. Maddie said she thinks Libby has a man, but she doesn't know who it is."

"Anything else?" Bea asked.

"No. But you were right. Mrs Wilton was really pleased I made the effort to say thank you, and she said it was lovely to hear a guest actually say they liked the food. She said she didn't think some guests appreciated how hard they all worked downstairs. Then she complained about them bringing their own food, leaving towels all over the floor, and drying their wet shoes in their rooms on radiators rather than leaving them in the boot room. She said some of this batch of guests didn't know how to behave." He pulled a face. "Then she asked me if I had any favourite food, and when I said sticky toffee pudding, she promised to make me one for tonight." A big grin spread across his face, and he licked his lips. Bea laughed. No one looking at Perry's tall slim frame would ever believe his love of desserts. He never exercised. In fact, he hated it, especially running, which she loved. Yet he never put on an ounce.

The connecting door opened. Bea's stomach dropped. *I bet it's Fitzwilliam.* She rose. She needed to find Owen Buckey.

DCI Richard Fitzwilliam edged into the room and closed the door behind him. He cleared his throat. "Lady Beatrice, can I borrow you for a minute, please? I can really do with your help."

33

1:45 PM, MONDAY 11 JANUARY

Lady Beatrice closed her eyes. *Is he serious?* After what he'd said to her earlier, how did he have the audacity to ask for her help? Summoning her strength, she opened her eyes and glared at him.

He flinched slightly and ran his hand through his hair. "Er, look, I'm sorry I said what I did earlier. I really do value the help you've given me... the help you've all given me... these last few days. But I'm in here" —he gestured towards the closed door behind him— "interviewing Owen Buckey, who is being uncooperative and doesn't seem to appreciate the serious trouble he could be in if he doesn't talk to me. I'm confident you'll be able to get through to him."

She smiled smugly. *So he wants my help, does he? Well, he'll have to do better than that pathetic apology.* "So you don't mind I'm a deranged Sherlock Holmes then? Or am I Dr Watson in your little scenario?"

Perry gasped. Fitzwilliam winced. "Look, I'm sorry, but—"

She bit down on her bottom lip. "But what, Fitzwilliam? I

don't appreciate that you've been doing this for how many years was it… fifteen?… and so you know everything."

He coloured. "That's not what—"

"You said you didn't need us to help you figure out who the killer is, but now it seems you do!" She glowered at him. *How dare he make me feel like I had no value to him and now comes crawling back…*

Beside her, Simon hissed, "Bea, behave!"

She looked away and took a deep breath, a painful tightness in her throat. Simon was right. This wasn't how she'd been brought up. *You never show how much it hurts. Pull yourself together, Bea.* She glanced up at Fitzwilliam. He was looking down at the tartan rug he was standing on, his shoulders slumped. *Is he mad at me?* He didn't look it. Instead, he looked like a young boy standing outside the headteacher's office waiting to go in. "I'm sorry, Fitzwilliam. That was uncalled for on my part," she said as she walked towards him. "If you still want me to, I'll come and talk to Owen." Standing before him, she had a sudden urge to reach out and touch his arm. He looked up, and their eyes met. She smiled tentatively.

He slowly smiled back. "Thank you, Lady Beatrice. That would be very helpful."

He dropped her gaze as he walked over to them. "Spicer has been busy, so let me tell you where we're at. As you suspected, Owen Buckey *is* a fan of Urshall United. He's a member of their supporters' club. It seems to be a family tradition, as so are both his brothers and his father, as well as numerous cousins and uncles. His family still lives in Hackney, where his father owns a pub and several barbers. The local CID have Owen's older brother on their radar as a possible runner for The Hack Crew, known as THC. They're involved in street drugs, protection rackets, paid disruption services, and moneylending."

"Oh my giddy aunt, that's some serious stuff," Perry said, holding his hand to his chest.

"Indeed," Bea agreed. This was more than football hooligans. But how did it fit into Ben Rhodes's death?

"Yes, it is, Perry. And although they're a local outfit at the moment, City CID believe they have ambitions to expand into other geographical areas."

"So do you think Owen might be a secret member of The Hack Crew, and he killed Ben after getting upset he purchased his family's favourite football club?" Bea asked.

Fitzwilliam shook his head. "We think THC lent money to Ben Rhodes to purchase the shares in Urshall United. Although Max Rhodes won't tell me who provided the funds to his brother, he has confirmed whoever it was was behind some serious threats made recently when Ben Rhodes failed to pay his first repayment, along with an extortionate amount of interest, on time."

Perry gasped. "So you think *they* had him killed, but Owen did it?"

A brief flash of irritation crossed Fitzwilliam's face, then it softened. "We're not at that stage yet, Perry. But it gives us an indirect link between Owen Buckey and Ben Rhodes. I've asked him about it, but he says he hasn't seen his brother for years and isn't aware of what he's up to. He claims to know nothing about THC. I asked him again about his movements yesterday morning. He says he was in the laundry room clearing up after the shoot. I can see from his body language he's lying about something, but now he's clammed up on me completely."

"Let's go then," Bea said, grabbing her empty coffee cup.

She smiled at Perry and Simon. "I'll catch up with you as soon as we're done."

She moved towards the connecting door, stopping by the table to pour herself a refill of coffee. Now she had a chance to really prove her worth to Fitzwilliam. *Don't blow it, Bea...*

———

Sitting in an armchair in the middle of the room, Owen Buckey sprang up when they entered the room. "My lady," he said, giving a brief nod as Bea walked towards him.

Ever the professional footman, she thought. *Is he really a killer?*

"Owen, please take a seat." He slowly lowered himself into the chair, perching on the edge. She knew no member of staff was comfortable being seated while a member of royalty was standing, so Bea quickly sat on the sofa opposite him. Fitzwilliam moved to the end and leaned against it. She looked at him, and he nodded. *Oh my gosh, he's giving me the lead.* "So, Owen, I understand the chief inspector here has been asking you some questions about members of your family and their involvement with an organisation called The Hack Crew."

"Yes, my lady." He remained still in his seat, his hands resting in his lap.

"It's your brother who works for them, I understand?"

"I don't know, my lady. As I said to the chief inspector here, I haven't seen my family for two years." His eyes darted to his feet. When he looked up, his cheeks were stained pink. "I disappointed my father when I chose not to go into the family business like my brothers. He couldn't understand why I wanted to work for someone else." He twisted his mouth to the side. "We went in different directions, my lady.

When my mother left two years ago, I had no reason to go back to Hackney."

"So you didn't know of your brother's involvement with this group?"

"No, my lady."

She glanced at Fitzwilliam. His chin tilted down; he was frowning.

"All right. So moving on to yesterday. You retrieved all the wet and dirty coats and boots and took them to the laundry and drying room downstairs. Is that correct?"

Owen's eyes widened for a few seconds, then he looked down. He nodded at the same time as he rubbed at an invisible spot on the knee of his trousers.

Fitzwilliam's right. She'd seen this behaviour before with her mother's maid, Naomi, when she'd been praying Bea wouldn't ask her a direct question that would divide her loyalties. He didn't want to lie to her, but why? *Is he protecting someone?*

"What time did you go downstairs, Owen?"

He raised his head but avoided her eyes. "I did two or three trips, my lady, from about eleven-fifteen until around eleven forty-five, then I was in the basement sorting everything out until about twelve forty-five when I was due upstairs to help Brock set up lunch."

"And did you see anyone during that time?"

He shook his head, still averting his eyes.

"So just to be clear, Owen. No one can vouch for where you were between twelve-ten and twelve forty-five, the time during which someone killed Mr Ben Rhodes."

He rubbed his hands together and cleared his throat. "Er, no, my lady."

She let out a sigh. She didn't want to bully him into co-operating, but she needed him to tell her the truth. "Owen, I don't think you realise the seriousness of the situation you're currently in. The police can link you via your brother to an organisation they believe wanted to harm Mr Rhodes. You have no alibi for the time of Mr Rhodes's death. They will therefore assume you are in some way involved. Do you understand?"

Owen took a sharp intake of breath, then looked at her, his eyes wide. "I had nothing to do with Mr Rhodes's death, my lady. You must believe me," he pleaded.

"Then you have to help me, Owen. I promise you won't be in trouble if you just tell the truth."

He looked down at his lap, where his hands were clasped so tightly together they'd gone white. *Come on, Owen. Just tell us…*

He let out a heavy sigh and looked up. "I wasn't in the laundry area the whole time, my lady."

"So where were you?" Bea asked softly, trying hard to control the impulse to rush him.

"I went upstairs to the second floor. I went to the house-keeping room in the east wing and met Libby Carpenter."

Bea wrinkled up her nose and looked away. *Oh no, not in the housekeeping room. Don't they have rooms they can go to?*

Owen quickly continued, "We were watching the match, my lady. Urshall versus Liverpool. Urshall is my team, and Libby's a big fan too. I was supposed to be on duty, but I'd finished all my work, so —"

"And you've been told off for this before, haven't you, Owen?"

He slowly nodded his head. "Yes. That's why I couldn't say anything. Both Libby and I have been in trouble before, and I don't want to make it worse for her. I'm so sorry, my lady." He hung his head and stared at the floor.

Bea raised an eyebrow at Fitzwilliam, and he nodded. "Well, thank you for telling us, Owen."

"Am I going to be sacked, Lady Rossex? I love working here..." He trailed off, a catch in his breath.

"As long as Libby can corroborate your story, Owen, then I see no reason why Mr Brock or Mrs Kettley need to know, do you?"

He raised his head and smiled. "Thank you, my lady."

"But I don't expect it to happen again, Owen. Do I make myself clear?"

"Yes, my lady."

34

A FEW MINUTES LATER, MONDAY 11 JANUARY

DCI Richard Fitzwilliam let out a long deep breath as the door closed on Owen Buckey. "Thank you, my lady. That was masterclass in non-aggressive interrogation."

Lady Beatrice smiled. "Well, thank you, chief inspector. In fairness, I think I had an advantage in that he simply didn't want to lie to me."

Fitzwilliam shook his head. "He doesn't want to lie to a member of the royal family, but he's happy to lie to the police!"

She grinned. "I find that a lot."

He laughed. "Well, I should be grateful you're here then." His brown eyes were soft and sparkling, the creases in the corners making him look more happy and relaxed than she'd seen him look all day. Then his face clouded over. "I really am sorry for what I said earlier, you know." He shrugged. "I worry about you getting into a dangerous situation and getting hurt."

About to open her mouth to retort that she wasn't his responsibility to worry about, she stopped when she realised that, indeed, that was almost the definition of his job!

"I also think I'm getting stuck in my ways," he continued. "I'm so used to it being just Spicer and me. We know how each other works, and we just get on with it."

Yes, she thought, *that's because Spicer knows how to manage you.*

"Anyway. I'd be happy if we could continue to work together to solve this. I'm not ashamed to admit I'm a bit stumped right now."

Me too!

"Yes," she smiled. "We'll all be happy to help. Shall we find Perry and Simon? They'll be dying to know what happened."

He nodded, and they walked across the room together. "What we really need is Daisy to find us a big juicy clue." He looked around. "Where is she, by the way?"

"She's with my grandmother. Ever since she lost Pluto, she's been stealing Daisy from me whenever she gets a chance."

"Maybe you need to buy her another dog," Fitzwilliam said, opening the door for her.

"My mother suggested that, but she refused. She said she's too old, and when she dies, the poor dog will be left to run wild around Francis Court like Alfie does."

Fitzwilliam laughed. "Well, she has a point. Your parents' dog is almost feral."

She stepped through the door, smiling. "He's just a free spirit, that's all."

Perry and Simon, who were still sitting at the table, their heads close together, stopped talking and looked up at the same time.

They're wondering if Fitzwilliam and I are friends or enemies right now. She stifled a groan. *Are we really that bad?* She swung round to look behind her at Fitzwilliam, who had stopped at the table and was pouring himself a cup of coffee. *What is it about this man that gets under my skin so badly?*

"How did it go?" Perry asked, his eyes shining with excitement.

She walked around the back of the empty chair opposite Simon and sat down facing Perry. "We got there in the end. Owen Buckey was in the second floor east wing house-keeping room with Libby Carpenter."

Perry screwed up his face. "Ew!"

She rolled her eyes. "Watching the football together."

"Oh, really…" Perry said, smirking.

"Well, we need to confirm it with Miss Carpenter," Fitzwilliam said, taking the seat next to Bea. "But whatever they were up to, as long as they were together, that's all we need to know."

Perry made a snorting sound and covered his mouth with his hand.

Simon gave his partner a look, then returned his attention to Fitzwilliam. "So Owen Buckey and Libby Carpenter now have alibis, and all other staff and guests have alibis. Have I missed someone?"

"Well, there's Clive Tozzi. He has no alibi but also no motive, and of course, two or more of the McLeans, who we know have a powerful motive, could be in it together." Fitzwilliam rotated around to face Bea and gave her a smile.

Great! *He decides to consider them* now *when I'm fairly confident it's no longer true.*

"She doesn't think that anymore, do you, Bea?" Perry said.

Bea glared at him. *I can't tell him, remember? I promised Fergus!* He screwed up his eyes and mouthed, "Sorry," to her.

"Why not, Lady Beatrice? With so few options left, it's beginning to look more and more like a possibility." Fitzwilliam took a sip of coffee, still staring at her.

Rats! She looked over at Simon. He raised his eyebrows and shrugged.

"Erm, I just don't think it's likely, that's all," she said, smiling tightly.

"Well, I think it's more likely than the butler having done it, don't you?" Fitzwilliam said, a grin tugging at the corners of his mouth.

Out of the corner of her eye, she saw Simon tilt his head and mouth, "Tell him." *What? I can't. Unless… unless I tell him in such a way I don't* actually *tell him*. She rubbed her forehead. "So here's the thing, Fitzwilliam. I may know something I can't tell you because I promised someone I wouldn't. What I can say is this thing I know means I believe all the McLeans have a real alibi."

He tilted his head to one side, his brow furrowed. "Is this something else you overheard?"

"No!" she cried indignantly, ignoring the voice in her head telling her she *had* overhead Fergus and Ed. Worse than that, she'd run down the corridor and snuck into the room next door to find out what they were saying. *That's not even overhearing, is it? That's eavesdropping.* Heat burned her cheeks. She leaned back in her chair and crossed her arms. "I had a confidential conversation with someone, and that's all I can say." Hold on… that wasn't *all* she could say. "But what I can tell you, because no doubt Spicer or Fred can verify it, is the McLeans sold seventy percent of their shares *before* the share price fell through the floor. They didn't lose anywhere near as much money as we thought, and what they *did* lose, they can write off against their tax bill, so the net impact is minimal," she said triumphantly. Seeing the sceptical look on Fitzwilliam's face, she added, "According to my source."

"And you consider your source is reliable, do you?" he asked.

She nodded. "It's someone I trust."

"Okay, well, I'll get Spicer to check it out."

She touched her throat. She'd expected him to dismiss her statement without at least a name.

He looked over at Perry and Simon. "And did you two come up with anything new while Lady Beatrice here was talking to her secret informant?"

She winced, but when she snapped her head around to glare at him, he turned and winked at her. She suppressed a sigh. *I just can't make this man out...*

"I spoke to Mrs Wilton, the cook, and her assistant, Maddie, but apart from telling me Owen was a huge Urshall United fan, which you already know, I didn't find out anything else other than we're having sticky toffee pudding tonight for dinner," Perry replied.

"Well, that's good to know," Fitzwilliam said, grinning.

"So we're back to Clive Tozzi being the only person without an alibi..." Simon said with a sigh.

Fitzwilliam's grin disappeared. "It would appear so. I've got DS Spicer trying to find out what she can about him, but that's all I have right now."

Perry sighed. "Simon always tells us there's a point during a case where you think you've hit a brick wall and you want to give up, then suddenly something new comes to light and—"

The phone on the table in front of Fitzwilliam vibrated, then rang. Bea leaned over slightly. The name 'Spicer' flashed up on the screen. Fitzwilliam stood up. "Well, let's hope this is that call then. If you'll excuse me a minute, please." He pressed the call received button. "Fitzwilliam," he barked.

Bea watched him saunter over towards the table. *I hope this is something useful, or else, we really have hit a brick wall.*

35

FIVE MINUTES LATER, MONDAY 11 JANUARY

"Can you hear what he's saying?" Perry Juke whispered, leaning across the table towards Lady Beatrice

Lady Beatrice shook her head as she watched Detective Chief Inspector Richard Fitzwilliam pace in front of the table by the wall. "No," she whispered back. "But he's getting faster. Is that a good sign?" She raised an eyebrow at Simon Lattimore.

"Oh, I got the name Clive Tozzi," Perry said in hushed tones. "But that's about all."

"Maybe Spicer has more info on him. Is it possible he's the killer?" Bea suggested.

Simon shrugged.

"He's coming!" she hissed as Fitzwilliam put his phone back in his pocket and walked back to the table.

He rubbed his hands together, then sat down. They all looked at him. He gave a tentative smile. "Well, it seems our friend, Mr Tozzi, has some explaining to do…" He picked up his coffee cup and took a sip. They leaned towards him.

Come on, get on with it! He was as bad as Fred.

"Well?" Perry said, his eyes sparkling.

"That was DS Spicer."

Yes, yes, we know that.

"She did some digging on Clive Tozzi. When she contacted the agency that Ben Rhodes used, the woman she spoke to there said Clive was a last-minute replacement for the person originally assigned to the job. She said Clive's background is ex-military, and as he speaks French, he spends most of his time working in Monaco and Cannes doing body-guarding duties over there. He occasionally comes to London, and when he does, he'll take brief assignments anywhere in the UK. She told Spicer it hadn't been her who'd organised the job, but she mentioned she'd been surprised Clive had been available as his mother had recently died in Spain, and she'd thought he'd been taking some time off to organise her affairs."

So? Bea stifled a groan. *Is this going anywhere?* She caught Perry's eye, and he pulled a face.

"So then, Spicer, who likes to be thorough, sent over a picture of Clive to confirm they were talking about the same person—"

Perry slapped his hands to the sides of his face. "It wasn't the same man!"

Fitzwilliam nodded. "Exactly. The woman at the agency didn't recognise him at all. She then rang the real Clive Tozzi, and as expected, he was in Spain."

"Indeed," Bea said. "So who was it who assigned him to the job?"

"Well, here's where it gets even more interesting. She looked on their system, and the user who'd assigned Clive was someone who'd left three months ago. Turns out they are slow in deleting old users. The woman is trying to get hold of the ex-member of staff, but Spicer thinks it's more likely that someone hacked their system and just randomly assigned a user to the booking."

"So we've no idea who this person who claims to be Clive Tozzi is?" Simon said.

Fitzwilliam stood. "No. But I'm about to find out. Lady Beatrice, would you care to join me?"

Would I? She sprang up. "Indeed."

"Lattimore, this man could be our murderer, so we need to keep an eye on him and make sure he doesn't run. Will you round up a handful of security guys and post them at all exits of the castle, please? Could you also ask them to find the uniformed constable and send him to me? Then will you and Perry find Clive Tozzi and bring him next door?"

Simon stood. "Yes. No problem."

Perry hesitated, then looked at Simon. "But if he's the murderer, do we really want to go and get him on our own?"

Fitzwilliam, unsuccessfully suppressing a smile, said, "If it makes you feel safer, take a security guard with you."

Simon gently grabbed his partner's arm and heaved him up. "There's no need. We'll be fine, Fitzwilliam. Come on, Perry. Let's go and tackle a murderer."

Perry gave Bea a worried look as he followed his partner out of the room. He paused just before the door and looked over his shoulder. "If I don't come back, I bequeath you my shoe collection…"

36

3:30 PM, MONDAY 11 JANUARY

"Mr Tozzi, thank you for coming. Please take a seat."

DCI Richard Fitzwilliam gestured towards the armchair in the middle of the room. Clive Tozzi looked around, his gaze drifting past the half-open door to the Card Room until he landed on Lady Beatrice in a chair by the window.

Is he really the murderer? She met his gaze. His flickering dusk-blue eyes didn't look menacing to her. His expression was one of confused alarm, as if he knew this was more than just a friendly follow-up chat. He averted his eyes. *He knows something's up...*

He sat down, and Fitzwilliam returned to his favoured position, perched on the arm of the sofa opposite. He leaned over and placed his phone on the table. "How's your French, Mr Tozzi?"

Bea stifled a giggle. *Great start!*

Clive Tozzi leaned back in his chair and frowned. "Why?"

"Well, I understand you spend most of your time working in Cannes and Monaco. That must be great, all those beautiful people and lazy sunny days. *Vous devez trouver l'Ecosse très froide, n'est-ce pas?"*

Tozzi narrowed his eyes. "I don't know what you're on about, mate."

Bea sat up straight. *This is brilliant.* She'd never seen Fitzwilliam so posed and in control. A shiver ran down her spine.

"Let's not waste any more time, shall we? We both know you're not Clive Tozzi. Why don't you tell me who you really are?"

Bea suppressed a gasp. *Talk about going in hard!* Fitzwilliam was normally much more subtle. But then she'd not seen him interview a potential killer before.

The shaven-headed man's eyes popped open wide, and he swallowed loudly. "Er, I don't know what you mean."

"Mr Tozzi is currently in Spain dealing with his recently deceased mother's estate. So who are you?"

The man clenched the arms of the chair tightly, his teeth gnawing on his lower lip. He glanced upward, his eyes darting from side to side. "Look, it's not what you think. I didn't kill him, I swear!"

Bea inched to the edge of her chair.

"Then tell me who you are." Fitzwilliam crossed his arms and leaned back slightly.

The man sighed heavily, then said, "My name is Declan Wince."

"Thank you, Mr Wince. And what do you do?"

Declan Wince now gripped the sides of the chair so hard his knuckles turned white. He shook his head. "I can't say."

"You can't say? Mr Wince, you are in serious trouble. You have no alibi for the time of Ben Rhodes's death, and you've already lied about who you are. You're well on your way to being arrested for murder, so I suggest you *can* say, Mr Wince."

The man snorted. "You don't understand. You may as well arrest me. At least I'll be safer in prison than I will be if the people I work for find out I've said anything to you."

The Hack Crew! Bea only just stopped herself from jumping up. *He must work for THC. Does that mean they sent him to kill Ben?*

"So you work for The Hack Crew, do you, Mr Wince?"

Colour drained from the man's face so quickly it looked like someone had opened a valve and let out all his blood. His shoulders tightened, and he said in a rasping voice, "I can't tell you."

Fitzwilliam uncrossed his arms and huffed. "Well, then let me tell you what *I* think." He rested his hands on his knees. "You work for THC. They sent you here to scare Mr Rhodes in person because he failed to make his first payment to them on time, and he didn't respond to the threatening calls and text messages." He leaned forward. "Am I right, Mr Wince?"

His eyes widened, but he said nothing.

"So I'm right so far then."

Can he really tell? Or was he just trying to goad the suspect into saying something?

"You're one of THC's heavies. You're sent to frighten people into paying. Someone hacked into the security agency's system and allocated you in the guise of Clive Tozzi, who doesn't normally work in this country, to this job in Scotland looking after Mr Rhodes." Fitzwilliam paused, leaning back.

Declan Wince rubbed the back of his head but still said nothing.

Fitzwilliam continued, "You saw your opportunity yesterday when Mr Rhodes said he was having a bath. Did you hold him down to scare him? Waterboarding is what they call it, isn't it…"

Wince made a moaning sound.

"But it went wrong, didn't it, Mr Wince? You held him down for too long… He suddenly stopped thrashing around. He didn't come back up after you took your hand off his head. That's when you realised you'd killed him, Mr Wince, didn't you?"

Wince jumped up. "No!" he cried. "He was already dead when I got there!"

Bea slapped her hand up to her mouth.

Fitzwilliam slowly stood. "Sit down, Mr Wince."

He slumped back into the chair and rubbed his hairless head with his hand.

"Now tell me what happened," Fitzwilliam said quietly.

Wince let out a slow breath. "I went into his room at about twelve-fifteen. I was just going to have a chat with him, you know, to explain why it was important he paid the money he owed. When I walked in, he wasn't in the main room, but the light was on in the bathroom. I went in, and I could see his knees sticking out of the water. I called his name, but he didn't answer, so I went around to the alcove. I saw him under the water." He shook his head. "I tried for a pulse, but there wasn't one. There was nothing I could do." He dropped his head. "I realised if anyone found me in there, they would think I'd killed him, so I left sharpish and went back to my room."

Oh my gosh. Is he telling the truth? His arms were folded in his lap. He looked more relaxed now, like someone had lifted a weight off his shoulders. But he was the only person without an alibi. So if he hadn't done it, then who had? Bea shifted in her seat. His story seemed so unlikely. What was the chance he'd stumbled over the dead body of someone he was here to hurt?

"What was the temperature of the water?"

She started. It seemed Fitzwilliam might believe him.

"It was still warm."

"And did you see anything different that first time to when you were there the second time with Max Rhodes?"

"Like what?"

"Like if anything was added or removed. Did you see anything in the room other than the bathtub and Mr Rhodes"

"I don't know. To be honest, I wasn't really looking. There was some water on the floor. I had to be careful not to step in it. I didn't want to get wet feet. I don't remember seeing anything else, but I guess something could've been there."

"And did you touch anything?"

He shook his head. "No."

"And can you confirm you work for THC, Mr Wince?"

Wince flinched. He slowly shook his head.

Fitzwilliam rose and walked up to the connecting door, which was ajar. "Constable," he shouted. The uniformed police officer who had been stationed outside the bedroom of Ben Rhodes the day before walked in. "Yes, sir." He followed Fitzwilliam as he trudged across the room and stopped in front of Declan Wince.

Bea stilled. *What's going on?*

Fitzwilliam looked down at the pale man in front of him. "Declan Wince, I am arresting you for the murder of Ben Rhodes. You do not have to say anything. But it may harm your defence if you do not mention when questioned something which you later rely on in court. Anything you do or say may be given as evidence."

The man let out a long low sigh, then stood.

So Fitzwilliam doesn't believe him after all then? Her chest ached, and she looked down at the tartan rug under her feet.

"Mr Wince, as I cannot move you to a police station straight away, you will be locked in a bedroom with a police officer on guard outside until we can get you processed. You will have access to food and a bathroom. The constable here will take your phone and personal possessions and ensure they are kept safe and transported with you to the station."

Wince nodded.

"Constable, please take Mr Wince away."

The tall PC took out a pair of handcuffs, gently pulled Declan Wince's arms behind his back, clipped them on, and led him from the room.

Bea rose from her seat and let out a deep breath. "Goodness, that was intense."

Fitzwilliam nodded. "Yes. It went slightly better than I'd hoped after he refused to confirm he worked for THC."

She walked towards him, smiling. "Well, at least you have your man, chief inspector."

He met her gaze but didn't return her smile. "I hope so."

37

EVENING, MONDAY 11 JANUARY

Perry Juke stood up and kissed Lady Beatrice on the forehead. "We're going up now. Goodnight."

"Really?" She pulled back the sleeve of her dark-green jumper and glanced at her watch. "But it's early yet. We haven't even had coffee."

Simon Lattimore rose. "Sorry, Bea, but I have to write at least one more chapter tonight." He kissed her on the cheek.

"Why do you have to go too?" she asked Perry.

He scratched his smooth chin. "Er, I need to… call… my parents. And then I've got a film I'm halfway through, so…" He trailed off as he moved to join his other half.

Bea looked over at Detective Chief Inspector Richard Fitzwilliam, who was currently on his mobile phone over by the fireplace, and frowned. "Don't leave me on my own with him," she hissed.

Perry smiled. "You'll be fine. Now the case is all wrapped up, he seems to be in a good mood."

He was right. They'd had a pleasant meal in the Card Room this evening. Fitzwilliam and Simon had told them stories of silly mistakes criminals had made that had got them caught and things the police had almost missed that had finally solved the case. Fitzwilliam had been relaxed and surprisingly entertaining. But even so…

"Please, just wait and have a quick coffee with me, then I can go up too," she whispered.

"Sorry, no can do," Perry said as he grabbed Simon's arm and led him away from the table. They waved goodnight to Fitzwilliam as they passed him, and he waved back. As they reached the door, Perry looked back, caught Bea's eye, and winked.

She stifled a gasp. Heat rose up her neck. *He's leaving me here on my own with Fitzwilliam deliberately!* She took in a deep breath. *You wait until I get my hands on you tomorrow…*

The door opened, and Brock walked in carrying a tray. Next to a coffee pot and cups sat four glasses, a decanter of whisky, and a bottle of Tia Maria. "Lady Rossex, your coffee." He glided towards the table along the wall and placed the tray down. He scanned the room. "Mr Juke asked for the drinks. Is he not here, my lady?"

Oh, Perry! She couldn't help but smile. Would he ever give up trying to pair her off with any single man he could find? She peered over at Fitzwilliam. Maybe he wasn't single anymore. He'd been on the phone for a while, chatting and laughing with the person on the other end. Could it be the new girlfriend? Not that she cared, of course. She could only wonder what was going on in Perry's head if he thought she and Fitzwilliam were a match. The man was volatile at best, rude at worse, and even somewhere in the middle, he was fairly annoying with his disapproving looks.

"He's gone up, Brock. But you can leave them there anyway. Thank you."

"My lady." The butler bowed and silently left the room.

Bea rose and sauntered over to the coffee pot, then poured herself a large black coffee.

"… well I'm glad you're managing all right…" Fitzwilliam had his back to her, facing the enormous marble fireplace that dominated the other side of the room. "… hopefully tomorrow; worst case, the day after…" He shifted his weight, putting one hand in his trouser pocket. "… Yes, me too, but I'll stay an extra few days to make up for it…"

Ah, so it was the 'friend' he'd been staying with somewhere on the estate.

"… I'll let you know, but yes, it would be handy if you brought the car. I don't fancy wearing or carrying all that stuff back…" The other person said something, and he threw his head back, letting out a deep throaty laugh.

Bea gave his back an incredulous stare. *Does he really laugh like that?* She'd certainly never heard it before. *But then*, she reasoned, *I'm hardly a friend, am I?* He was probably different with his friends.

A scratch at the door diverted her attention. She put down her half finished coffee and moved towards it. The door opened, and a white furry bundle bounded into the room. *Daisy!* What was she doing here? She bent down to greet her little dog as a man cleared his throat. As she looked up, William gave her a tentative smile. "I'm so sorry, Lady Rossex, but it seems Daisy escaped from The Queen Mother's apartment. We've been looking for her everywhere, and then I saw her scratching at the door, so I thought it best to let her in."

Bea looked at Daisy across the room, who was now throwing herself at Fitzwilliam. "Thank you, William. I'm so sorry she's been trouble. Can you let Her Majesty know Daisy's fine? I expect she'll be worried."

"Yes, my lady." With a brief glance at Daisy, who was

now on Fitzwilliam's lap, trying to lick his face, he left the room.

"Daisy!" Bea hurried across the room. "I'm so sorry, Fitzwilliam." He looked up, grinning. Daisy sat on his lap facing him, her tail swishing across his knees. "Look, I'd best go," he said into the phone. "I'll call you tomorrow." He ended the call and discarded his phone on the seat next to him. "Hello, Daisy," he said to the little terrier, who jumped up and placed her paws on his shoulders, her tongue out ready. He grabbed her around her middle, put her down next to him, and looked up at Bea. "Where did she come from?"

"Don't ask! It appears she escaped from my grandmother's rooms and made her way down here to find me, I assume." She picked up her naughty dog. "You're going to get me in so much trouble with Grandmama, Daisy-Doo." Daisy spun her head around and licked Bea's ear. "Yuck!" she said, laughing, and gently put her on the floor. "There's coffee or whisky or both?" she said to Fitzwilliam as Daisy jumped up onto the sofa and curled up next to him.

"Both please." He patted the top of Daisy's head. "Do you want me to…" He scrambled up.

Bea raised her hand. "No, you stay there. I'll get it."

A few minutes later, she was back with a coffee, two glasses, a pair of tongs, a small jar of ice, the bottle of Tia Maria, and the whisky decanter on a tray. *I'll just join him for one drink, then I'll make my excuses and leave.* She placed the tray on the table. "The coffee's for you," she told him as she picked up the bottle of Tia Maria, added some ice to a glass, and poured the dark liquid over it. She took her drink and sat down opposite him in a leather armchair.

"So are you worried you've got the wrong person?" she asked. Since his slightly odd comment about hoping he'd got the right person earlier this afternoon, Bea had doubted it herself. Clive… no, Declan had been convincing with his description of how he'd found Ben Rhodes already dead.

Fitzwilliam stopped, the coffee cup partway to his mouth. He put it back down on the table. "You'll laugh at me, I know. But something about him makes me think he's telling the truth." He shrugged. "I know he's not necessarily a nice guy. I imagine he has to do some awful things in his line of work. But he seemed like he was being honest." He leaned forward and dropped some ice in to the empty glass. "And also, I think someone who scares people for a living knows the line between pain and death. I find it hard to believe he would accidentally kill someone." He added a large shot of whisky. "So either he was there to kill Ben Rhodes and did it successfully, or he's telling the truth and someone got there before him." He picked up the glass and took a sip.

"But if it wasn't him, then who could it be? We've run out of suspects."

Fitzwilliam nodded. "And that's the other issue. So for now, I'm sticking with Declan Wince or whatever his name is."

Bea frowned.

Fitzwilliam continued, "Spicer can't find a record of anyone with that name who matches his age and nationality, and his fingerprints haven't come up on any of her searches. She's now going through City's records of known members of THC to see if she can physically identify him."

The coffee scent emitting from her Tia Maria liqueur as she raised the glass to her lips, made her inhale deeply and close her eyes. She took a sip, and the tension left her shoulders as the hints of caramel and citrus hit her tongue.

"Lady Beatrice?"

Her eyes shot open. Heat entered her cheeks. "Er, yes, sorry."

"I asked, what does your woman's intuition have to say? Have we got the right man or not?"

"My woman's intuition?" she spluttered. "I thought you held little store in something so intangible?"

During past cases, he'd been keen to dismiss her 'feelings' about people even when they'd proven to be spot on.

He smiled slowly. "Well, I think you've proven over the last nine months that there's something to be said about instincts or whatever you want to call it."

Well, that's a bit of a turnaround.

"Like you, I feel like Clive or Declan or whatever his real name is, was convincing when he told us how he'd found Ben's body… but…" She hesitated. What did she really know? After their last case together when she'd got it so wrong, maybe she couldn't trust her gut-feeling any more? There were no other suspects, and the man Fitzwilliam had arrested was clearly a criminal.

"But what, my lady?"

She let out a deep breath. "I'm not sure my woman's intuition is up to much these days…"

"Why do you think that?"

"Come on, Fitzwilliam; we both know I made a fool of myself over Seb. All the signs were there that he was using me to get more publicity for himself and his restaurants, let alone the other stuff…" She looked into her glass, then took another sip.

"Are you still blaming yourself for what happened?" he asked softly.

She shrugged. "I'm blaming myself for having poor taste in men…"

He grinned. "Well, I won't argue with you there. He was as smooth and as charming as a Disney villain."

She laughed. "Well, you tried to warn me. So maybe it's you who has woman's intuition, not me."

He laughed too, then relaxed back into the sofa. He looked around the room with its wall-to-ceiling shelves stacked with books, games, and magazines. Then his gaze drifted up to the shining gold ceiling with wooden hexagons overlaid and sighed. "Do you ever get used to this grandeur and opulence?" he asked.

She smiled. "I've been around it since I was born, so I guess it doesn't feel out of place to me, but I can still appreciate how amazing it is."

"Do you remember DCI Reed?"

She started. *Where did that come from?* Detective Chief Inspector Angus Reed from PaIRS had headed up the investigation into her husband James's death fifteen years ago. "Yes, I remember him. He's Scottish, isn't he?"

He nodded. "Did you know he was a walking encyclopaedia when it came to palaces, castles, and stately homes?"

"No."

"I remember him telling me the history of the Painted Hall at Francis Court one time. I wonder if he spent much time here. I bet he'd love this room."

"Is he retired now?"

Fitzwilliam's face fell. "No. He died last year."

"No! Oh, I'm so sorry. He wasn't very old, was he?"

"He was fifty-seven."

"What happened, if you don't mind me asking?"

"He had cancer. They diagnosed him in June, and he was dead by October. And do you know what the ironic thing is? Five years before, his wife had cancer, and he'd taken a six-month sabbatical from work to look after her. She made a full recovery. Now she's on her own." He shook his head. "Adler and I still visit her. She's got a flat at Gollingham Palace. They let her stay after Reed died. She's still lost without him."

Adler? That's an unusual name.

"Is Adler a colleague?" she asked.

"Yes, don't you remember her? She was also part of the PaIRS team, along with me and DCI Reed, who investigated the earl's death."

"I don't think I met anyone on the team other than you and Reed."

"She was a DS at the time, like me. Emma Adler. You'd like her; she's ballsy. She's also a DCI now. She heads up one of the other investigation teams. It's her I'm visiting here. She broke her leg a little while ago. She's here recuperating." He chuckled. "Well, she should be. Instead, she's trying to do too much. It was all I could do to stop her from coming here with me yesterday even though she's in plaster from her foot to above her knee!" His smile was full of affection as he leaned over and patted Daisy.

Bea took another sip of her drink to combat the dryness of her throat. *He must really care about this Adler if he's come all this way to see her. Are they lovers as well as work colleagues?* A pulling sensation in her gut made her move forward in her seat. *Well, if he's found someone who can put up with his know-it-all manner, then good for him!* She knocked back what remained of her drink and rose. "Well, Fitzwilliam, I need to apologise to my grandmother for Daisy's escapade before she turns in for the night. So if you'll excuse me."

He jumped up. "Of course." He smiled. "Thank you for your help today."

"You're welcome," she said, turning to her little dog still

sprawled out on the sofa. "Come on, Daisy. You've got some grovelling to do."

———

Opening the door to her rooms, Lady Beatrice waited for Daisy to pass through, then let it go with a satisfying *clunk*. She turned the key in the lock and let out a sigh of relief. *What a day!* She watched her little dog trot across the room. At least her grandmother hadn't been too upset about Daisy's antics, although it was still a mystery to everyone how she'd got out. Anyway, Daisy was forgiven, and Bea had been asked if (well, told really) Daisy could go back tomorrow morning. As much as she'd wanted to say no, one look at Queen Mary's face and she'd agreed. *We really will need to get her a dog whether or not she likes it, or Daisy will soon be the size of a house.* She'd talk to her mother about it when she got back to Francis Court, and they could hatch a plan.

Her phone rang. *Who's that at this time of night?* She fished her mobile out of the back pocket of her black jeans and saw her cousin's name flash up on the screen. Of course, who else would ring at this time of night? "Caro," she said. "This is a pleasant surprise."

"Darling," her cousin replied. "I hear you're snowed in."

"Yes, although it's stopped snowing now. We're just waiting for it to warm up so it'll clear."

"How dreadful. You should be here. It's twenty-nine degrees today."

"No, this is much more fun."

Caroline tutted. "Anyway, I rang because we've been away on a meditation day retreat, and would you believe we had to check our phones in when we arrived? I can tell you now, I wouldn't have agreed if I'd known. Anyway, I only got it back an hour ago, and it hasn't stopped pinging with message after message. Is it true? Is Ben Rhodes dead?"

"Yes, I'm afraid so, Caro. I'm so sorry. I know he was a friend of yours."

"Well, it's Max I know much better than Ben, but even so. I can't believe it." She was silent for a few minutes, and Bea slowly made her way to her dressing room. She placed the phone on her dressing table and set it to speaker. "And is it true it happened there at Drew Castle?"

"Yes," Bea said, hoping her cousin wouldn't ask for too many details. She wasn't sure she should say anything more. The police had reported nothing yet about how he'd died or that it had been murder. It wasn't her business to release the information. She'd not even told her mother despite being badgered by her this afternoon. She didn't want to risk it getting into *The Society Page*.

"So what on earth happened to him, Bea?"

"I'm really sorry, Caro, but I can't say at the moment. PaIRS are here investigating, but it's being kept quiet while they talk to the family and stuff."

"Is Max there?"

"Yes."

"How's he handling it? I texted him a short while ago when I heard the news, but he hasn't got back to me yet."

"He's a bit shaken, as you can imagine."

"Poor Max. I know he complained about Ben and his behaviour, but he'll be devastated. They were close."

"What did you think of Ben, Caro?"

"I only met him a handful of times. He and Fergus McLean were thick as thieves last year, so Fergus brought him to the house a few times. Then there was the drug thing—"

"What drug thing?"

Caro sighed in a bored-heard-it-all-before way. "When he was in Athens a few weeks ago, the police caught him driving erratically, and they found drugs on him. It was only a small amount, but he got cautioned. A mutual friend was staying with him and had to turn up at the police station to pay some sort of fine to get him out. Probably a bribe more like. Apparently, Ben didn't seem too bothered by it. He was too slick for my liking. Oh, and a bit of a diva as well. I remember the first time he came for dinner. I'd no idea he was gluten intolerant as no one had told me, so the first I knew about it was when he arrived. The kitchen staff rallied around and made him something gluten-free, but then he had the audacity to moan because I couldn't offer him a choice. I much prefer Max. Oh." She gasped. "I feel terrible saying that now he's dead."

Bea smiled wryly. *Why do we feel that something we would happily say behind someone's back when they're alive suddenly becomes inappropriate because they're dead? It's not like they change between the two states.*

"So is the devilishly handsome DCI Richard Fitzwilliam there?"

Bea snorted. "What? When did I ever say he was handsome?" She had, of course, told Caro about him after their cases together last year. But only to complain about how boorish he was.

"Ah well, I had a chat with Mummy about him over Christmas. He's overseeing something to do with her trip with Daddy to India in May, and they had a meeting with him. She said he was awfully nice and devilishly handsome. Those were her exact words."

Bea scoffed. "Well, I think the Duchess needs glasses then!"

Caro laughed. "I'll tell her you said that! But seriously, is he being as dreadful to you as he was last time?"

Bea took a moment to think. "We've only had the one falling out so far, which is good compared to our normal track record."

There was shouting in the background. "I'm sorry, Bea, but I must go. We're off to cocktails at some friend's villa. Please give Max a big hug from me. I'll ring you tomorrow. Bye, darling."

Bea sighed as the screen went dark. Cocktails by the pool, no doubt. Maybe next year, she and Sam should take up Caro's offer and spend Christmas and New Year with her. No snow, no draughty old castle; instead cocktails on the beach in twenty-nine degrees. *Bliss*...

38

MID-MORNING, TUESDAY 12 JANUARY

"So you don't think he's the murderer?" Perry asked Lady Beatrice, a frown on what was visible of his forehead under the woollen hat he was wearing. As they rounded the corner of the castle, he pulled the zipper of his coat up even further as the biting wind caught them.

Oh my goodness. Whose silly idea had it been to go for a walk in the snow? *Ah, mine...* She'd been seduced by the bright sun and the thought of being outside after being cooped up for two days. Now, as she pulled her hat even further down her head and re-wrapped her scarf around her neck, she realised it was way too cold to be outside.

She nodded. "And I don't think Fitzwilliam really thinks Clive, Declan, whoever he is did it either."

"But if it wasn't him, then who could it be? Everyone else has an alibi." He rubbed his hands together, then shoved them in his pockets.

"I know. That's the problem. But it just doesn't feel right."

"Okay, well then, let's revisit everything. We've done it in previous cases when we got stuck, and it's worked. Maybe it will again."

"But we need Simon to do that."

"Well, we don't have Simon at the moment. He's writing, and I promised we wouldn't disturb him. So it's just you and me. Come on; we can do this."

He's right! We can do it. They just needed to talk through all the suspects and alibis and hope they'd missed something. "First motive. Fred has confirmed the McLeans lost very little in the deal in the end, so let's say their motive has disappeared. Then we have fanatical football fans. Although I know very little about football and what motivates people who do, I still just don't think it's credible an individual would kill Ben for that. Next there's the money Ben borrowed from THC. We know they wanted it back, so if Clive isn't our killer, then it's unlikely the loan is the motive for his death. That leaves us with a more personal motive. I don't think we've really considered that enough."

Perry nodded. "You're right. So why else would someone want to kill him?"

"Let's discuss what we know about Ben Rhodes. I have a feeling this is all to do with his personality."

Perry stopped and gave her a look. "Okay, that's new, but yes, let's give it a go." He started walking again. "I'll start. So we know he borrowed money from some dodgy guys to buy shares in a football club that they whacked a load of interest on, and he then couldn't afford to pay it back. We know he asked Max to help, but Max didn't. We know he had a fling with Fergus but broke it off supposedly for Fergus's own good. Er, what else?"

"We know his ex-finance guy's son was the one to start the rumours leading to the price-drop of the shares Ben then bought for a rock-bottom price," Bea added.

"Do you really think it was a coincidence? Because the more I know about Ben Rhodes, the more I think he could have been in on that," Perry said.

"That's it, isn't it?" Bea said as they walked up the stone steps leading from the formal gardens to the path level with the house. "We've got to know a lot about Ben Rhodes as a person. He bought a football club he couldn't afford, *and* he didn't even like football. He expected his brother to bail him out. He cheated on his wife. He was tardy. He took drugs. He was the kind of person who caused a fuss about a food allergy even though he'd not mentioned it to anyone in advance. He was involved with a criminal organisation—"

"Hold on, back up. What food allergy?"

"Oh, sorry, I forgot to tell you about that. Caroline said he had an intolerance to gluten. He went to hers for a dinner party but had told no one. Then, even though the cook made him something gluten-free at the last minute, he complained because they didn't offer him a choice."

"I wonder if that's what Mrs Wilton was alluding to when she mentioned guests bringing their own food?"

"Maybe. But what I'm trying to say is, let's be honest, Ben Rhodes was a liability."

Perry nodded. "I see where you're going. So who would want to get rid of him?"

"Exactly!" Bea cried. "And let's ignore alibis at the moment considering the time of death might be earlier than we first thought if Clive, Declan, whoever he is is telling the truth."

"Okay, well first off, I'd say Fergus McLean. Ben ghosted him, and Fergus was really upset about it. Did he go to talk to Ben, Ben told him it was definitely over, and Fergus lost it?"

Bea blew into her hands. "It's possible. Although they had only been seeing each other for a few months. Fergus seemed to be more hacked off about being ignored than he did about the relationship being over. But yes, he has to go on the list."

"Okay, so how about his wife? She might be better off financially now that he's dead?"

"True. And maybe she's got life insurance on him?"

"Yes, but hold on, Bea. How could his wife have killed him? She isn't here."

"I know. That makes it challenging. Maybe she had an accomplice?"

"Max?"

"Interesting. Could be. Of course, Max is the other one who could've wanted Ben out of the way."

"You think Max killed Ben?"

"I don't know, but Ben must have been a real pain as a brother and was potentially about to drag the previously well-respected Max into this messy business with THC. Maybe he had enough of being embarrassed by his brother and wanted him gone." Bea paused as they reached the main entrance to the castle. "It doesn't sound too farfetched, does it?"

Perry let out a deep breath, sending out a mist of cold air that enveloped him "Well, now that you say it, no."

———

"This is such a treat," Lady Beatrice said as she grabbed a mini marshmallow with her tongue and chomped it up. "Yum. What beats a hot chocolate on a wintry day?"

"Ummm." Perry could not reply, his nose buried deep in the oversized cup of chocolaty milk.

Curled up by the blazing fire in the Card Room, Bea snuggled into the chair as the warmth invaded her body. She looked over at Perry, his eyes closed as he luxuriated in the heat.

"So," he said in a lazy voice. "Forgetting the money and the football stuff. We have Max, Ben's wife Gemma, and Fergus who we think could have a powerful motive to kill Ben Rhodes. So where do we go from here?"

"I think we need—"

A scratching at the door made them start.

Daisy? But she was with Grandmama. *Oh, no. Did she escape again?*

Bea shot up out of her chair, hurried to the door, and pulled it open.

Sitting with her paw up, Daisy darted through Bea's legs before she had a chance to stop her.

What's she got in her mouth? "Perry, catch her!" Bea cried as she turned round. There was no need to worry. Daisy dropped what she was holding and jumped up onto Perry's lap.

"Got her!" Perry said, grinning as he held the little white terrier in his arms, moving his face out of the way of her pink tongue.

Shaking her head, she marched over. "Daisy, you little Houdini. How did you get out?" As she got closer, she looked down at the floor where Daisy had dropped some sort of packaging. She bent down and picked it up. The yellow packaging was open at one end and chewed at the other. Bea turned it over. Emblazoned on the front was *Gluten-Free Peanut Butter Cookies* with a brand name Bea recognised as belonging to an upmarket food store in London. She peered inside. It was empty. She looked over at her little dog. Had she eaten them all? Or had she merely stolen the empty wrapping?

"What is it?" Perry asked.

"It's just an empty biscuit packet. I've no idea where she...." *Gluten-free? Ben Rhodes had a gluten intolerance?*

She stared down at Daisy. Had she got into Ben's room? But she couldn't have. It was still locked, wasn't it?

Perry stood and put down his empty cup. "Bea, I'm going to go up and get changed now. I'll meet you back down here for lunch."

"Indeed. Well, I'd better let Grandmama know Daisy is safe. I don't think I want her going up there anymore if she's just going to escape every time. It causes too much worry for everyone."

"Well, do you want me to take her to my room then?" Perry picked up the heavy wax jacket, gloves, scarf, and boots he'd been wearing earlier and put them over his arm.

"Would you? That would be fabulous. Thank you."

Perry rose, picked up Daisy, and left the room, saying, "We'll see you later."

Bea looked down at the empty packaging in her hand. How had Daisy got it? Maybe a rubbish bin somewhere? *Oh, Daisy, are you so obsessed with food, you're now scavenging in bins?* Sighing, she put it down and ambled across the room. *And now to face Grandmama...*

Just as she opened the door, William appeared in front of her. "Oh, my lady. I'm so sorry. Daisy has gone missing again."

"It's all right, William. We found her—" Bea began.

"William, it's okay. She's with Mr Juke." Mrs Kettley came rushing down the corridor, stopping abruptly when she saw Bea. "Oh, Lady Rossex, sorry."

"It's all right, everyone. Daisy came and found us. Perry has now taken her up with him."

"That's a relief." Mrs Kettley turned to the footman. "William, please ring up to Queen Mary's rooms and let them know we've found Daisy." William nodded and scurried off towards the main hall. "I don't know how she's getting out, my lady."

"Don't worry. The Queen Mother will leave tomorrow as long as the thaw continues, then things will be a lot quieter. While I have you, Mrs Kettley, can I show you something, please?"

The housekeeper nodded and followed Bea into the room.

"Is Ben Rhodes's room still locked?" Bea asked as she led Mrs Kettley over to the table in front of the fireplace.

"Yes, my lady. The police said we should be able to have it back tomorrow."

Bea picked up the packaging. "Daisy brought us this a little while ago. She must have picked it up on her journey from The Queen Mother's suite to here. I thought it might have come from Mr Rhodes's room as I know he was gluten-intolerant. But if the room is locked, then…" She shook her head. "I don't like the idea of her raiding bins…"

"It could have come from Mr Rhodes's room, my lady."

"But I thought you said it was locked?"

"Not Mr Ben Rhodes but Mr Max Rhodes. When we had to move him from the west wing to the east wing after they sealed off the crime scene, I noticed he had a bag of food, and a lot of it was in that yellow packaging, my lady." She shook her head. "Why guests need to bring their own food is beyond me." She huffed and crossed her arms. "Mrs Wilton can accommodate many food preferences. They only have to ask. It's just bad manners, if you ask me."

Why would Max Rhodes have food for Ben in his room? Was he keeping it for him?

"Will that be all, my lady?"

Or did he also have an intolerance? They were twins, after all… and being gluten-free is hardly rare. But still…

"Mrs Kettley, have you noticed any other empty packets like this anywhere?"

The housekeeper shook her head. "Only in the bin in Mr Rhodes's room."

"Mr Ben Rhodes or Mr Max Rhodes?"

"Mr Max Rhodes, my lady."

Bea's mind was a jumble. An idea started gathering speed in her brain. It seemed incredible, but it also explained a lot. She needed to talk to Fitzwilliam. "Thank you, Mrs Kettley. You've been most helpful. Just one last thing. Mrs Wilton told Perry a few days ago about guests drying their shoes on a radiator. Which guest was she referring to?"

She crossed her fingers behind her back as Mrs Kettley gave her the name. It was the one she'd been expecting.

39

12:00 NOON, TUESDAY 12 JANUARY

Lady Beatrice hurried down the corridor. *Where is he?* Her stomach churned as she opened the door to the anteroom. Empty. *Is my theory crazy? Will Fitzwilliam laugh in my face?* She darted a glance at the next room. The library. She opened the door. *Rats!* Empty. She saw the door was ajar to the Breakfast Room on the other side. She ran over and poked her head around the door frame. Empty. Her chest felt like it was about to squeeze the life out of her. *Focus, Bea.* At breakfast, hadn't Fitzwilliam told Simon he wanted to write up some notes about the case? The study? On wobbly legs, she raced along the corridor, then paused. Voices. They were coming from the room Simon was writing in. The door was only half closed. She rushed towards it. Flinging it open, she shouted, "Simon, have you seen—" She stopped. Detective Chief Inspector Richard Fitzwilliam and Simon Lattimore paused in mid-conversation and turned to stare at her. Her heart raced. She took a deep breath and looked Fitzwilliam in the eye. "I think Max Rhodes is the killer!"

Perry Juke looked at himself in the mirror. *That's better,* he thought as he studied his reflection. The light-blue and white collar of his shirt was just poking out of the top of his navy-blue cashmere jumper, the bottom of which hung over his pressed blue jeans. He nodded, picking up the outdoor wear he'd borrowed from Lord Fred, and left them on a chair. Daisy jumped off the bed and trotted towards him. "Shall we have some lunch, Daisy?" he asked the little terrier, picking up his designer brogues and slipping his feet into them. "All that fresh air has made me hungry." He stood, and with a last glance in the mirror, he ran his fingers through his spiky blond hair and opened the door. Daisy proceeded him out. As he closed it behind him, he heard footsteps close by. He turned around and saw a man of about his height walking towards him.

Perry smiled. "Are you on your way to lunch too?"

Max Rhodes stopped by his side and nodded.

———

DCI Fitzwilliam frowned at Lady Beatrice as he rose. She held up her hand before he could say anything as she closed the door behind her and walked towards them. "Please just hear me out."

Simon, who had risen when she'd walked into the room, bent down and swivelled his chair around as he sat down again. Now facing away from the window, he held his arm out to indicate the chair beside Fitzwilliam. "Okay, sit down and tell us."

I hope I'm not about to make a complete fool of myself. Her heart raced as she lowered herself into the chair and turned to face the two men. *Let's start with the easy bit first.* "If the man you arrested is telling the truth, then no one has a confirmed alibi because we don't know the time of death, right?"

Fitzwilliam frowned. "Well, he sent a text message to his brother at eleven minutes past twelve."

"But how do we know the message came from Ben? All we really know is it came from his phone." Her left knee bounced, and she slapped her hand on it. "Remember when you interviewed Clive Tozzi or whatever his name is? He said he didn't see the phone on the floor by the bath when he found the body the first time—"

"What he actually said was he couldn't remember seeing anything other than water." Fitzwilliam pointed out.

"What if that's because there was no phone there?"

"So what you're suggesting is the killer took the phone and sent the message to provide themselves with an alibi?"

"Yes!" she cried, shifting forward in her seat. "And that person was Max Rhodes. He was also first on the scene when Ben's body was officially discovered, so he could have just dropped it by the bath then. Clive said he had to push Max out of the way to get in so he could check for a pulse, so Max must have gone into the room first."

Fitzwilliam gave a small nod. "I guess it's possible," he said thoughtfully. "But wouldn't he have heard the clatter of the phone if Max did drop it?"

She opened her mouth, then closed it again. "Well, er… maybe he placed it down rather than dropped it…"

Shoes! "And then there are the wet shoes…"

They both shrugged, and heat rose up her neck. Her confidence was failing. Was she just reaching? *Well, I've started. I might as well finish…*

"Mrs Kettley complained that rather than leave their shoes in the boot room to be dried with everyone else's, a guest had left theirs on the radiator in their bedroom. I just asked her about it. Guess who it was?"

"Max Rhodes?" Simon said.

"Indeed. He probably got water on them when he was holding his brother under while Ben thrashed around." She shuddered.

"By why would Max want to kill his brother?" Simon asked.

"Think about it. Ben was becoming a liability and a potential embarrassment for the respectable businessman, Max. All that bad press over the football club, a wife determined to spend his money, being hounded by some not very nice people for loan repayments, drugs, and an open FCA investigation into insider dealing. If he was dead, it would all go away."

"And Max wouldn't be tarnished by any of it," Simon added. "Yes, I can see that."

Fitzwilliam rose. "Well, Lady Beatrice, that's—"

She jumped in, worried he'd brush her off like he'd done all the cases before. "There's more, Fitzwilliam." She closed her eyes for a second, trying to calm the rapid beat of her heart. *Come on, Bea, just tell them.* She opened her eyes. "What if you're Ben Rhodes, and you wanted it all to go away?"

They stared at her. She blew out a breath. "You kill your twin and pretend it's you who's dead."

40

MEANWHILE, TUESDAY 12 JANUARY

"Lady Beatrice and I were walking outside," Perry Juke told Max Rhodes as they stood outside his room. "It's freezing out there, I can tell you."

"Does it look like the snow will be gone enough tomorrow so we can leave?" Max asked, sounding slightly bored.

Well, this is awkward. Perry shrugged. "It's thawing, but it's just turning to ice." *Why isn't he moving?* "But then, what do I know? I'm not an outside person at all. I mean, don't get me wrong, I can appreciate the beautiful countryside as much as the next person." *You're babbling...* "We live near the sea on the Fenshire coast. It's breath-taking. But I prefer to admire it from a coffee shop than be out in it." *Stop now, Perry.* "Not like Lady Beatrice. She loves it. She goes running on the beach all year round." *He's going to die of boredom if you don't stop!* Perry took a breath.

Max grinned. "I feel you. What's wrong with these crazy people who run? If God wanted us to move that fast, he'd have given us wheels, eh?"

Perry smiled politely. *Shall I pretend to forget something and go back into my room? Then maybe he'll go on without me? Where's Daisy?* As he looked to his left, his stomach dropped. The swing door was open. Rats! He'd propped it open when he'd been carrying all of Fred's clothing *and* Daisy. He'd forgotten to close it behind him. Had she already gone downstairs? Hearing a noise, he looked right, and with great relief, he spotted her further along the corridor in the opposite direction to the one they needed to go in. She was sniffing under a door. Thank goodness he had an excuse to leave.

———

"You think Max Rhodes is actually Ben Rhodes?" Fitzwilliam asked, a look of incredulity on his face.

"Yes. It all makes sense."

"Based off some drying shoes and a text that may or may not have been sent by the killer?" Fitzwilliam rubbed the back of his head, then looked up. "But there are no other fingerprints on the phone other than Ben's. And everyone's shoes got wet with all this snow. That's why most have been left to dry in the boot room. So not really compelling, is it?"

Oh no! It was going the way she'd feared it would. She needed to un-jumble everything in her brain. What else was there? She looked down at her hand. *You idiot!* She unfurled her fingers to reveal the screwed up packet Daisy had found. "And there's this!" she said, thrusting the empty wrapper at Fitzwilliam. "Did you know Ben Rhodes had a gluten intolerance?"

Smoothing out the cramped packaging, Fitzwilliam shook his head.

"Well, he did. Anyway, Daisy found this from some-where, and I asked Mrs Kettley, thinking it must have come out of Ben's room at some stage, but she said Max Rhodes has a bag full of gluten-free food in his room."

He sighed. "A lot of people eat gluten free – either due to intolerance or for dietary reasons, Lady Beatrice. Max could easily be one of those people."

She suddenly recalled something else. "But I remember now on the first night here when I sat next to Max at dinner. He ate the bread with his smoked salmon. But at breakfast the next morning, Ben didn't eat anything with gluten in. Don't you see? Max is actually Ben!"

————

Perry Juke shifted his weight as he looked at Daisy down the hall. "Sorry, I must go get—"

"Do you go to the gym?" Max stared at him. "You look like you work out."

Perry gulped. *Oh my giddy aunt! Is he coming on to me?*

————

Fitzwilliam let out a groan. "I don't know what to think," he said, looking from Lady Beatrice to Simon Lattimore. "It all seems so farfetched. But then…" He shook his head. "Lattimore, what's your view?"

"Well, it's certainly out there as a theory. But it's possible Max Rhodes is actually Ben. I guess with identical twins, they could swap with each other, and no one would know. They have the same DNA after all."

Bea cleared her throat. "I have a question. Do identical twins have the same fingerprints?"

Fitzwilliam tilted his head to one side. "No. That's a good point. But we'd need to have—"

Bea felt a little breathless. "Caro said the police picked up Ben Rhodes in Athens a few weeks ago and found drugs on him. They cautioned him, then let him go after he paid a fine or possibly a bribe. Wouldn't they have fingerprinted him?"

Fitzwilliam's face broke into a smile. "Yes! If they gave him a caution, there should be a record. I'll get Spicer on to it now." He jumped up and grabbed his phone.

"Well done, Bea." Simon said, patting her arm. "I think you just might be on to something there." He glanced at his watch. "It's lunchtime. Where's Perry?"

"Oh, he went to get changed. He said he'd be back for lunch…" She checked her watch, then picked up her phone. "I'll chase him up."

41

STILL MEANWHILE, TUESDAY 12 JANUARY

"Daisy!" Perry Juke shouted at the white terrier as he walked towards her. He wanted to go and have lunch. He wanted to get away from Max Rhodes, who was emitting a slightly predatory vibe. And Daisy was fixated on the door down the corridor. Perry moved quicker towards her. "Daisy!" She was scratching at the bottom of the door. As Perry got level with it, he glanced at the square of card in the brass holder. Max Rhodes. He turned to find the man himself right behind him.

Max frowned. "What's the dog doing to my door?" He bent down and reached for Daisy.

In one swift scoop, Perry grabbed her. "Sorry, she's a terrier, you know. They like to dig."

Max nodded, then with a sly grin said, "Well, as we're here now, do you want to come in for a pre-dinner drink?"

Er, no. I'm hungry, and you're creeping me out a little. "Er, I think Lady Beatrice and my partner are waiting for me." He hoped the mention of Simon would deter Max if he was having any ideas.

"Oh go on, just the one. I'm sure they'll wait." He twisted the handle, and the door opened.

Daisy immediately threw herself out of Perry's arms and ran in. "Daisy!" Perry shouted. "Come here."

Max Rhodes grinned, his eyes shining. "Well, it seems the dog has decided for you…" He stood by the open door and gestured inside.

Daisy! That's it. No more bacon for you! "I'm sorry. I'll just go and get her." Perry walked into the room to see Daisy running out of an open door on the left-hand side with something yellow in her mouth.

Max Rhodes swore and ran past Perry, aiming for Daisy with his arms outstretched. She dodged to his right and headed for Perry. Perry bent his knees and grabbed her just as she was about to jump at him. He held her with one hand and pried the object from her mouth with his other. He recognised it immediately. He stared at the packaging, frowning.

"I'll take that." Max swiped the packet from Perry's hand.

"Why do you have gluten-free biscuits in your room?" Perry asked, his brow still furrowed. "I thought it was Ben who had the intolerance?"

Max froze, staring down at the packet. "We're both intolerant," he blurted.

Perry's phone beeped. He bent and returned Daisy to the floor. He looked at the screen.

Bea: *Where are you? We're waiting to go to lunch. I think we've had a breakthrough — Max could be Ben, and he killed the real Max. Hurry! xx*

A wave of dizziness hit Perry. *Oh my giddy aunt!* He looked down at the message again, struggling to read it as his hands shook uncontrollably. *I'm in a bedroom with a murderer!* He looked up and caught Max's gaze. *Please don't kill me...*

42

AT THE SAME TIME, TUESDAY 12 JANUARY

"Has he replied?" Simon Lattimore asked, his eyebrows drawn together.

Lady Beatrice shook her head. "No, but he's probably on his way. I wouldn't worry."

"But it's not like him to be late for food," Simon said as he stood. "I think I'll just pop up and check—" *Bang!*

Bea and Simon started as Fitzwilliam slapped his hand down on the desk a second time. *Bang!*

Bea's heart jumped. *What on earth is going on?*

"That's great Spicer, good work," Fitzwilliam shook his head. "No, I can't believe it either." His eyes met Bea's. "Yes, she is. Right, well, I need to talk to our friend, Mr Rhodes. I'll ring you later."

Still holding her gaze, he cocked his head to one side. "Well, believe it or not, you are right, my lady. The fingerprints we took from the dead body do not match those held on record for Ben Rhodes."

She gasped. *Oh my goodness!*

"But those on record match the ones we took from Max Rhodes."

Simon took a step back. "So it's Max Rhodes who's dead?"

"Yes, and Ben Rhodes is very much alive and kicking," Fitzwilliam replied, dropping his arms to his sides.

Even though it had been her suggestion, Bea's mind was still scrambling to make sense of it all. "And he killed Max?"

Fitzwilliam raised his hand. "We don't know that—"

"But the phone," she cried.

"I will need to speak to Tozzi about that. And even then, it's not evidence Ben Rhodes took it." He moved towards the door. "All I can do right now is interview Ben Rhodes and find out why he's been pretending to be his brother. Any ideas where he might be?"

"Well, it's lunchtime. He's most likely going to be in the Breakfast Room, I would think," she pointed out. "Perry might be there too, Simon. We'll come with you."

"Sure," Simon said as they headed for the door.

———

Ben Rhodes snatched the phone from Perry's Jukes hands. *What the?* "Hey!" Perry shouted, reaching out towards him. "That's mine."

Ben pressed his lips flat as he stepped back to avoid Perry's flailing arms. He stared down at the screen and swore, his head jerking back as he scanned the room.

Perry's chest tightened. *What am I going to do?* He looked behind him, where Daisy was now sniffing around the open door. *Run, you idiot!* He tensed his muscles, ready to spring. He was too late. Ben had already begun to move.

Perry's pulse raced as he dragged his shaking body after him. *Daisy!* "Daisy, get help!" Perry shrieked, hoping against hope Daisy still remembered the command Sam had taught her last year. It had worked for Bea in the past, but would it work now for him?

A white streak of fur disappeared through the frame as Ben grabbed at the door and slammed it shut. Perry's muscles went weak, and he stopped dead in his tracks. He straightened and pressed his palm to his heart. *Please get help, Daisy. I think he's going to kill me*! He looked up and came face to face with Ben Rhodes. A raised vein was visibly throbbing on Ben's forehead. *Yes, he's going to kill me…*

———

"He must be in his room then," Lady Beatrice said as they stood in the empty Breakfast Room. The aroma of chicken soup filled her senses, and Bea's stomach rumbled. *Maybe we should have lunch before we talk to Max… no, Ben Rhodes?* "Should we—"

"Perry's not here either," Simon Lattimore said, looking down and checking his phone. "I'm going to go up and find him." He headed towards the door.

Bea turned to Fitzwilliam. "Do you want lunch first before you tackle Ben Rhodes?" she asked hopefully.

He shook his head. "I'm not hungry yet. I can wait."

Well, I don't know if I can! She grimaced. "Indeed. Then let's find him."

Is that a smile tugging at the corner of his mouth? She followed him and Simon out of the room.

———

"Well, Perry," Ben Rhodes said, his eyes darting around the room. "Now your friends have discovered my little secret, I'm faced with a dilemma."

Perry stifled a gasp, gawking at the man blocking his way. *So he really is Ben, not Max?*

Ben rubbed the back of his neck. "This isn't how I planned it." His voice wavered. "I hoped to get out of here tomorrow undetected, then disappear abroad, heartbroken after the death of my brother." He huffed, his lips moving as if he was trying to find the right thing to say. He threw up his hands. "Now I need another plan," he said in a sharp tone.

Perry's heartbeat thrashed in his ears. *How am I going to get out of this?* He glanced at the door. Ben paced back and forth in front of it. *How can I get past him?* He wished he were faster and stronger. Then he could overpower him. Or maybe if he just had the training like Bea had on her kidnapping prevention course. *What did she do with Alex Sterling's killer?* He racked his brains. *Didn't she kick him in-between the legs or something?* Perry looked at Ben again. *How on earth can I get my leg up that far?*

Ben stopped pacing, and his eyes narrowed as he stared back at Perry. He slowly walked towards him, his eyes holding Perry's gaze. He blinked. Once. Twice. "I think you may be my only way out, Perry…"

———

Rounding the corner and walking into the cavernous foyer, Lady Beatrice, Simon Lattimore, and DCI Richard Fitzwilliam stopped when a bark alerted them to Daisy haring down the sweeping staircase in front of them. She stopped four steps from the bottom and barked again.

"Daisy!" Bea smiled as she hurried towards the stone steps. She looked up expecting to see Perry following, but no one was behind the little terrier. Her scalp prickled. Daisy barked again, still not moving from the stairs. *Where's Perry?* She turned to the others, frowning.

Simon rushed forward. "Where's Perry, Daisy?" She barked and turned to jump up the next step, then looked back at them. She barked and jumped up the next one.

"She wants us to follow her!" Bea cried, beginning to run. *Oh, Perry. Are you okay?* She launched herself at the bottom step, a chill dragging up the back of her spine. She focussed on the white bundle of fur in front of her and ran.

————

Perry Juke flinched as Ben Rhodes slowly walked towards him, his arms out on either side. *Is he going to grab me?* Perry inched back with every step forward Ben took. *Thud!* The back of his knees hit the side of the bed. Perry stopped. He could hear Bea's advice in his head. *Don't sit down. It will make you even more vulnerable.* His eyes widened as Ben, his jaw clenched, lunged towards him. *This is it!* Perry's vision blurred. His body felt heavy. *Why was I too old-fashioned to ask Simon to marry me? If I had, then at least he'd have the legitimacy of being a widower...*

————

As Lady Beatrice reached the top step, she felt someone beside her. She turned and saw a red-faced Richard Fitzwilliam panting next to her. A smugness overtook her fleetingly as she realised she'd beaten him up the stairs; then as her foot hit the tartan carpet of the landing, she took in a lungful of air and sped after Daisy as the little dog turned right and raced along, through the open glass swing door of the east wing, barking loudly. *Perry, we're coming!*

But before she could get through, Simon pushed past her and hurtled down the corridor after Daisy. As Bea moved to follow him, Fitzwilliam was at her shoulder. *I'm next!* They squeezed through at the same time. Then she barrelled past him, following Simon and Daisy. Simon stopped in front of a room on their right and tugged open the door, but Daisy kept on running, barking. Bea and Fitzwilliam carried on after her.

———

The sinking sensation ceased abruptly as Perry Juke heard the faint sound of barking in the distance. *Daisy!* His eyes shot open as Ben Rhodes dragged him towards the bedside table and jerked open the drawer with his other hand. Perry looked down and wished he hadn't. *Oh my giddy aunt!* The light from the window glinted off the silver blade as Ben extracted the knife.

"What are you doing?" Perry spluttered as he tried to wrench his arm free. He flinched as Ben's hand crushed his bicep. Pulling Perry before him, Ben raised the knife so it was in front of Perry's face and whispered in his ear, "You're my insurance policy, Perry. Don't do anything stupid, or I promise you, you'll regret it."

43

A FEW SECONDS LATER, TUESDAY 12
JANUARY

Richard Fitzwilliam's hand shot out from behind Lady Beatrice and clasped the brass door handle. Daisy, still feverishly barking at the door, was on her hind legs scratching wildly at the wood. "Step back!" Fitzwilliam commanded, heaving open the door. *Please be all right. Please be all right*, Bea chanted in her head as Simon shouted, "He's not in our room!"

His running footsteps got louder as he joined them just as Fitzwilliam threw the door open. "Daisy, wait!" Bea commanded.

The three of them bundled in, then stopped as one as the door slammed into the wall. Bea's muscles tensed. *Perry!*

Ben Rhodes held Perry Juke in front of him like a human shield. Restraining both of Perry's arms with one hand, he held a knife in the other, the tip of which sat precariously close to Perry's neck. Beside her, Simon gasped, and Fitzwilliam took in a heavy breath. Perry's eyes bulged. He didn't blink. She met his gaze. *You'll be all right. We'll get you out of this, I promise.*

"All of you, just stay where you are," Ben said, his eyes narrowed. "I don't want to hurt your friend here, but I will unless you do as I ask."

Simon went to step forward, but Fitzwilliam threw his arm out, blocking him. Bea grasped Simon's hand. "He'll be okay," she whispered. He squeezed her hand in reply.

"So, Ben, what is it you want?" Fitzwilliam asked, his voice sounding calm and confident.

"I want to get out of here. But I'm not talking to you." He nodded in Fitzwilliam's direction. "Or you." He nodded at Simon. "I'll only talk to Lady Beatrice."

What? Why me? She looked at Perry. *I'll do it.* Fitzwilliam took in a breath to speak, but Bea grabbed his arm. "Leave it with me."

"Yes, listen to the lady," Ben said. "So I want you gentlemen to take out your phones slowly and place them on the floor in front of you."

Fitzwilliam and Simon hesitated. "Now!" Ben shouted and yanked Perry, who whimpered softly. They did as he asked. "Right, now I want you both to slowly move to the bathroom door over there." He pointed to the corner nearest them. "Go!" The two men shuffled towards the room. "Go in…." he instructed in a clear voice. They walked in. "Now close the door behind you. If I see the door open, I will kill him. If I hear any noise that suggests you are moving around, I will kill him. Do you understand?" Both men nodded. Fitzwilliam caught her gaze. She smiled as reassuringly as she could. *It will be fine.* In her peripheral vision, she saw Simon mouthing something to Perry. "Now!" Ben hollered, and the door slowly closed.

Bea took a deep breath. She trawled her memory for what she'd learned on the kidnapping course she'd attended a few years ago. They had devoted one day to negotiating with a kidnapper to get someone released. She remembered being taught a step-by-step process. *But what was it?*

"So, my lady." Ben's eyes flicked between her and the bathroom door. "I need to get out of here."

Agree with them. She was sure that was one rule. *Don't interrupt them. Something about leaving pauses. Let them talk. Let them know you're listening. Oh, and wasn't there something about repeating what they said back to them?* Her heart was beating out of her chest. *Focus, Bea. You have to do this for Perry.*

"Indeed." She nodded. She held his gaze until it darted over to the bathroom door again.

Say nothing. Let him talk.

"When did you work out I was Ben, not Max?" he asked.

"When my cousin told me Ben was gluten intolerant, but Daisy brought me a gluten-free wrapper from your bedroom and when I heard you left wet shoes in your room to dry."

Ben swore under his breath. "It wasn't supposed to be like this, you know."

She nodded encouragingly. If she kept him talking, was there a chance he would get tired and loosen his grip on Perry and the knife?

"I just needed to get out of the situation I'd got myself in. The guys from THC play rough, you know. They added a stupid amount of interest on to what I'd borrowed from them to buy the club." He shook his head. "I borrowed twenty-five million over four years, which should have been about six hundred thousand a month with interest, and suddenly they wanted one point five million for the first repayment. It's daylight robbery."

Bea nodded. "Indeed. That sounds completely unreasonable."

"Exactly! So I refused. I told them I'd tell the FCA about Nathan's son working for THC and how they'd set up the whole share-crash. They just laughed and told me to go ahead. They said my association with them would make me culpable too and then, not only would I get jailed and fined, but I would still owe them money. And, of course, the interest would go up even more."

She shook her head. "That's dreadful."

He let out a deep breath, then a slow smile. "Max and I have been swapping places all our lives, you know. If one of us didn't want to do something and the other didn't mind, we'd just swap." He gave a short laugh. "How do you think he got that Swedish model to agree to go out with him in the first place? I turned on the charm, took her out a couple of times. I warmed her up for him so he could take over." He shrugged as best he could. "Of course, when she got fed up with spending his money and realised how boring he was, she binned him." Bea nodded. "He was so pleased when he got invited here by your brother. He loves old places like this and all the pomp and ceremony. And when he heard about the death threats I was getting, he suggested I come too to get away from the 'crazy Urshall United fans'. He didn't know it was THC threatening me."

Ben lifted an eyebrow at Bea. She darted a quick look at Perry. His eyes had glazed over, and he was still. *Hang on, Perry.* She smiled back at Ben. "You played him perfectly."

He smiled smugly, then his face clouded over. "But then he found out who I'd loaned money from and told me I needed to fix it." He bared his teeth and waved the knife around. "It's all very well saying that when you've got millions in the bank, but he knew I didn't have the extra money easily at hand. I told him about the ridiculous interest rate they want to charge and asked him if he'd help me out until I could sell some shares." He huffed. "He said he'd think about it."

One hand still gripped Perry tightly, but the one holding the knife had dropped and now hovered just above Perry's shoulder. *Can I get to Ben and knock it out of his hand before he realises? But then he might stab Perry in the neck. No, I'll have to wait until he's more relaxed.* Bea nodded. "And did he think about it?"

"That's why I went up to his room before drinks. He was getting ready to have a bath. Did you know we'd swapped rooms? I always prefer a shower to a bath, but Max liked to have a good soak. Said it relaxed him." He gave a menacing grin. "Not on Sunday night it didn't." He snorted. "Anyway we had a whisky together, and I asked him if he'd decided. And do you know what?"

"What?"

"He said he was very sorry, but I needed to deal with the consequences of my poor choices, and he wouldn't help me out this time. He had the cheek to suggest I mortgage the house in Surrey or sell the flat in Athens."

Bea shook her head. "That must have been hurtful." She moved an inch closer to them.

"Exactly." Ben lowered the knife a little and flicked it back and forth. Bea tried to catch Perry's eye. She needed him to be fully alert for when she was ready to move, but his face was directed at the floor, his eyes closed. "I remember looking at him and thinking if only I was in his shoes, I wouldn't have anything to worry about. No money-grabbing wife who won't give me a divorce. No stupid football club where everyone hates me. No bullies chasing me for money. And considering Max didn't want to 'make a fuss' asking the maids to switch our rooms, no one knew Max was in the one saying Ben Rhodes..." He closed his eyes for a minute and shook his head.

Bea moved a step closer, then cleared her throat, trying to get Perry's attention. Ben's eyes shot open. *Oh no, have I blown it? What can I do?* "Yes, some people have it so much easier than others do, don't they?"

"Yes! So really, it was his fault. He could have helped me, but when he refused, I had no choice but to help myself, you see."

"Indeed."

"So when he went into the bathroom, I waited until I heard him get in the bath. Then I wiped my glass and the decanter clean and went into the bathroom..."

Bea stared at Perry. Suddenly, he opened his eyes and looked at her. *I'm going to save you, Perry, but you have to do what I tell you.* She pleaded with him to understand. His eyes focussed on her face, and he gave a brief nod.

"He was lying there, his eyes closed. Not a care in the world. I walked around the bath. He opened his eyes and saw me, but there was nothing he could do. I was behind him in an instant, and I pushed his head down and held it..."

"Perry, move now!" Bea screamed as she launched herself at Ben's arm that was now hanging by his side, the knife loosely held in his fingers. "Fitzwilliam!" she shouted as she grabbed Ben's forearm and yanked it away from Perry. There was a second before Ben realised what was happening, then he lifted his elbow up and tried to shove Bea away. She hung on for dear life. *Is Perry safe?* She knew the knife was still in Ben's hand as she could see it. *Wham!*

A force hit her jaw so hard her whole body shuddered. Then pain ripped through her face, and she started to fall. She gripped Ben's arm as tight as she could. *You're coming with me!* She just had enough time to twist herself round before she hit the floor. The air was knocked out of her. She couldn't breathe. She let go of Ben's arm as a wave of nausea hit her. *Is Perry all right?* She closed her eyes. *Please let Perry be all right.*

44

AN HOUR LATER, TUESDAY 12 JANUARY

Lady Beatrice held the ice pack to the left side of her face and winced. She slowly flexed her jaw. *At least it's not broken.* Although she was going to have a cracking bruise and probably a black eye tomorrow. She glanced over at Perry Juke, sitting on the sofa opposite her, a tartan blanket wrapped around him and a hot chocolate in one hand. It was all worth it just to see him alive with no hole in his neck. Next to him, Simon Lattimore held Perry's other hand and sipped a coffee. He looked up. "Are you sure you don't need a doctor, Bea?"

She shook her head. "I'm fine, don't worry." At least that's what she said in her head. What she heard was a muffled, "Ifidoutorry." She lowered the ice pack, "ory,"

Perry sniggered. "Oh, Bea, I know it's not funny. But you look like you've gone two rounds with Rocky. Are you going to be okay, my super woman?"

Bea gave him a look. If he was joking already, hopefully he would recover from being held at knifepoint quickly. She reached out beside her and pulled the snoring Daisy closer to her side. She put down the ice pack, and her cold fingers picked up a large cup of steaming black coffee. As the hot liquid slid down her throat, the tension in her neck and shoulders dissipated. She snuggled back into the chair, feeling the rise and fall of Daisy's little white body on her leg.

She closed her eyes. Thank goodness Fitzwilliam had left the bathroom door open enough to hear her shout his name as she'd tackled Ben Rhodes. According to Simon, the two of them had managed to open it enough they could see through the crack and had noticed Ben Rhodes was getting tired. They'd been planning an offensive as soon as the knife got far enough away from Perry to no longer be a danger. She'd beaten them to it. But as she'd pointed out, it had been one thing getting the knife off him; she hadn't thought beyond that. Ben Rhodes was six foot and weighed probably twice as much as she did. Without Simon and Fitzwilliam bounding out of the bathroom and overpowering him, both she and Perry would have still been in danger.

Although Perry and Simon had been incredibly grateful to her, all Fitzwilliam had said to her as he'd helped her up off the floor was, "That was a brave but stupid thing to do, my lady." As if adding 'my lady' to the sentence had made it sound any less like she was being told off. She was glad that, apart from him having tried to persuade her to let him call a doctor to look at her face, she'd not spoken to him since. After Fitzwilliam had arrested Ben Rhodes for murder, he and two security guards had escorted the killer to a spare room, where he was currently being formally interviewed.

"Did you know Fitzwilliam has everything Ben Rhodes said to you recorded on his phone?" Simon said from across the table.

She frowned. How had he done that when Ben had made him and Simon leave their phones on the floor in the bedroom?

"He sneakily switched on the app he has that records interviews just before he put it face down on the floor."

That had been quick thinking.

"Hopefully it will help support the charge as, let's be honest, the other evidence is a little—"

Woof! Daisy jumped down from beside Bea as the door to the Card Room opened, and Detective Chief Inspector Richard Fitzwilliam strolled in. Daisy ran to greet him.

"There's coffee on the side," Simon informed him, then turned to Perry. "Do you want anything else, love?"

Perry licked his lips. "Well, I didn't have any lunch. Are there any scones up there?"

A smile tugged at the edges of Simon's mouth as he rose. "I'll have a look," he said, making his way over to the table on the side.

"And maybe a piece of chocolate cake?" Perry shouted over his shoulder. Then he looked at Bea and winked.

She tried to smile. *Ouch!* She picked up the icepack and returned it to the side of her face.

"Are you sure you're all right, Lady Beatrice? I really think you should see a doctor," Fitzwilliam said as he took the other armchair opposite the sofa. Daisy lay down by his feet.

She shook her head violently and was grateful when Simon, carrying a large plate with two scones, a patty of butter, a small jar of jam, and a generous slice of cake, said, "I've already offered. She's adamant that she's fine."

Bea nodded and gave them a thumbs up.

Fitzwilliam huffed. "What I don't understand is, even when it's Perry here being held at knifepoint, you seem to be the only one who actually got hurt!"

She wanted to reply, "Just lucky, I guess," but it would

hurt too much. *He does have a point though.* This wasn't the first time she'd been injured during an investigation.

He shook his head at her, then took a sip of his coffee before he put it on the table in front of him. "So Ben Rhodes is safely locked up and being guarded by two police officers. CID hopes to come and collect him later, weather permitting."

"And Clive Tozzi?" Simon asked.

"Mr Tozzi, who we've now found out is really called Jacky Prince, is wanted for an assault on a shop owner in Hackney. We're handing him over to City police and someone is on their way to get him as we speak. In the meantime, he remains locked up here."

Fitzwilliam picked up his coffee again and looked over at Perry, who was about to put half a scone topped with butter and jam in his mouth. "And how are you feeling now, Perry?"

Perry reluctantly lowered his hand and shrugged. "I can't seem to get warm." He pulled the blanket tighter around himself with his other hand. "But apart from that, I'm doing fine, thanks." He smiled, then took a bite of the scone.

"That's shock, which is perfectly normal in the circumstances. I have to say you did an amazing job of keeping calm in there. That really helped to get Ben to relax and let his guard down. You should be extremely proud of yourself."

"Thanks," Perry said through a mouthful of food.

Fitzwilliam swivelled his head and looked at Bea. "And I've no idea where you learned those negotiating skills, but I know specialist officers who do that for a job, who wouldn't have done it as well as you did, Lady Beatrice."

The back of Bea's eyes prickled. *That has to be the nicest thing he's ever said to me.*

"However, I have to say your decision to tackle him on

your own was foolhardy. You could have been badly injured or even killed by that knife."

Bea's shoulders slumped. Of course he couldn't just say a nice thing without countering it with a telling off! She lowered the ice pack and glared at him. If only she could talk properly, she'd tell him—

"Did Ben Rhodes confess in full to his brother's murder?" Simon blurted out, giving Bea a warning look.

"Yes. Once he realised the game was up, he made a full statement. He admitted to using his phone to send the text message to Max's phone, which he took for himself. He wiped his prints off his and put it in Max's hands a few times so it looked like his phone, then left it on the bathroom floor when he went to find the body with Mr Prince."

Perry swallowed the last of his scone and said, "You know, I wouldn't be surprised if he thinks he'll be better off in jail after all."

Fitzwilliam tilted his head to one side. "I wouldn't be so sure. THC probably has enough contacts in jail to make sure his stay is very uncomfortable."

"And what about the FCA investigation?" Simon asked. "Will they try to prosecute him for insider trading?"

Fitzwilliam shrugged. "Rhodes claims he didn't know about the connection between the boy and THC until after the deal was done. Also, unless he's prepared to testify, which I doubt he will be, then I'm not confident what we have in his statement is sufficient for them to do much with it."

Simon sighed and looked out of the window. "You know, if we didn't get snowed in and Ben got stuck here, he may well have got away with it, and Clive... I mean, Jacky Prince, would have struggled to prove his innocence."

Fitzwilliam nodded. "Without Rhodes's confession, we wouldn't have had sufficient evidence to charge him with murder even if Prince could have proved he wasn't guilty. And let's not forget Daisy's contribution." The little terrier's ears pricked up, and she opened her eyes. "Without her finding the biscuit packaging and coming to get us when he took you, Perry, we'd never have made the connection." He reached down and patted the dog's white head. "Well done, Daisy. Once again, you proved yourself to be smarter than all of us put together."

Bea picked up the icepack again. She was proud of her little dog. *But I do think that's going a bit far.* She glanced over at Fitzwilliam. He raised his coffee cup to her and winked.

45

LUNCHTIME, WEDNESDAY 13
JANUARY

"Can I join you?" Brett Goodman, a plate of food in one hand and a drink in the other, stood by the side of the table where Lady Beatrice, her brother Lord Frederick Astley, and Detective Chief Inspector Richard Fitzwilliam sat by the window in the Breakfast Room. Daisy, curled up under the table between Bea and Fitzwilliam, opened an eye, then, clearly judging the new addition not to be worth moving for, she went back to sleep.

"Yes, of course, Brett," Fred said, indicating the chair opposite him.

"Beatrice." Brett grinned at Bea as he sat down next to her.

Oh my gosh, that smile…

She wanted to smile back, but her face was still stiff and aching on one side. Smiling made it hurt. At least she could talk properly today, and she'd escaped the black eye she'd been dreading.

"When are you leaving, Mr Goodman?" Fitzwilliam asked, then hesitated. "Er, I mean, your colleague left earlier, so I'm surprised to see you still here."

Bea stifled a giggle.

Brett picked up his knife and cut his venison burger in half. "Because of the delay here, I need to go straight back to Washington DC. The quickest route for me is from Edinburgh via Dublin, then straight to DC. Eve is going back to London. My flight's not until this afternoon."

"Ah," Fitzwilliam mumbled and carried on eating his game pie.

"So, my lady. I never had a chance to tell you I knew your husband." Brett Goodman popped a mouthful of burger into his mouth.

Brett knew James? But why would James know someone in the CIA?

"You surprise me, Brett. How did you know each other?"

Brett, wiping his mouth with his napkin, shot a look at Fred, who was giving him daggers.

What's going on? She looked across at Fitzwilliam, who was staring open-mouthed at Brett Goodman, then at her brother, who refused to meet her eye.

"Well?" she snapped at Brett, then flinched as pain shot through her jaw.

"Er." Red spots had appeared on his coffee-coloured cheeks. "Er, Fred?"

"What's going on, Fred?"

Fred covered his face with his hands and swore.

"Frederick Charles Astley, you'd better tell me now, or—"

He dropped his hands. "Can you just forget he said anything?" he asked hopefully.

"No, I can't. Now spit it out!" Ouch! Being mad was hurting like billy-o.

Fred glanced at Fitzwilliam, who was next to him. Fitzwilliam shrugged. "It's too late now," he said.

She glared at Fitzwilliam. *So he's in on this too?*

"Okay," Fred dropped his voice and leaned in. "Remember how I said I did some stuff for MI6?"

"Yes," she said hesitatingly. "You're an SO. Is that the right term?"

He nodded, then turned and scanned the empty room. "Well, so was James," he whispered.

Grabbing onto the tabletop, Bea felt as if she was having an out-of-body experience. *James a spy? How is that even possible? Why didn't I know?* Thoughts spun in her head, making her feel giddy. A glass of water was thrust into her hand from across the table, and Fitzwilliam hissed, "Drink!" The cold liquid left a delicious soothing trail as it slipped down her throat. She took a deep breath and slowly let it out.

She put the glass down, her eyes now focused on the man in front of her. "You knew?" she whispered.

Fitzwilliam cleared his throat. "Er, yes. They told us during the investigation into his accident in case we came across anything that was related." He rubbed the back of his neck. "Sorry."

"But why didn't you tell me?"

"We were sworn to secrecy. I couldn't tell anyone." He met her gaze. He looked genuinely sorry.

She focussed on Fred. "And you! How long have you known?" she shouted.

Daisy gave a low *woof* from under the table. Fitzwilliam reached down and patted her on the head.

Fred lifted his chin. "Only since I became one." He held up his hand. "And before you ask, I didn't tell you because I would've had to tell you how I knew, and of course, I couldn't."

She grabbed her hair in her hands and pulled it over her face. James had been a spy? Her eyes prickled. *Why didn't he tell me? Who was the man I was married to?* She no longer knew anymore.

"Are you okay, Beatrice? I'm so sorry I upset you. I wasn't aware you didn't know."

"Of course she didn't know, Brett," Fred hissed. "We're not allowed to tell anyone. It's too dangerous."

"I know that. But once he was dead, surely it made no difference?"

Looking up from her hair through watery eyes, she said, "Exactly! So why didn't someone tell me?"

Fred reached diagonally over the table and grabbed her hand. "I'm so sorry, Bea. I don't know why we weren't told at the time." Her eyes met her brother's, and she slowly nodded.

Taking a deep breath, she hooked her hair over her ears and wiped under her eyes, avoiding the swollen red patch around her jaw. She turned to Brett Goodman. "Sorry, Brett. You weren't to know. Now, you said that you knew James. Did you know him well?" She smiled encouragingly at him as she reached for her coffee cup and took a gulp.

"I was over here as the CIA-MI6 liaison back then. I first met James when he was being evaluated as a possible SO. My speciality is psych evaluations, so they often asked me to sit in on interviews to give a second opinion. I liked him immediately. He was twenty-three, only five years younger than me, and he gave out such a good vibe. He was so enthusiastic about having an important role to play not just within the royal family but for his king and country. And he was very bright." He smiled. "Not that I need to tell you that, of course. Anyway, we clicked, and when he passed selection, they assigned me to brief him on the CIA and our role. We hit it off and stayed in contact." He shook his head. "I was in the States when I heard about the accident. I was wrecked. It was a few weeks before that that I'd spoken to him. I couldn't believe it turned out that that would be the last time."

"You spoke to him that close to his death... er, was he okay?" Did Brett know about his relationship with Gill? Had James talked to him about it? Something had been bothering him around that time, she recalled. Had it been something to do with running away with Gill? She studied Brett carefully, but he didn't seem to be uncomfortable or embarrassed.

"Now that you mention it, no. He was worried about something he'd come across when he'd been in Miami a couple of months before. He wouldn't say what it was on the phone." Brett smiled at her. "You get paranoid about these things when you're in our line of business. Anyway, he wanted to see me, but I was in the States and it was close to Christmas. I told him I couldn't get over until the New Year. I suggested he talked to his MI6 contact, and he asked me if I thought he could be trusted. I can't remember who it was back then, but I remember saying yes. He said he would set up a meeting but wasn't sure if he would say anything or not until after we met." He shrugged. "And that was it, the last time I spoke to him."

Bea sat quietly for a moment. She recalled that night, the week before Christmas, when she'd overheard her husband on the phone late at night telling someone he needed to see them. After what had happened with the accident, she'd assumed it had been Gill he'd been talking to. Could it have been Brett? "Was this the week before Christmas? On a Sunday?" she asked, her skin tingling.

"Er, yes, I think it was. I remember I was in Cape Canaveral on the east coast visiting friends. We were just getting ready for an early dinner."

That must be it then. It would have been late evening here, and she'd been on her way to bed, so that fitted. Her muscles felt weak. *So James wasn't talking to another woman, after all...*

"Mr Goodman, did you say anything to anyone after his accident? You know, that you spoke to him, and he was concerned about something?" Fitzwilliam asked.

Brett shook his head. "No, I don't recall that I did. I assumed whatever it'd been, he'd passed on to his contact. I didn't think it was relevant to the accident, you know?"

So Brett obviously didn't know James had been supposed to be meeting his MI6 contact the morning after he died. *I wonder what it was about Miami that was bothering him so much?*

"It must have been a hard time for you, Lady Beatrice. With all that ludicrous speculation in the press that he was having an affair. I hope you don't believe any of that stuff. I knew your husband. He loved you and your life together. He wouldn't have risked that."

Bea swallowed. That was kind of him to say. Unfortunately, it seemed he hadn't known her husband any better than she had.

She nodded. "Thank you. Yes. It was difficult back then. But it was a long time ago. I've learnt to move on."

She was grateful when the phone in front of Fitzwilliam rang. He looked at the screen as he picked it up. He rose. "If you will excuse me, I need to take this." He strode away to the other side of the room.

Fred stood too. "I need to get packing. My flight's from Edinburgh as well. Do you want a lift, Brett?"

"Yes, please, bud. That will save me from having to get a taxi."

"Great. Meet you down here in an hour?"

Brett nodded.

"Sis, I'll talk to you later, okay?" He crouched down and

reached under the table. "Look after your mum, Daisy; she's a bit tired and emotional," he quipped.

How dare he! This is partly his fault! She opened her mouth, but she was too late.

"I hope the Perry and Simon thing tomorrow goes smoothly," he said, then winked and walked off.

Bea took in a sharp intake of breath and let it out slowly. Turning to Brett, she smiled. "Well, you must think this has all been a little... odd? Sorry, it was a bit of a shock, that's all."

He held up his hand. "Please, there's no need to apologise, Beatrice. Of course, if I'd have known, I would have kept my crazy mouth shut!"

"Well, I'm glad you didn't." She smiled.

He smiled back. "I'm due to be back over in London next month. Maybe I could take you out for dinner?"

Her tummy fluttered. If only she wasn't off handsome and charming men... No, it wasn't just that. If only he hadn't known her husband so well... *How do I let him down, gently?* "Thank you, Brett, for the invitation. But I'm sorry. I'm not dating at the moment."

He nodded. "And it would feel weird, huh? Knowing I was friends with your husband."

She smiled. "Yes, and that too."

He rose. "I get it. But you know, if you ever change your mind, Fred has my number." He leaned over and took her hand. Kissing it gently, he said, "Goodbye, Beatrice. I hope we meet again soon."

Heat rose up her neck as he dropped her hand and strolled off. She sighed. Maybe she should rethink—

"What was all that about?" Fitzwilliam asked gruffly as he sat down opposite and placed his phone on the table. "Does he think he's some sort of American prince?"

She laughed. "He was just being charming."

"Smarmy, more like," he muttered as he took a sip of coffee.

What do you know? You wouldn't know charming if it came up and bit you!

"So that was Adler. I said I should be able to get away later today. I just have a report to write. The internet at the cottage isn't great, so I'll do that here. Then I should be done."

"Is the cottage far away?"

"It's probably only about a mile, although the other afternoon, it felt a lot further."

He grinned, and she smiled back. He sounded happy to be getting back to his 'friend'. She leaned back in her chair and folded her arms. She could organise one of the Land Rovers to take him and all his snow gear back... Or she could leave him to walk home... She suppressed a smile. Then he'd be too tired to—

"But they're going to come and pick me up, anyway."

They? He'd only mentioned Adler...

"Well, actually, it will probably just be Izzy."

Izzy? *So he's got two women?*

"I don't imagine she'll want the hassle of trying to get Adler in and out of the car for such a brief trip."

Do they all work together? That must be awkward. She couldn't help herself. "So is Izzy also a colleague?"

Fitzwilliam shook his head, smiling. "No. She's Adler's wife."

Wife? She uncrossed her arms and shifted in her seat. *Oh... now that's embarrassing. Just as well he didn't know what I was thinking.* She'd jumped to a wrong conclusion about him. Again. *I must stop doing that.* "Er, I have an idea. Why don't you invite them both to dinner here tonight? They could then take you home after? It's the least we can do to say thank you after prying you away from them."

"Are you sure that's not too much trouble?"

"No, not at all. We've still got plenty of food here. It might all be game related, but there's lots of it."

"Well, if that's the case, then I'll give them a ring now and see if they're up for it." He picked up his phone and walked away.

What have I done? Now I've got to spend an evening with Fitzwilliam and two people I don't know, and *I have a face like a baboon's backside.*

She grabbed her phone and began to type. *I just hope Perry and Simon aren't sick of pheasant yet.*

46

EARLY AFTERNOON, WEDNESDAY 13 JANUARY

The Society Page online article:

Police Make a Shocking Statement Regarding the Reported Death of Ben Rhodes

Banerdeenshire police released a statement a short while ago saying that after a thorough investigation into the reported death of Ben Rhodes, they had incorrectly identified the victim. The dead man was, in fact, Max Rhodes (38). In an even more shocking twist, they announced they had arrested Ben Rhodes and charged him with the murder of his identical twin brother. Max Rhodes's family has received the news and will make a statement later today.

Ben Rhodes's wife Gemma, now suddenly no longer a widow, is being comforted by friends and has so far refused to talk to the press.

Meanwhile, fans of Urshall United took to social media to express their disbelief at the events of the last few days. One football supporter wrote, 'So Ben Rhodes is alive, and he killed his twin brother? You couldn't make it up if you tried!'

Another was more concerned about how this would affect their club. 'So if Ben Rhodes is alive, then does he still own the club? Can he run it from prison?' A spokesperson for Urshall United said they were still digesting the news and would make a full statement once they have sought legal advice.

———

Lady Beatrice's chest felt tight as she descended the main staircase at Drew Castle, Daisy by her side. She stopped and adjusted her little black dress. *Is it too short? Am I over-dressed?* She rubbed her hands together. *It will be fine.* Perry and Simon would be there. Glancing downward, she saw the main foyer with its dark tapestries depicting battles on the walls and the display of old long barrel guns making a crescent shape above the entrance. Would Fitzwilliam's friends be comfortable with such an aggressive demonstration of power? As she'd said to Fitzwilliam the other evening, she was used to being surrounded by the narrative, often with war-mongering undertones, but what did it look like to an outsider? She looked up at the intricately-carved white-painted ceilings and down to the portraits lining the walls of the staircase showing the ancient lineage of the castle and the family who had lived here for centuries. Was it an ostentatious display of wealth or a celebration of history? She'd always seen it as the latter, but would others see it differently?

If only Fred hadn't rushed off to catch a flight back to London. She suddenly realised she would be outnumbered tonight; the only royal at dinner. The only one who knew what it was like to grow up in this environment. For a minute, she even wished her grandmother was here rather than safely back at Foxhall. Then she checked herself. The formality The Queen Mother's presence would bring was the last thing she needed tonight. She shook out her shoulders and hands. *Come on, Bea. This is who you are. You shouldn't feel ashamed of it.* She stuck her chin up and swept down the stairs. As they reached the bottom, Brock appeared by her side.

"I have set drinks up in the Drawing Room, Lady Rossex, and dinner will be served in the Green Dining Room."

Perfect. The Green Dining Room, sitting only a maximum of twelve, was a much more intimate setting than the Grand Dining Room. "Thank you, Brock, that's perfect." She glanced at her watch just as the doorbell clanged, and Daisy gave an excited *yap*. She took a deep breath in, then let it out slowly as Brock sailed towards the door.

———

Two hours later, seated around the centre of the wide polished wooden table, Bea scolded herself for having been so silly earlier; everyone was relaxed and enjoying themselves. *I needn't have worried.* She studied the three people opposite her. Emma McKeer-Adler (Fitzwilliam appeared to refer to her simply as Adler) and her wife Isobel ("Please call me Izzy") were either side of Richard Fitzwilliam, who was leaning forward, talking to Simon Lattimore on her right. Adler, sitting at a slight angle to the table to facilitate her prone right leg resting on a tartan-covered stool, listened to the two of them, a faint smile on her face. A small diamond nose stud caught the light, standing out sharply against her dark skin. She didn't seem at all like the surly and ambitious chief inspector she'd imagined. Was that because she'd assumed she would be a female version of Fitzwilliam? Bea suppressed a smile. *Yes, that was probably it.*

Izzy was deep in conversation with Perry, who was sitting opposite her on Bea's left. With her smiling round face and her short blonde hair, she looked like someone you would talk to about your problems while she made you a nice cup of tea. She'd told Bea while they'd been having drinks that she made ceramics and had actually met Adler while restoring one of the collections at Gollingham Palace. *And there was me, worried our surroundings would intimidate her tonight.*

After William and Brock cleared the last of the plates, they left the room. "That was delicious, Lady Beatrice," Izzy said as she picked up a chocolate mint and popped it into her mouth. "Was the pheasant from your brother's shooting party over the weekend?"

Bea nodded. "Yes, they had a fruitful day on Sunday, I believe."

"Oh my giddy aunt!" Perry said, thumping his hand to his chest. "We might have just eaten something that was shot by a murderer!"

Everyone turned to stare at him, and he blushed. "Obviously, I mean a murderer of humans, not of animals... they're all animal killers..." He trailed off and grabbed his wineglass. "Sorry," he said, taking a large glug of Malbec.

Bea stifled a giggle. Next to her, she could feel Simon shaking. He coughed and composed himself. Opposite her, Fitzwilliam picked up his glass, his brown eyes sparkling, and took a sip.

"Izzy, guess what? I've met Simon before," Adler said, leaning across Fitzwilliam. "We worked together fifteen years ago. We were both on the investigation into the Earl of Rossex's death—" She stopped abruptly, and wide brown eyes stared at Bea. "I'm so sorry, my lady, I—"

Bea held up her hand. "Please, there's no need to apologise. My husband's death was fifteen years ago. We can talk about it without me going into a swoon, I promise." She grinned at the rather startled Adler. "In fact" —she eyed Fitzwilliam across the table— "has Fitzwilliam brought you up to date with what we found out recently about James's death?"

Snapping her head around to look at him, Adler raised an eyebrow. "No, he hasn't."

Fitzwilliam leaned back and frowned. "I didn't think you wanted it out there for general consumption." He crossed his arms and stared at her.

Oh no, it was all going so well, and now I've hacked him off. I need to fix this…

"Of course, I don't. Sorry. I appreciate your discretion. But I think maybe if we shared it with Adler and Simon, who were both involved in the original case, they may have something to add that will help make sense of it all."

Perry cleared his throat beside her. "You mean there's stuff you haven't told us?"

She shrugged. "You know some of it, but I don't think I've brought you completely up to date. To be honest, I promised myself I was going to move on and forget all about it." She looked at Fitzwilliam and gave him a wry smile. Fitzwilliam nodded. "So I think it's the right time to share it all." She turned to Izzy. "Izzy, I trust I can rely on you not to repeat what I'm about to say to anyone outside this room?"

"Yes, of course, my lady."

"Great," Bea said and started with a summary of the letter her husband had written to her on the night he'd died. She told them everything she and Fitzwilliam had found out about James's accident over the last nine months. She even told them about James's relationship with MI6, although it turned out Adler already knew. The only thing she left out was what Brett had told her; it would involve them knowing he was

CIA, and that would link him to Fred, who she'd promised she wouldn't reveal his secret.

When she finished, a stunned silence descended, then Adler spoke. "So Gill Sterling, the passenger in the earl's car who died with him, was being paid by someone to compromise the earl?"

Bea frowned. "Er, no, that's not what I said…"

Adler tilted her head to one side. "But that's what it all points to, surely? The pretending to be beaten by her husband to get his sympathy, telling James she would run away with him when she clearly had no intention of doing so, the large amount of money she had in her bank account from an untraceable source, and the second phone suggesting that's how they communicated with her. Have I missed anything?"

Oh my gosh. Bea held her hand up to her throat. Adler had hit the nail firmly on the head. That was *exactly* what it looked like.

"I wonder if it was the papers who were paying Gill Sterling. Imagine the press they could get from a kiss and tell," Simon suggested.

Bea winced. He grabbed her arm and whispered, "Sorry."

She patted his arm with her hand and smiled. "It's okay. And it's a valid observation. Maybe it is that simple."

"Hold on," Adler said to Fitzwilliam. "Why don't you talk to Chief Superintendent Tim Street?" She turned to the others. "He's a senior officer at PaIRS and was the one who told us about the earl's involvement with MI6."

"I have already, Adler," Fitzwilliam replied.

"Oh?" Her mouth fell open.

"He hasn't been able to find out anything either. The last conversation I had with him, he told me to drop it and move on."

"Oh," Adler said. "That's a shame."

Fitzwilliam nodded. "We seem to have come to a dead end."

Bea studied his face. She knew from what he'd said to her before that he hated loose ends. Was he really going to give up on this? And now that Brett had told them James had been worried about something he'd found out in Miami, surely that was a new lead that could be explored? His eyes caught her gaze. She wished she knew what he was thinking behind those brown eyes. He looked away, and her heart sank. *He's giving up, isn't he?*

The door opened, and Brock appeared. "Coffee is laid out in the Drawing Room, Lady Rossex, when you and your guests are ready." He gave a quick bow and stood by the door.

"Thank you, Brock." She turned to her guests. "Shall we retire to the Drawing Room? We also have a fine selection of whisky," she said, looking directly at Fitzwilliam.

————

"Thank you so much for a lovely evening," Izzy McKeer-Adler said to Lady Beatrice, tucking her arms into the full-length faux-fur coat William held open behind her. "I'll bring the car right to the door," she shouted out to her wife, who was still slowly making her way towards them.

Emma McKeer-Adler stopped by Brock, and handing her crutches to him in exchange for her white puffer jacket, she smiled at Bea. "Yes, thank you. It's been great. Perry told me just before they left that your next job is at Gollingham Palace?"

Bea nodded. "Yes. We're hoping to be finished here next week. After a week at home completing a few things, we should be ready to start."

"Well," she said, putting her jacket on. "I hope to get this thing" —she pointed to her cast— "off in two weeks and then I'll be back to work, even if I'm restricted to the office for a while. So maybe Izzy and I can return the favour and have you over for dinner at our place. It's not as impressive as this." She looked up. "But Izzy's a superb cook, and after a few glasses of wine, you tend not to notice the lack of suits of armour." She grinned, nodding her head towards the imposing silver knight, complete with sword, standing guard outside the entrance to the Grand Dining Room on her right.

Bea laughed. "It must be nice not to have to do all that polishing."

It was Adler's turn to laugh as she took her crutches back from the butler. "Thank you," she said to him as she turned and headed for the door.

There was a clatter as Richard Fitzwilliam reached the bottom of the stairs and the straps on his backpack hit the end of the bannisters. Just behind him, Daisy jumped off the last step and followed him towards Bea.

As he arrived by the glass door, Brock held out his arms. Draped over them was the large yeti-looking coat Fitzwilliam had arrived in three days ago. *Was it only three days? It seems like weeks.*

"Will you be wearing this coat, chief inspector? Or would you like me to put it in the car with the snow boots and skis?" the butler asked.

Fitzwilliam looked amused as he said, "Thank you, Brock. It can go in the car, if you don't mind."

"Yes, sir." Brock turned and, feeling his way to the door handle, disappeared outside in a mound of fur.

"Well, Lady Beatrice. Thank you for dinner, and thank you for all your help on this case," he said, a twinkle in his eye.

Bea held his gaze. *Shall I ask him if he's going to pass the new information we got from Brett Goodman on to CS Tim Street?* She opened her mouth, then hesitated. He would know what to do. She didn't want to be accused of telling him how to do his job again! She smiled. "You're welcome, Fitzwilliam. I hope you can now enjoy a few days with your friends before you have to go back."

Fitzwilliam nodded, then crouched down to Daisy. "And of course, Daisy, we couldn't have done it without you." He ruffled the wiry fur on the little terrier's head, then straightened up. Shifting his backpack on his shoulder, he turned and headed for the door.

Bea bent down and scooped Daisy up.

"Oh, and Lady Beatrice?"

She looked up, the white bundle in her arms. He stood with his hand on the door handle, smirking. "I hope if I see you at Gollingham Palace, it's to have a coffee with you rather than view a dead body you've found."

She smiled. "Me too, Fitzwilliam. Me too."

47

JUST BEFORE SUNSET, THURSDAY 14 JANUARY

Lady Beatrice's stomach churned. She checked her phone again. The message she'd sent Perry was still on her screen, but it hadn't been delivered.

Bea: *Can you come and meet me in my apartment? I want to go over tomorrow's plans. xx*

They only had fifteen minutes before sunset, and Perry was missing.

"Where is he?" she cried, throwing her hands up in the air.

"Bea!" Simon Lattimore grabbed her arms. "Calm down; he'll be here."

She wriggled free. "But he's not even read the text. If he's late, then the sunset will be over, and it will ruin everything!" A muscle in her cheek twitched, and she slapped her hand over it.

Simon smiled indulgently. "It won't be ruined, Bea. The

only thing that can ruin it is if Perry says no." He pulled a face.

She shook her head. "Well, that won't happen."

"Then we have nothing to worry about, do we?"

She took a heavy breath. *He's right. It will be fine.* She darted a glance at her phone in her hand. Oh my goodness, the message had two ticks now. Dots appeared just underneath it.

"He's replying!" she shouted even though Simon was only inches away from her. He stepped back, smiling while she stood frozen, her eyes on the screen. *Beep.*

Perry: *Okay, on my way. xx*

"Oh my gosh, he's coming." She grabbed Simon's arm. "You need to go. Do you have the ring?" He patted the front pocket of his jeans and nodded. "Good. Right. So the balcony doors are open, and there's a rug you can kneel on so you don't get dirty—"

"Bea, we've already been through this several times. I—"

"There's a bottle of champagne just inside the balcony door in an ice bucket. You'll have to open it yourself." She took a deep breath and carried on. "I'll open the door and push him in, then you—"

He tugged on her arm. "Bea! Stop. I know. We've planned it beautifully. Now let me go, or I'll still be here when he arrives."

She shook her hands at him. "Yes, go. Go!"

As he hurried across her sitting room, waving, she shouted after him. "Good luck!"

Bea scuttled over to the small sofa by the window and

picked up her little dog. "Oh my giddy aunt, Daisy!" Burying her head in Daisy's white fur, she felt an overwhelming urge to scream. *Get a grip, Bea!* She put the wriggling Daisy down and looked out of the window. The sight before her couldn't be more beautiful. A large orange ball burnt low in the sky, the dark spiky outline of trees and hedges standing out against the lilac background. The haze of pink shimmered over the blanket of snow still covering most of the ground, broken only by the grey shadows of tree trunks. A lump came to her throat. *It's perfect...*

The thud of Daisy jumping off the sofa made her turn. Perry walked into the room, his tall lean frame encased in a navy-blue jacket with a fine red thread running through it, creating squares in the material. The ruby-red buttons stood out against the white T-shirt he was wearing underneath, and along with the dark-blue denim jeans he wore, his look was the ideal blend of formal and casual. He bent down to pet Daisy. Bea hurried over, her stomach a mass of butterflies.

"Perry! You're here."

Perry straightened. "Of course I am. Are you okay? You look a tad flushed?"

"Yes, yes. I'm fine." She grabbed him. "I want to show you something in the other room. I need your opinion," she blurted out.

He resisted. "Oh my giddy aunt! Look at that view." He froze, facing the window, his mouth open.

Her skin prickled. *Not now, Perry. I need you to move.*

"Yes, yes. It's lovely. Let's go." She tugged on his arm. He didn't move.

"I don't think I've ever seen anything so—"

She yanked at his jacket. "It's even better from the other room."

He reluctantly turned. "Okay, I'm coming."

She pushed him ahead of her, and they left the room, Daisy following.

The Upper Drawing Room was only three rooms along from her suite. Feeling hot and dizzy, she focused on the door that was slightly ajar ahead of her. *I just need to get him in and then it will all be all right.* She halted outside the door. She'd practiced this so many times. *Here goes...*

"Oh." She patted the back of her jeans. "My phone." She whipped it out, keeping the screen facing away from Perry. She studied the blank screen. "Oh, it's mother," she said in a stilted voice. "Why don't you go on in without me? I'll be there in a minute."

Perry frowned. "Er, okay."

"Hi, Ma," she said, balancing her phone under her chin while she grabbed Daisy with one hand (*No, you don't, little girl!*) and gave Perry a gentle shove with the other. As he cleared the door frame, she pulled the door shut behind him.

Lightheaded, she released Daisy and let the silent phone drop into her hand. *Did I get away with it?* She smiled. It didn't matter now. She took a deep breath and let it out. *It's up to Simon now.*

She pressed the screen on her phone, selected a number, and hit FaceTime. Seeing herself in the camera while the call connected, she winced. *Oh my gosh, I look deranged.* Pink splotches covered her face, her red hair stuck up in tufts, and her eyes were so wide she looked like she'd been shot. She quickly smoothed down her hair and blinked.

"Mum!" Sam's smiling face greeted her, and her shoulders instantly dropped. She grinned back at her son. "Has it happened yet?" he asked eagerly.

"It's happening right now behind this door." She flicked the camera around. "He's only been in there for a few—" The sound of a cork popping made her squeal. Daisy barked. "I think that's it!"

The door was thrown open, and a grinning Simon poked his head out. "Do you want to come—"

He stood aside as Bea rushed into the room, still holding her phone in front of her. Daisy ran ahead, barking. Perry stood by the window, tears streaming down his face. He saw her, and his wet face split into a massive grin.

Simon gently took the phone from her hand and whispered in her ear, "Thank you."

A tear began running down her cheek as she lunged towards her best friend and enveloped him in a bear hug.

"I'm so happy, Bea, I could burst." Perry mumbled into her hair, squeezing her tight.

"So am I," she said, trying to catch her breath as the tears refused to stop.

They remained entwined for a few seconds, then Perry pushed her away from him, still holding her arms. "That was some of the worst acting I've ever seen!" His eyes shining bright with tears, he burst out laughing.

Wrenching one arm free, she wiped it across her face. "I know," she said, sniffling and laughing at the same time. "And would you believe, I practiced it too?"

Daisy jumped up in between them, and Perry crouched down. "Would you like to be a bridesmaid, Daisy? You'd look so cute in a little blue dress." He wiped one hand under his eye and patted her with the other.

Bea looked around for Simon. He was over by the window, her phone in front of his face, chatting. *Sam!* She walked over and slid her arm around Simon's waist. "Hey, Sammy," she said to her grinning son as Simon put his arm over her shoulders. She hugged him tight.

"Hey, Mum. Simon and I were just talking about wedding

food. He says I can help choose the menu." She smiled. Simon's passion for food was rivalled only by her son's.

"I think we should ask Ryan Hawley to cook. I could ask him if you want, Simon?"

At least something good had come out of the disastrous food festival at Fenn House last year. Her son had struck up a friendship with his food hero, Ryan Hawley, TV celebrity and executive chef at Nonnina, the prestigious restaurant in Knightsbridge. Ryan had visited Sam's food club at school, and just before Christmas, he'd invited her, Sam, Simon, and Perry to dine at the chef's table at Nonnina, where she'd had the best meal she'd ever had in her life.

"We can talk about it when you're next home, buddy," Simon said.

Perry appeared behind them, holding Daisy and waving her paw at the screen. "Hey, Sam."

"Perry! Congratulations. I can't wait for the wedding!"

Perry laughed. "Me too!"

"Okay, darling. We are going now because I know you have homework to do. I'll see you in less than two weeks, and I can't wait. I love you."

"Bye, everyone." Sam waved. "Love you too, Mum."

She unwrapped herself from Simon and took the phone. She wiped her face and took a deep breath. "I think we need champagne and then you can tell me all about it."

48

AFTERNOON, MONDAY 18 JANUARY

The Society Page online article:

Wedding Bells for Author and Celebrity Chef Simon Lattimore

We hear from a reliable source that the author and celebrity chef, Simon Lattimore (39), and his long-term partner Perry Juke (34) are engaged to be married. We understand the proposal took place at Drew Castle, the King's estate in Scotland, where the couple have been staying for the past few weeks while Mr Juke and his business partner Lady Beatrice (36), the Countess of Rossex, have been working on a refurbishment project. A wedding date is yet to be announced.

Lady Beatrice and Perry Juke have almost completed their work at the castle, where they have been giving several family suites on the second floor a makeover, and are due to leave later this week. Their next project is a renovation and restyle of various guest suites at the King and Queen's official residence, Gollingham Palace, in Surrey.

It is understood Lady Beatrice will return to Francis Court via the boarding school Wilton College in Derbyshire, where she will visit her son Samuel Wiltshire (14). Lady Beatrice's brother Lord Frederick Astley (38) has already departed Drew Castle and has returned to London, while Queen Mary The Queen Mother (82) remains at her home on the estate, Foxhall.

After the tragic events that took place at Drew Castle last week, which resulted in the death of the entrepreneur, Max Rhodes (38), his twin brother Ben (38), owner of Urshall United, attended court this morning and was remanded in custody. No request for bail was made. The murder case has now been referred to the High Court of Justiciary in Scotland, and the trial is expected to begin later in the year. Ben Rhodes's wife Gemma (35) did not attend the court hearing, and it is rumoured she has left the couple's home in Surrey and is staying with friends in Portugal.

———

I hope you enjoyed *A Dead Herring*. If you did, then please consider letting others know by writing a review on Amazon, Goodreads or both. Thank you.

Will Lady Beatrice finally get to the bottom of her husband's fatal accident? Read the next book in the A Right Royal Cozy Investigation series *I Spy With My Little Die* available on preorder in the Amazon store or wherever you get your paperbacks.

Want to know how Perry and Simon solved their first crime together? Then join my readers' club and receive a

FREE short story Tick, Tock, Mystery Clock at https://www.-subscribepage.com/helengoldenauthor_nls

If you want to find out more about what I'm up to you can find me on Facebook at *helengoldenauthor* or on Instagram at *helengolden_author*.

Be the first to know when my next book is available. Follow Helen Golden on Amazon, BookBub, and Goodreads to get alerts whenever I have a new release, preorder, or a discount on any of my books.

A BIG THANK YOU TO...

Thank you to my friends and family who provide me with support as I continue along the journey of being an author. A huge thank you to you all for your enduring encouragement and commitment to support me.

To my husband Simon, who is hoping that if I really make a go of this he can retire early, thank you for your patience every time I say I can't do something with you because I have a deadline.

To my parents Ann and Ray, who are still with me through every step of the process, from beta reading to final eyes. Your support is invaluable.

To my beta readers Lis, Leila, and Lesley, thank you for your insightful and constructive feedback.

To my editor Marina Grout; my sounding block, my encourager, and now my friend, you make what I write become the best version of itself.

To my lovely friend Carolyn Bruce for being that critical additional set of eyes for me before I press that final button to publish.

To Alfie and Margot, who want to bark when I'm trying to work and fall asleep just as I'm about to take a break. I love your company, I just wish it was a little less noisy!

And last, but most definitely not least, to you, my readers. Your emails, social media comments, and reviews mean so much to me, and I appreciate your time and attention. I must mention two readers in particular, Nicky M and Karen

Nichol, who won a competition to name a character each in this book. Thank you both for taking part, and I hope you enjoy seeing your name in print.

To you all — please continue to get in touch, I'm always keen to hear from you. There is more coming from Lady Beatrice, Daisy, Perry, Simon, and Fitzwilliam, I promise.

As always, I may have taken a little dramatic license when it comes to police procedures, so any mistakes or misinterpretations, unintentional or otherwise, are my own.

CHARACTERS IN ORDER OF APPEARANCE

Richard Fitzwilliam — detective chief inspector at *PaIRS (Protection and Investigation (Royal) Service)* an organisation that provides protection and security to the royal family and who investigate any threats against them. *PaIRS* is a division of *City Police*, a police organisation based in the UK capital, London.

Emma McKeer-Adler — detective chief inspector, investigations team PaIRS.

Isobel 'Izzy" McKeer-Adler — Emma's wife.

Nigel Blake — Superintendent at *PaIRS*. Fitzwilliam's boss.

Lady Beatrice — The Countess of Rossex. Seventeenth in line to the British throne. Daughter of Charles Astley, the Duke of Arnwall and Her Royal Highness Princess Helen. Niece of the current king.

Benedict 'Ben' Rhodes — guest, younger twin brother to Max. Businessman and owner of Urshall United FC.

Queen Mary The Queen Mother — wife of the late King. Mother of HRH Princess Helen and grandmother of Lady Beatrice.

Lord Frederick (Fred) Astley — Earl of Tilling. Lady Beatrice's elder brother and twin of Lady Sarah Rosdale. Ex-Intelligence Army Officer. Future Duke of Arnwall.

James Wiltshire — The Earl of Rossex. Lady Beatrice's late husband killed in a car accident fifteen years ago.

Gill Sterling — the late wife of Francis Court's estate manager. Passenger in car accident that killed her and James Wiltshire.

Sam Wiltshire — son of Lady Beatrice and the late James Wiltshire, the Earl of Rossex. Future Earl of Durrland.

Charles Astley — Duke of Arnwall. Lady Beatrice's father.

HRH Princess Helen — Duchess of Arnwall. Mother of Lady Beatrice. Sister of the current king.

King James and Queen Olivia — King of England and his wife.

Lady Sarah Rosdale — Lady Beatrice's elder sister. Twin of Lord Frederick Astley. Manages events at Francis Court.

Robert (Robbie) Rosdale — Lady Sarah's eldest son.

Perry Juke — Lady Beatrice's business partner and BFF.

Simon Lattimore — Perry Juke's partner. Bestselling crime writer. Ex-Fenshire CID. Winner of cooking competition *Celebrity Elitechef.*

Sebastiano Marchetti — Famous Italian chef, known as Chef Seb. Lady Beatrice's ex-beau.

Maxwell 'Max' Rhodes — guest, elder twin brother to Ben. Prominent businessman and multi-millionaire.

Elger Hinz — Max Rhodes's ex-girlfriend and model.

Gemma Rhodes — Ben Rhodes's wife.

Daisy — Lady Beatrice's adorable West Highland Terrier.

Pluto — The Queen Mother's recently deceased chihuahua-pug cross.

William Featherstone — head footman and deputy butler at Drew Castle (reader suggestion from Karen Nichol).

Maddie Preston — kitchen maid at Drew Castle.

Mrs Erin Wilton — cook at Drew Castle.

Mrs Megan Kettley — head housekeeper, Drew Castle.

Hector McLean — guest, neighbouring landowner and retired businessman.

Fergus McLean — guest, Hector's son.

Edward 'Ed' Berry — guest, Hector's son-in-law and Rose's husband.

Lady Caroline 'Caro' Clifford — Lady Beatrice's cousin on her mother's side.

Rose Berry — guest, Hector's daughter.

Jacob Brock — butler at Drew Castle.

Owen Buckey — footmen at Drew Castle.

Brett Goodman — guest, CIA rep.

Eve Morrison — guest, MI6 rep (reader suggestion from Nicky M).

Hope Adler — Emma McKeer-Adler's daughter at university in Edinburgh.

Tim Street — Chief Superintendent at PaIRS.

Clive Tozzi/Declan Wince/Jacky Prince — security for Ben Rhodes.

Tina Spicer — Detective Sergeant at *PaIRS*.

Libby Carpenter — head maid at Drew Castle.

Steve/CID Steve — ex-colleague of Simon Lattimore at Fenshire CID.

Alfie — The Duke and Duchess of Arnwall's five-year-old border terrier.

Alex Sterling — the late Francis Court's estate manager. Husband of Gill Sterling.

Ryan Hawley — Executive Chef at Nonnina and TV chef.

ALSO BY HELEN GOLDEN

Can Perry Juke and Simon Lattimore work together to solve the mystery of the missing clock before the thief disappears? FREE novelette when you sign up to my readers' club. See end of final chapter for details.

First book in the A Right Royal Cozy Investigation series. Amateur sleuth, Lady Beatrice, must pit her wits against Detective Chief Inspector Richard Fitzwilliam to prove her sister innocent of murder. With the help of her clever dog, her flamboyant co-interior designer and his ex-police partner, can she find the killer before him, or will she make a fool of herself?

Second book in the A Right Royal Cozy Investigation series. Amateur sleuth, Lady Beatrice, must once again go up against DCI Fitzwilliam to find a killer. With the help of Daisy, her clever companion, and her two best friends, Perry and Simon, can she catch the culprit before her childhood friend's wedding is ruined?

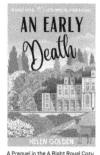

The third book in the A Right Royal Cozy Investigation series. When DCI Richard Fitzwilliam gets it into his head that Lady Beatrice's new beau Seb is guilty of murder, can the amateur sleuth, along with the help of Daisy, her clever westie, and her best friends Perry and Simon, find the real killer before Fitzwilliam goes ahead and arrests Seb?

A Prequel in the A Right Royal Cozy Investigation series. When Lady Beatrice's husband James Wiltshire dies in a car crash along with the wife of a member of staff, there are questions to be answered. Why haven't the occupants of two cars seen in the accident area come forward? And what is the secret James had been keeping from her?

A murder at Gollingham Palace sparks a hunt to find the killer. For once, Lady Beatrice is happy to let DCI Richard Fitzwilliam get on with it. But when information comes to light that indicates it could be linked to her husband's car accident fifteen years ago, she is compelled to get involved. Will she finally find out the truth behind James's tragic death?

EBOOKS AVAILABLE IN THE AMAZON STORE, PAPERBACKS FROM WHEREVER YOU BUY YOUR BOOKS

Printed in the USA
CPSIA information can be obtained
at www.ICGtesting.com
LVHW090202160224
772029LV00012B/103